KT-382-452

Praise for THE FINISHING LINE

'If you liked *Four Weddings* . . . you'll love *The Finishing Line*. Owen Slot's first novel is a Richard Curtis-esque romantic comedy about three friends racing to get married'   *The Times*

'Bloody good read . . . a great insight into what makes men tick'   *New Woman*

'Funny and touching'   *Cosmopolitan*

'His mates are getting married and the singleton Will feels left on the shelf. Is he the male Bridget Jones? Perceptive and amusing'   *More!*

'Touching read . . . we'd like some more – it's charming and funny'   *Heat*

'A refreshing change . . . A wryly amusing look at being the last single man standing. Perfect beach reading'   *Liverpool Daily Post*

'Fun'   *Independent on Sunday*

About the author

Owen Slot is Chief Sports Reporter for *The Times*. He won the Sports Reporter of the Year in 1998, 2001 and 2002. He lives in London and *The Finishing Line* is his first novel.

OWEN SLOT

The Finishing Line

FLAME
Hodder & Stoughton

Grateful acknowledgement is made for permission to print the lyrics from the following copyrighted works:

'American Pie' words and music by Don McLean © Copyright 1971 Mayday Music, USA. Universal/MCA Music Limited. Used by permission of Music Sales Limited. All Rights Reserved. International Copyright Secured.

'Don't Give Up On Us' words and music by Tony Macaulay © Copyright Universal Music Publishing Limited. Used by permission of Music Sales Limited. All Rights Reserved. International Copyright Secured.

Copyright © 2003 by Owen Slot

First published in Great Britain in 2003 by Hodder and Stoughton
A division of Hodder Headline
First published in paperback in 2004 by Hodder and Stoughton

The right of Owen Slot to be identified as the Author
of the Work has been asserted by him in accordance with the
Copyright, Designs and Patents Act 1988.

A Flame Paperback

1 3 5 7 9 10 8 6 4 2

All rights reserved. No part of this publication may be
reproduced, stored in a retrieval system, or transmitted, in any form
or by any means without the prior written permission of the publisher,
nor be otherwise circulated in any form of binding or cover other
than that in which it is published and without a similar condition
being imposed on the subsequent purchaser.

All characters in this publication are fictitious and any resemblance
to real persons, living or dead, is purely coincidental.

A CIP catalogue record for this title is
available from the British Library

ISBN 0 340 82463 8

Typeset in Sabon by Palimpsest Book Production Limited,
Polmont, Stirlingshire

Printed and bound in Great Britain by
Clays Ltd, St Ives plc

Hodder and Stoughton
A division of Hodder Headline
338 Euston Road
London NW1 3BH

For Juliet, with love

ACKNOWLEDGEMENTS

Many thanks to Ant Harwood who rescued this book from under a pile of dust and to Philippa Pride who helped blow off the cobwebs, also to Tom and Claudia Bradby for your unceasing encouragement, to Simon Beccle, Sammy Pollock, Simon Hill-Norton, Mark Lucas and Endemol UK. But particularly to Juliet; this would never have happened without you.

Part One

1

My name is Will Tennant. Today is Sunday 29 March and I have just woken to some very good news.

I have found a human body lying in my bed. The body is female and, judging by the pile of clothes on the floor, it is naked. The good news is that I am lying next to it and I am naked too.

Such situations are fairly rare but I know nevertheless what to do: I have to let her sleep. The longer she sleeps, the longer she stays, and the longer she stays, the more complete her arrival. If, for instance, she were to leave at six a.m., she would clearly want to disown the whole experience; she would think that I am a hideous mistake and she would have no qualms about letting me know as much. And I could do without that.

What time would I settle for? A nine o'clock departure would be fine, albeit inconclusive. At least nine o'clock would give the incident a sort of authenticity. If she leapt from my lair and fled, dressing herself in a panic, wobbling in and out of inappropriate shoes all the way to the front door and blabbing breathlessly about a brunch date in Barnes, I could walk away with some sort of credibility. I wouldn't be in deficit at least – and as long as I don't come out down, I can handle it.

There is some courtesy in a nine a.m. exit. Six o'clock would be bad news, nine is borderline but courteous, ten thirty might mean she likes me, and eleven thirty means she probably thinks I like her too. Get to lunchtime and I might even find myself with a relationship on my hands. Christ.

But right now I think I can indulge in some shameless self-congratulation: the body next to me is that of no ordinary female. It is outstandingly good-looking, for a start, and I don't think my opinion here is excessively influenced by it having landed up naked next to me. OK, she's not your standard, long-legs magazine cover – not everyone's pin-up; we've always known that. What I'd not realised until now, as I make the most of this unique opportunity to study it from about nine inches away, is what a sweet nose she has. It is small and irresistible. I want to stroke it. How can we not have spotted it before? I thought it was the big innocent eyes, now underscored by smudged black eyeliner, that were the attraction, and the dollops of thick blonde hair, like vanilla ice-cream, that are now spread across her face, and her small mouth with the slightly upturned top lip. But it's the nose. God, I want to touch it. I could kiss it very gently and then maybe it'd wiggle at me as a sign of approval. I'd better not. She'd wake up, scream and run out of the house naked. And then she'd struggle to get a taxi.

Right now she's purring away and, while she's unconscious at least, she seems contented. She is giving all the indications of finding me – naked, remember – and my bed a pretty happy place to be.

So, somewhere along the line, I am entitled to some credit. What the occasion really demands is a packed grandstand around the bedroom with everyone on their feet, applauding effusively and hurling their hats into the air. Overall, though, this would not serve the cause because the chances are that she would be woken up. As for me, I can neither raise my bat nor take a bow in recognition because, on this fine morning, I am forced to celebrate almost motionless. I wrap the duvet around my legs with sufficient care to ensure that she won't be disturbed and beyond that I'm not prepared to risk the slightest movement, apart from a blink in joyful disbelief as my digital alarm-clock counts out the glorious evidence: 9.42, 9.43, 9.44, 9.45.

What is she going to make of all this when she wakes? My bedroom is not exactly a showcase designed to seduce nocturnal visitors: they are too infrequent to make that its sole defining purpose. Nevertheless, I would like to think that the place reflects well on me. There are four shelves loaded with books, a few of which are translations from foreign texts, all of which I have read and none of them because I studied them at university. Next to the bookshelves stands Elvis, a life-size cardboard cut-out of him in his early good-looking days, thrusting out a cardboard guitar, his right arm rising having hit the note. On Elvis's cardboard head, rather incongruously, is one of my baseball caps. It brings him more up to date with modern fashion – at least, that's how I explain it. My prize possessions, though, are on the walls: three black-and-white framed prints by the photographer Herb Ritts, one of Bob Marley, one of Magic Johnson, the third of two naked women in an artistic pose. Overall, so far, I think I come out pretty well.

On the downside, however, there is a pile of dirty washing strewn across one corner of the room. That's a shame. But the symmetry is mildly entertaining because, in the opposite corner, there is another pile of clothes, which belongs to my current bedmate.

10.02 a.m. Still no stirring from the female body. What joy. As the minutes mount, so too do my shameless mental laps of honour. This is *brilliant*, I think, and I, for the moment, am brilliant too. I feel great, on top of my game. Jake and Alex will hail this as one of the all-time great achievements. Even if she runs out on me now and I never see her again, they'll be impressed because it's 10.09 a.m. This is, without doubt, the pinnacle of my achievements with womankind. Even if there haven't been that many. Well, there was that girl at university. No, this one beats even that. And the heavy relationship at law school? Not a patch on this. How long will this ridiculous ego-trip last? C'mon, get a grip. Does she really like me? Why *should* she really like me? Is she going to deflate the whole experience by running out the minute she wakes up? Don't worry. The clock now says 10.15 a.m. Everything is fine. Everything is far, far better than fine.

10.15 a.m. I never dared think I'd get this far. I creep out of bed, still not disturbing her, and head down the dimly lit landing for the sitting-room, treading carefully to keep noise to the minimum. If there was ever a self-indulgence to be had, it is now: 10.15 a.m. has arrived, I'm going to leave the girl in bed and watch her, instead, on television.

I walk into the sitting-room. Jake is sprawled across the sofa, his long legs draped over the end. He stares at me in a way that suggests wonderment. It is as if he is frozen. Either that or he doesn't recognise me, which would be strange because he is my best mate and he has also been my flatmate and tenant for five years.

Finally, and emphatically, Jake speaks: 'You absolute bastard.'

'What do you mean?' I reply, feigning surprise.

'Don't come over all modest on me. You and that girl, it's unbelievable.'

'Sorry, I'm just not with you.' I'm with him every step of the way.

'What you have just done,' he continues, 'is very hard to believe. You with her,' he now points at the television, which isn't even switched on, 'happens in films. Not real life.'

Then he drops his deadpan seriousness, breaks into a smile and starts to rant: 'God, I'm so fucking jealous. I really can't believe it. I simply can't. And you! Why not me, for God's sake?'

'Well, look at you,' I reply jokingly, gesturing at his body. 'You think she'd go for that?'

'Maybe not. But you don't look much better your-self.'

He's got a point, a good one. Jake often does. And now I am scanning him nervously. This is a guy girls tend to like because of his sandy hair and friendly, young face – he can still pass himself off as a teenager. But today he looks a wreck, as hung-over as I feel. His hair is splattered forward, he is wearing an old Nike T-shirt, boxer shorts with Father Christmases on them, and a thinning blue towelling dressing-gown. His voice is croaky, he hasn't showered, and if I moved an inch closer I'm sure I'd be able to confirm that his breath smells. And he's right. My dressing-gown's a lighter shade of blue, my T-shirt's got a surf logo on and my boxer shorts are covered with teddy bears in sunglasses, but otherwise I look and probably smell exactly the same. Most Sunday mornings this is fine, and in fact it has been the happy status quo for a large percentage of Sunday mornings over the past five years. But it is not fine today. If the Sleeping Beauty was to rise from her bed (my bed, remember, isn't it fantastic?) and discover us, she'd disappear as quickly as if she'd woken up to find me kissing her nose.

'I'm proud of you, anyway,' Jake says, though my mind is already wandering. Look at us. We're a disgrace. We've waited five years for someone like her to stay the night and we're so unprepared that we're about to greet her in two pairs of infantile boxer shorts.

'Am I jealous?' he continues. 'Yes. Absolutely. I am utterly consumed by jealousy. But I do have it in me to squeeze out a little bit of pride too, you complete and utter bastard.'

'Jake. Ssh!' I tell him to turn the volume down, by flapping my hands and nodding towards my bedroom.

'No!' he exclaims.

'Yes.'

'She's still here in Davenport Road, in number fifty-seven, in our flat?'

'Yup.' I'm enjoying it now. Jake's mock disbelief is perfect. What a friend.

'What? She's really here? We're sitting here watching television and the star of the show is in bed down the landing?'

'Jake, keep your bloody voice down. She'll find us if you don't shut up and then we'll be in real trouble.'

'In one of our beds? OK, not mine. But still, it is one of the beds in our flat. That surely gives me some sort of claim to greatness too.'

'Ssh!'

'You're a genius,' he says, undeterred, holding his head in apparent amazement. 'But why the hell aren't you curled up with her?'

'Two very good reasons. Actually three. First, I wanted to come in and bask in my glory. Second, I tell you,' I'm showing off childishly now, 'she's got this amazing nose and the temptation to kiss it was getting too much.'

'Really?'

'Shut up. I haven't told you the third and most important reason.'

'Oh, what's that, then?'

'I wanted to ask you to hide behind the sofa when she comes in. Either that or go and clean your teeth and put some clothes on. She'll probably run away the moment she wakes up anyway, but I don't think you and your underwear are likely to persuade her to stay.'

'Don't be so silly. We both look lovely. Come on, let's watch her on the telly.'

So Jake turns it on and we do what we frequently do on a weekend morning. We watch ITV children's television, a cooking programme called *Starters For Starters*, only this time the star of the show is snoring into my pillow.

Sometimes Jake and I watch *Starters For Starters* twice in a weekend, on Saturday morning and then the Sunday-morning repeat. This is a bit desperate, I know, especially because neither of us has the slightest interest in culinary matters. The closest we have ever come to taking down a recipe was last year when I rang the relevant ITV broadcasters asking to buy a book of *Starters For Starters* recipes that I could give Jake for his birthday. They didn't have one, so I settled instead for a publicity photo of the presenter, Jenny Joffee, which served merely to fuel the fantasy.

You see, we cared not for cooking but for the cook. And all this may not be terribly cool for a pair of thirty-two-year-olds, but we never took it seriously: we just liked her because she was ours. We have long been proud of that, ever since one bleary-eyed Saturday morning when we stumbled across her in episode two of series one. Spotting her so early in her TV career, and in a slot in the TV schedules that few of our contemporaries were likely to notice, helped us claim her as our own: our discovery, our girl.

If you're single, it's good to have a girl to talk about, and somehow the joke never wore thin. This was helped by Jenny – we were on first-name terms pretty quickly – being such a star turn on the box: amusingly self-effacing, smiley, approachable, a girl-next-door hybrid of everything that is children's television. And we liked the way she ran her finger round her mixing bowl then licked it. Some trademark, that, for children's TV. There can't have been many other viewers who so appreciated her programme's erotic content.

It was the sixth episode of *Starters For Starters*, a lesson on how to make toffee, that sealed her place in our hearts. There was little special about the programme except its cute subtitle *Joffee Makes Toffee* – and that Joffee's toffee failed. On the Sunday, we watched again to see if the title had been changed to *Joffee Makes Treacle*. It hadn't.

Right now, though, I'm too fidgety to concentrate on the programme. Jenny is on television making lemon mousse, Jake is watching her and I am looking around at the room, taking in the pile of CDs and half-read newspapers on the floor, and yesterday morning's cereal bowls on the coffee table, which are stuck to an old copy of *GQ* next to last night's almost-finished bottle of wine and the Bengal Elephant ashtray – which clearly belongs to the curry-house up the road and is half full of cigarette butts. I had never thought of us as stereotypical bachelors before. Nor had it struck me that the antique, still-working Sodastream Jake's mother gave him, and the framed poster of the original Charlie's Angels on the wall above the fireplace were not as amusing and ironic as we had long supposed.

What would a TV star like to see in a bloke's flat? Maybe there should be a bit more chrome and some tall designer chairs beside a breakfast bar. Maybe I should move house quickly, so that when Jenny wakes up I can tell her that my real chrome residence is in Notting Hill. Then she would excuse our dilapidated sofa, which has foam spilling out of its cushions, and I could explain that I don't normally live with this half-dressed shambles who is still extracting pleasure from her children's TV programme.

Suddenly my mind is awakened by a terrible thought. 'Oh, hell, Jake,' I say, panicking.

'Yes.'

'That publicity photo of Jenny I gave you. Where is it?'

'You know where it is.'

'I seem to have forgotten.'

'It's on the pinboard in the kitchen, behind the Bengal Elephant takeaway leaflet and the postcard of those breasts Alex sent us from Thailand.'

I go into the kitchen and take down the photo of Jenny, which is exactly where Jake said it was. She looks much better in my bed than in the photo. I return to the sitting-room, with it in my dressing-gown pocket and wonder where to dispose of it.

Jenny is still on the TV, now whisking up her lemon

mousse. Jake still hasn't changed his clothes. I take one more look at our decaying failure of a penthouse and burst into action. I clear the cereal bowls, I take out last night's wine bottle and the ashtray. Then I start on the mountain of cascading CDs, and give up, crushed by the realisation that I am merely on the foothills. This is one for the industrial cleaners. The game is up. We must be better prepared next time we get a TV star in for the night.

I try to relax in front of the television, but none of the usual television conversation can apply as we sit in front of *Starters For Starters* because never during our one-series-long adulation had we considered that our dream might come true. Fantasies generally don't. In the seventies, I wanted to bed Charlie's Angels, but hadn't managed it with a single one, not the lovely Jaclyn Smith, not Farrah Fawcett or Kate Jackson, and not, at best, with all of them at the same time. During my teenage years, my desires started with Chris Evert and Debbie Harry, then exploded in all sorts of dangerous and inexplicable directions, taking in such extremes as Sharon Gless from *Cagney and Lacey*, Isabelle Adjani in *Subway*, either Krystle or Fallon from *Dynasty* – or even, since I couldn't separate them, the pair of them in a degenerate double act – and almost every gameshow hostess who ever draped herself over a jackpot car. I hadn't slept with any of them either. Nor had I considered what they would think of my flat if they woke up in it one morning.

So, now that we are in our early thirties with our

hearts set on Jenny Joffee, why should it be any different? Yesterday morning, like the aforementioned others, she was fantasy. Then yesterday afternoon she appeared at the same wedding as the pair of us. And now, Sunday morning, she is in my bed. She is fact.

I can hear someone coughing down the landing. I can hear the water running from the bathroom tap. It is 10.35 a.m. It seems that Jenny Joffee is awake.

2

Yesterday everything was simpler. I liked making jokes that my friends laughed at, I liked having good-hair days because I've always thought I had good hair, I liked it when London transport conspired to get me home from work in under forty minutes and I liked going to the pub with Jake and Alex every Sunday night. I liked Elvis Presley, Mary Chapin Carpenter, Coldplay, XFM, sushi, Boddington's, Tolkien, Armistead Maupin, *The West Wing*, and Channel 4 American sitcoms. None of this is unusual and neither has it changed. In the immediate aftermath of Jenny, though, it is fair to say that it all finds itself in a different perspective. Because yesterday I had no defining part of my identity – I wasn't Will Tennant 'Elvis man', or Tolkien Tennant – I was a conglomeration of the above, plus lots more. I was Will Tennant, lawyer, single man – surprisingly so, is the general consensus – good sense of humour, good hair. A good catch? Good Will Tennant.

And there I was, sitting between my friends Jake and Alex in the middle of a packed congregation in a grand church in the City of London. We were asking our usual pre-wedding questions: How do people reach the extraordinary decision to get married? How do they know? Will it last? Why is it always one of them and not one of us? On this occasion Peter and Di were taking what is accurately referred to as 'the plunge', but I could see their forerunners dotted around the church in happy-looking pairs. There are now so many of them that we are heavily outnumbered.

Suddenly we were stopped in our tracks. Peter, the nervous groom was looking at his watch when there was a clatter as the door at the back of the church opened. We all turned round, expecting to see Di, the bride. But instead a short pretty blonde was standing there, clearly not knowing where to sit and blushing in the knowledge that two hundred pairs of eyes were on her. I knew immediately that it was Jenny and I noticed simultaneously that my heart was beating rather fast.

The next few seconds, I swear, passed in slow motion. Some of the congregation giggled, some even tutted, although I think hardly any had a clue that a B-list television celebrity had just walked in. I didn't miss a thing: I noticed how those dollops of blonde hair poked out from under the brim of her purple velvet hat, which she was touching nervously to try and hide her face; I liked her shiny silver trouser suit; I registered the slight upturn in her top lip and that those large, innocent eyes seemed to emit a light of their own. I also took in every aspect of every one of her self-conscious footsteps from the door to her seat. The silence next to me suggested that Jake and Alex were following exactly the same train of thought. Only when Jenny sat down did life resume its previous pace accompanied by an outbreak of whispered exclamations and boyish giggling.

So that was me yesterday: single Will Tennant, good hair, getting a little left behind in the game of life and chuckling like a schoolboy because one of my fantasies had walked into the church. And now I am someone else. I am Will Tennant who sleeps with the stars. For the moment I quite like it.

'So what do we do now?' I asked Jake and Alex at the wedding reception.

'Stand around and admire her,' replied Jake. 'Consume lots of champagne and get sufficiently drunk to pluck up the courage to talk to her.'

'Not a bad idea,' I replied, holding out my champagne flute for a refill from one of the waitresses. The place was swarming with them – it was wonderful. We were in a large oak-panelled room with a high, ornate ceiling and there was a deep echo of small-talk. And Jenny Joffee.

'She looks great, doesn't she?' said Alex dreamily as, like spotty adolescents, we studied her across the room. 'Do you think she's normal? I mean, what do we talk to her about? Do you talk to a telly star about telly? I'm not sure where to start.'

'You're just going to plough on over there and dive in, are you?' I asked Alex.

'We can't just stand here and talk about it.'

'I can,' said Jake, who could.

'We can't just do nothing,' I acknowledged. 'This is a sort of Judgement Day.' Fantasising over this girl had been rather lovely and easy when we hadn't met her. But now, in the same room as her, an unforeseen pressure was exerting itself on us. It would have been too feeble to do nothing, but feeble was certainly easiest.

'Oh, come on!' said Jake. 'Don't tell me you two are going to go all macho. The thrill of the chase? For fuck's sake! Isn't it exciting enough just to be here with her?'

'No, it isn't,' I said. 'It's seize-the-day time. All that crap.'

And with that I remained rooted to the spot and watched enviously as Alex wove his way to Jenny.

Typical Alex: stocky, below average height and packaged with an attitude that seems to match his build. Few people have ever managed to knock *him* off course. He was like that when the three of us met at Nottingham University and he has remained so ever since. The only changes are that his Yorkshire accent has dulled a bit, his waistline has expanded and so has his wallet, which was notoriously empty when we were students. Like me, he is a lawyer – but I suspect a slightly better one.

He's good with girls too. When it comes to pursuing women, I'm not equipped with the reserves of bravery and machismo that are necessary to bound up and talk to a TV star who doesn't know me. I've always wanted to be one of the blokes in the adverts who spring bunches of flowers on strange girls whose perfume they happen to like, but it's just not me. No matter how good the perfume.

But if there's one real-life perfume-ad guy on this earth, it's Alex. One of the reasons I like Jake so much is because he is even less perfume-ad man than me, and I find that reassuring. We could be locked into this reception for a week and he still wouldn't talk to Jenny.

One of the reasons I like Alex so much is because he occupies the other extreme: he shows us that everything is possible. Alex is living proof that we can be preposterously smooth perfume-ad men after all.

And one of the reasons I like both of them is that neither of them is married. We became a triumvirate at college, long before the marriage thing became an issue, although anyone who meets us for the first time might think we had been forced together by Darwinian natural selection. While some people, like Pete and Di, get paired up, we are a little club, increasingly exposed and selected, it seems, to survive untainted by wedlock. In fact, we haven't even come close. While all these others are busy marrying each other, we didn't have – until now – so much as a girlfriend between us.

Jake has been single for pretty much all his life, and he's been pretty for all his single life too. There's no real reason for him to be so hopelessly and consistently unattached. It's a bit of a mystery. If any of us could be described as a looker – and I may be no expert on these things but you tend to get the message – then it's him. Alex is shortish, dark, with a sort of rugged appeal, and Jake could hardly look more different. He is the tallest of us – as usual, I'm somewhere in the middle – and looks slim and fit; he has this youthful fresh face and he does a good line in self-deprecation. Somehow, though, the ability to relax in the company of women has passed him by – a psychoanalyst would probably point here to his attractive, overbearing mother. The answer to the obvious question – is he gay? – is no. He's just too damn nice and when girls show an interest, which they do, he invariably fails to realise it.

Thanks to Jake setting the bar so low, I am a comparative Lothario. I read once that the average western male gets to sleep with nineteen different women in his lifetime. Well, if I try my hardest, I might get there. I just wonder if any of them will remain with me for life. Alex, on the other hand, probably shot past nineteen before he was nineteen; his dilemma is not that he can't find a girlfriend but that he can't stick with one.

It was no surprise, then, that it was Alex who was delighting Jenny with his hallmark anecdotes about trash culture from the seventies and eighties that we'd heard so often before. Alex lives so permanently in retro-culture that you almost feel sorry for him when he's confronted by something vaguely modern. Almost, but not quite: it's hard to feel genuine sympathy for the perfume-ad guys of this world. Especially when they're talking to Jenny Joffee. From where we were watching, Scott Tracy and *Thunderbird One*, Bodie and Doyle, Donny and Marie and the rest of his patter appeared to be doing quite a good job – until Jenny turned on her heels and marched off. Brilliant.

Alex was soon with us again. 'She called me a bastard,' he said, smiling in defeat.

'Couldn't have happened to a nicer guy,' said Jake.

'How on earth could she fail to succumb to your charms?'

'I don't know.'

'It looked from here as if you might be pulling it off.'

'I thought I was doing OK too. I seemed to hold it together, I was pretty brave, not too overawed.'

'What was she like?'

'Gorgeous. And she was pleasant to talk to, quite sharp, I suppose, funny, not all telly and intimidating.'

'Ooh, you're so brave,' jeered Jake. 'What on earth went wrong?'

'It would seem I made a horrendous mistake. I went and told her how much I liked her toffee recipe.'

The rest of the evening was all mine. The good news came in waves. First there was a further debriefing from Alex: Jenny was Di's second cousin, knew hardly anyone at the party and therefore 'might even talk to us again'. Second, and even better, I was sitting next to her at dinner. Third, the person on her other side at the table – Dylan Dale according to his place-tag – didn't turn up. I had her all to myself.

Best of all was the real-life version of Jenny sitting next to me. If anything, she looked more feminine than on television, possibly because her makeup made her face less round and innocent-looking, but more likely due to a bit of cleavage sitting up where the two sides of her silver jacket met. Funnily enough, we hadn't seen that on children's television.

She was, as Alex had said, easy company. She and I had a laugh at Alex's expense and I even persuaded her that the toffee mishap had a lighter side to it. This probably only went down well because she had drunk quite a lot of champagne, but it might also have been my inability to ply her with smooth perfume-ad-man lines. I was out there on my own, making conversation.

'So, do you fancy getting married some time?' I asked, picking up cunningly on the theme of the day.

'That's a bit forward, isn't it?' she replied, laughing. 'You've only known me a few minutes.'

'You must have some media star tucked away somewhere, waiting for you.'

'Not quite.'

'Don't tell me no one out there gets to see you licking the fairy-cake mix off your finger in real life.'

'There was. The empty seat next to me tells a tale, I'm afraid.'

'Dylan Dale?'

'Yup.'

'Well, you're better off without a bloke who has a name like that,' I said.

'You're probably right,' she replied, but looked sad.

'When did you split up?'

'Three days ago. We'd been together for over two years.'

'Do you want to tell me about it?' I said, changing my tone.

'Not unless you want to spend an otherwise enjoyable evening hearing how I was mesmerised by him and how stupidly long it took me to realise that he wasn't half what I thought he was. It was one of *those* – you know, quite heavy and everything.'

'What happened?'

'He was a fair bit older than me, and I was in awe of him. You know, experienced guy, quite big in TV, used to like spoiling me, taking me places. But he couldn't resist giving other girls in the business a helping hand too.'

'Ah. It's those older men, you see, they give us younger guys a bad name.'

'What?' she said.

'You'd be fine with someone who's only seven years older than you.'

'How old are you?'

'Thirty-two.'

'Oh, very good. How did you know I was twenty-five?'

'I saw *Starters For Starters* when you made your own birthday cake. It looked like a great party. Did Dylan get to go?'

'Listen, I'm supposed to be suffering post-relationship depression. You're not supposed to make fun of it,' she said, prodding my shoulder playfully.

'Oh, sorry. Are you OK, you know, really?'

'Sort of. I don't know yet. How long is it before you stop feeling all cluttered and heavy and crap inside, and always feeling like you might be about to cry?'

'Normally about three days.'

'Ridiculous! Haven't you ever had a major bust-up?'

'Yup. I went off my food for ten days.'

'Look, I'm being serious.'

'So am I.' I laughed. 'I went to see a doctor because I thought I had anorexia. He asked me if my emotional life had been turbulent and I clicked straight away.'

'Who was the girl?'

'Someone I met when I was at law school in Nottingham. Stephanie Honeyfield, Coventry City fan.'

'Why did you break up?'

'I found it a bit annoying that she was sleeping with one of my mates.'

'No! Did you really, really like her?'

'Yup. She supported Coventry City, was talented with horses – almost became a jockey, actually – she could beat me at table-tennis, which is very hard, and she had splendid breasts. They were really outstanding, a topic of conversation on their own.'

'Oh, fantastic.' Jenny was clearly well versed in the skills of sarcasm. 'And did that make her the perfect girl?'

'Nearly. She didn't have all the boxes ticked, though. She didn't laugh at my jokes, which is a heinous crime. She wasn't very good at quoting Shakespeare. And neither did she have her own TV show.'

'Very smooth.'

Me? Smooth? Wasn't that wonderful? And I continued to be quite smooth after dinner. Everyone else got up from their tables and started mingling but we just stayed seated, still chatting, apparently rapt. And then, when we hit our first real silence – me feeling awkward for the first time since the start of the meal and thinking that the spell had been broken – Jenny put her hand on my thigh, leaned over and told me it was about time I asked her to dance.

Fuelled by alcohol and a pang of self-confidence, I got to my rather unsteady feet. Jenny, I discovered, was even wobblier.

Somewhere in the room I knew that Jake and Alex would be looking on, as amazed as I was. Yet as Jenny flung herself around less and less self-consciously on the dance-floor, clearly not thinking much but certainly happy that the DJ had unearthed some of his old Madness LPs, I had one train of thought that I found impossible to derail. What do I do now? Can I make a pass at her? *Should* I make a pass at her? Is she *expecting* me to make a pass at her? Do people behave like this all the time in television or do they have the same body language as everyone else? Am I misreading this situation? Am I on the verge of looking foolish? What about this Dylan bloke? Is it too public to make a pass? How do I get her to slow down the dancing so I can attempt it?

Somewhere in the midst of it all, during a lovely trance-like dance number that I think was by Moby I found myself clutching the whirling television presenter in front of me. I don't know how this happened because the beat was so incessant that I couldn't find an appropriate pause, yet we came to a standstill in front of each other and I asked if I could kiss her.

No answer followed, not a yes, not a no, but instead

a lunge as Jenny locked her mouth on mine. Then, just when I thought everything was going brilliantly, she pulled back a bit, looked into my eyes and said, 'You're going to regret this.'

3

'Morning, boys.' It is Jenny.

What a vision. She's standing in the sitting-room doorway and all she seems to be wearing is my white shirt from last night, the tails of which come half-way down her thighs. I presume she has something on underneath, but I can only presume. Jake, I know, will want to talk about this later. I also know that he will be thanking me for years to come for presenting him with this heavenly half-naked telly vision.

'Hi,' I reply, in a voice that, I think, sounds fairly relaxed. I plunge my hand into my dressing-gown pocket and feel the photograph there. A slight flush is coming over my face. I try to push the photo down into the pocket so that she will not notice it, but it is already as deep as it will go. I fold it in half, hopefully without her noticing. If she sees me fiddling around in my pocket like this, with her standing half naked in front of me, she'll be straight out of the front door.

'Settle down and watch television with us,' says Jake, in an annoyingly provocative way. 'Look who it is!' he adds, pointing at the screen.

'Um, we were just checking that it really is you,' I explain weakly. God, how on earth can I have said that?

'Ah,' she replies, pulling down the shirt tails and standing on one foot. 'I didn't believe you when you said you watched it. Can you turn it over?'

'You mean watch it upside-down?' says Jake, and laughs at his own joke.

'Oh, no,' groans Jenny. 'Not the lemon mousse. It's terrible.'

'But look!' says Jake. 'There you are, taking one you prepared earlier out of the fridge. It's all fluffy and beautiful. Fantastic.'

'Thanks,' says Jenny, then turns to me. 'Is he always like this?'

'No. You've got him on a good day. Do you want a coffee?'

'Er, no thanks. But I wouldn't mind a shower. I'm afraid I can't get it to work.'

'There's a good reason for that,' I explain awkwardly. 'It doesn't. We're thinking of getting it mended.'

'Oh, are we? After two years? That's good news,' says Jake, funnier than ever.

This isn't going well, is it? There's a chilly awkwardness in the air. What I'd like is for Jenny to grab me by the hand and drag me back into bed, but that, it seems now, is even less likely than the shower coming back to life. At the very least I should be putting my arm round her, being a bit more familiar, making some sort of acknowledgement that only a few hours ago we were sharing something rather intimate, but I can't manage it. We are standing in my sitting-room as if we barely know each other.

'Jenny, what about another glass of wine?' says Jake.

'Wine? You must be mad, I feel terrible enough as it is.' She winces. 'I hope I wasn't too pissed last night. I wasn't, was I?' Which seems to suggest that her previous state of inebriation allows her to disown everything. Does it follow that if she had been half sober, she would never have done it? We'll deal with that later.

'No, you behaved impeccably,' I reply, relieved that I had found something half cool to say. That was quite cool, wasn't it?

'Yeah, I didn't do too badly,' says Jenny, looking me in the eye with a warm reassuring smile. That has to be good news.

But then she calls for a taxi and has a quick bath while she's waiting for it. Meanwhile, I stand around in my dressing-gown and teddy-bear boxers wondering what happens next. What do people in Television Land do when they have just slept together? Do they just move on because they have such wild and varied sex lives? Or maybe they just want to settle down too. It is only when she's fully dressed, heading for the door and out of my life, that I put a hand on her shoulder in an effort to find out. 'Jenny, you can't just vanish like this,' I say, trying to sound cool but heartbroken.

'Why not?' she asks, turning to face me.

'Because I don't want you to.'

'What would you rather I did instead?'

'Stay for lunch.'

'Sorry, I can't. I've actually got to go. And the inside of your fridge doesn't look very inviting.' She laughs. I must remember to keep it better stocked for the next media star who pops in for the night.

'Well you could give me your number, then.'

'I could. I'm not sure I should, though.'

'Even after a night with me? Very strange.'

'Yes. Even after a night with you.' And although we're both joking we're suddenly looking each other in the eye, with Jenny clearly not wanting to produce her number and sticking to her guns, me waiting for her to acquiesce, and the pair of us understanding the impasse.

'Look,' she says apologetically, 'I don't know why you'd want to ring me anyway.'

'Well . . . we don't know each other particularly well, but what little we do know, we quite like. At least, that's my impression. That, for me, is reason enough for wanting to ring you up.'

'I've only been single for four days. It would be madness. I'm not supposed to be giving out my number yet. I'm still all over the place. I'm supposed to be on a boyfriend-detox diet. I wouldn't be good for you. I'm sorry. Do you understand?'

'How do you know what would be good for me? I might like emotionally distraught television presenters.'

'I told you last night you'd regret it.'

'Look at it another way. Maybe I'd be good for you.'

'Oh, stop it,' she says, almost laughing. 'Can't you let me go?' And then she gives me a look that suggests she doesn't want me just to let her go. I might be misreading the situation, but that is how it appears.

'Look, how about this,' I say, with my last roll of the dice. 'Why don't you give me your work number and when I call you – say, on Tuesday – you'll have had two days to think about it?'

'Hmm.'

'Come on. That way it's in your hands. You can tell me on the phone that you don't want to see me. Or you could get someone else in the office to break the gruesome news. And you can even write down the wrong number if you want.'

'OK. OK. I'll give you my number.'

And with that she disappears. I am left treasuring the waft of an air-kiss in the vicinity of my left ear and clutching a piece of paper bearing a set of digits that masquerades as the phone number of the television studios where the girl I've just slept with works.

I ring the number and click into a recorded message: 'Hello, you have come through to Top Table Television . . .'

'Brilliant,' says Jake, in response to the successful telephone call.

'It's great, isn't it?'

Jake is lying on the sofa and I am bouncing up and down on it with one foot on either side of him. This is in celebration of my extraordinary achievement, and is also my grown-up way of repaying him for behaving like an idiot in front of Jenny.

'So we're going to see her again, then?' he asks.

'I don't know.' I am still bouncing up and down.

'Why not?'

'She says she needs to settle a bit.'

'Well, she could settle here with us and the paparazzi could camp on our doorstep, drink coffee from the coffee shop up the road, go through our bins and expose you for using too much hair gel. It all works rather well, doesn't it?'

'Hmm. I don't know.'

'You're not sure about this, are you? Even with the bouncing,' says Jake, his tone changing as the penny drops. His schoolboy joviality is replaced with something unusually (for him) serious. Accordingly, I stop bouncing.

'Well, you know.'

'Yes, I know.'

'But I haven't done too badly so far, have I?' I say gleefully to Alex and Jake. We are in the Dolphin, our regular Sunday-night pub, and we are still discussing Jenny. The chairs are nice and old and leathery, the décor is nice and old and leathery, and we are settled in a corner, a pint of bitter in front of each of us. I have to say that I like having my love life as the non-stop centre of attention. Particularly when it's Jenny we're talking about.

'No, you're a legend,' says Alex. 'Here, I've got something for you as a token of my admiration.' Grinning, he pulls out a plastic shopping-bag from beside his chair and puts it in front of me. I open it to find a wooden photo frame containing a black-and-white picture of

Jenny. It has been cut out of a newspaper – rather untidily.

'Thanks, mate, you're so thoughtful.'

'Isn't she lovely? Sorry it's a bit messy,' he explains, 'but it was in the *Mail on Sunday* and she had a bloke's arm round her waist. I thought I'd better chop that out.'

'A bloke with his arm round my bird?'

'Yup. It was someone called Dylan Dale. But the story was all about how they'd just split up. That's good, isn't it?'

It is indeed. I'd always thought their relationship was doomed.

'What time did she leave this morning?' asks Alex.

'Just before midday.'

'Err, excuse me, artistic licence . . .' interjects Jake.

'OK. Seventeen minutes past eleven.'

'Even without the artistic licence,' says Alex, acting astonishment, 'that's still quite a convincing stay. Why did she hang around so long?'

'She's using him to get to me,' says Jake.

'Very likely. But do you *like* her, Will?'

'I think I might.'

'Well, you have to see her again.'

And here we are, back at square one, where the conversation in the pub had started, where it had started the moment Jenny closed the door behind her. Do I pursue Jenny or cash in my chips now?

'I don't understand why it's even a question,' says Alex.

'That's because you're an unsympathetic, stunted, shamelessly successful shagger and completely missing the point,' interjects Jake. 'Will could quit now and he's ahead for ever. Will, this is a dream come true. You are the guy who slept with Jenny Joffee and no one can take that away from you. Why toy with it? I'd love to be you right now. You've achieved the unachievable, you've seen the glory, you've climbed Mount Olympus. But you can only go downhill from there. How many times do you think you can win the jackpot?'

'Are you saying he should just forget her?' asks Alex, almost aggressively.

'No, I hope he doesn't, not least because I quite like seeing her half naked in the flat in the morning and, you never know, maybe she's got a nice film-star friend who would like to settle down and go to movie premières in Leicester Square with me. But I can understand why there's some dilemma.'

'Thank you, Jake,' I say.

'Will?' Alex looks incredulous.

'Look, Alex, it's dead easy for a smooth bastard like you to say, "Go for it, nothing ventured nothing gained, you only get one shot at life." All that stuff. But put yourself in my shoes and it doesn't look that simple. It requires someone like Jake with a lifetime's knowledge and experience of being single to appreciate how much self-esteem I've just banked and that I risk freefalling straight into the red by deciding to "go for it" because "you only get one shot at life". I mean, the chances of me pulling this off are fucking minimal.'

'You're joking.' Alex is unmoved by my argument.

'Not entirely.'

'But that's no reason for just forgetting about her.'

'No, it's a small part of it.'

'What's the rest?'

'OK, Alex,' I say, leaning forward in my seat. 'To be quite frank, I suppose it's just that I'm at a stage where I'd quite like a relationship to work. I wouldn't mind having what Pete and Di have got and everyone else seems to have. So maybe it isn't that clever to go out with a TV star who is twenty-five, whose life I know fuck-all about, who says she doesn't want a relationship and who, when it comes down to it, would rather go out with a rock star than a solicitor. I guess what I'm saying is that while I'm not keen to have my hopes built up only to crash round my ankles, the stakes seem a bit higher here. I mean, this is Jenny bloody Joffee. This could really, really hurt.'

'Jesus Christ, Will, I don't believe it. From you, of all people,' says Alex, his eyes wide. 'You know what you're saying? You're going to be the next to drop. At least, it sounds dangerously as if you want to be.'

And with that comment, all the seriousness of my confession is gone. We refer to marriage as 'dropping', as if those who get married are shot down in battle, captured by the enemy, or in some way defeated – as if there are legions of would-be wives out there gunning down us lads as we fly past in our fighter planes. It romanticises us, the ones left standing, as if we, the survivors of this great battle, are embracing some noble cause, heroes continuing the fight. We would never say this to each other, it sounds too ridiculous, but it is curiously comforting to deal in such imagery.

But we know we're kidding ourselves. Peter's marriage came as a bit of a body-blow. It drives home the message that while our contemporaries are embracing change, Jake, Alex and I are standing still, immobile, rooted to the ground. Alex appears untroubled by this. He enjoys his life as a rogue and, so he says, has no desire to change it by following where everyone else seems to be going. Jake, at the other extreme, is so poor with women that the marriage debate doesn't impinge on him.

I am somewhere in the middle and a little perplexed. I've often wondered why anyone had to drop out of the sky in the first place. Were we not all quite happy a few years back, buzzing around above the clouds without a care in the world?

And now that everyone seems to be getting shot down, I wonder if the problem is that I'm flying my little plane out of range. Yet if that is so, which direction should I be going in to put it right? And if I head for Jenny, is anything likely to change? The least I can do is try it.

'So, what are you going to do, lover-boy?' asks Alex. He then finishes his pint and slams down the glass on the table provocatively.

'I don't know, but I'll come up with something.'

Somewhere deep inside, however, I am aware that a less impressive impulse is involved. It is unrelated to fighter pilots being shot out of the sky: a part of me can't resist

Jenny. And I'm not talking about an irresistible urge to see her or sleep with her again, I'm talking about my vanity. I need to know if she liked me or if I was a drunken mistake.

And, yes, there's an identity crisis going on here. I like being the guy who slept with a TV star, it makes me feel good, but I'm not sure if that's *me*. I'd love Jenny to confirm that it is. I'd love her to say I was a better lover than anyone in TV. Then I could play the Billy Joel role when he met Christie Brinkley and I could release a number-one single about being a back-street boy who's gone way above his station and made it with an uptown girl.

But there are three facts to consider here: first, it wouldn't be fair to inflict another song like 'Uptown Girl' on the world; second, Billy Joel had a bit of a lead on me when he met Christie Brinkley – he was a world-famous pop-star; and third, he split up with her anyway. Am I committing romantic suicide here? Am I looking to have Jenny confirm that I am not Billy Joel, not even in the short run, but just the same old Will Tennant after all?

4

Harvey Goode probably never stopped to think about us fighter-pilots up there in the sky. In fact, Harvey Goode has never shown much sign of stopping to think about anyone. That's probably why he's so successful: act first, think later sometimes – maybe on a good day – and, along the way, set up one of the largest telecommunications companies in the country.

I can't work out for the life of me how he built up so much wealth. I don't understand how Intertalk Ltd, his company, works. All I understand about Harvey is that the losers in his life are the women he marries. I know this because I am his divorce lawyer, or his 'matrimonial finance solicitor', which is the term we divorce lawyers use. I have been through one divorce with him and I'm about to have the dubious privilege of doing it again.

The first Mrs Goode – Emma, mid-thirties, jet-black hair, very good figure but could have done with a brace on her teeth – was married to another man when she met Harvey. If nothing else, Harvey has a sharp business brain: on the eve of the day that mobile phones achieved global domination, he was launching his own company selling mobile-phone accessories. Emma's husband was his main investor. Harvey was in his early forties, an entrepreneur fast-tracking his way to riches, exciting, jet-set, lightly tanned and pleased with himself. Even though Emma had won a scholarship to an Ivy League university in the States (I always forget which), she was still stupid enough to jump ship and join him. Once she was on board, he sold the phone business for twenty-two million pounds, washed his hands of her ex-husband and, before most people had heard of the Internet, he was building Intertalk, one of the earliest Internet empires. All very good, except one of the reasons why Harvey so enjoyed Dotcom Land was that Emma's younger half-sister was a twentysomething former catwalk model who had an idea for a retail website and needed backing.

Harvey couldn't have been more forthcoming: he gave her the money and much more, and he did so for many months. These many months ended, of course, when Emma rumbled them. It was simple: she rang her sister's flat for a chat and Harvey answered the phone. Emma walked out on Harvey, Harvey walked out on the sister and pulled his money out of her business. The business folded and so did the sister, ending up in a clinic with depression and an addiction to pain-killers.

Somehow the damage he inflicted on Emma was infinitely worse because just as this exploded in their faces Emma declared she was pregnant with his second child. She moved back in with him, convincing herself that she and Harvey could make their marriage work. Harvey, however, took a different line and convinced her instead that their marriage couldn't stand the strain of a second child and that, if they were to have any hope as a couple, she should have an abortion. This she did. Two months later, Harvey began divorce proceedings.

Harvey shared the whole story with me over a couple of meetings. He liked to portray himself as the victim, but his pain was far more evident when he discovered that the cost of his divorce would be – in order of importance – his house in Gloucestershire, an £800,000 lump-sum payment, £100,000 a year to Emma as maintenance for life, and his two-year-old daughter Lilly.

Here, on my desk, is the evidence that we are about to go through the whole miserable adventure again. Harvey needs to see me, the letter says, and his secretary will be calling to arrange a meeting.

With Harvey back on board, I currently have thirty-eight divorces on the go. Some are destructive, all are painful. My rather well-paid professional life is surrounded by the relics of failed relationships, a testament to how hopeless man and woman are at co-existing. It's a living that feeds off the pain and shattered dreams of others. At least, that's how Alex, who works for Drysdale, Lewis, Sage, puts it. He works in commercial law and informs me regularly that that's far more sexy.

My take on the business is this: I'm a professional at studying relationships from first hand, I'm paid to watch people and understand why they're so fallible and where they go wrong. Like a sponge, I soak up the evidence of human nature, sifting through it and learning from it. Yes, I find it fascinating. Yet it seems odd that, as a professor of human relationships, I'm not a little better at constructing my own. This is the observation that Sam, my feisty PA, makes with characteristic regularity. And she's right.

My life at Mellstrom Roberts, a slightly larger firm than Drysdale, Lewis, Sage (Alex would rather that this were not the case), has brought other, more positive spin-offs. I get a car, a pension, a large office to myself that overlooks the green quad of New Square at Lincoln's Inn, and the compelling Sam.

Sam is three years older than me, has three children and sometimes seems to be claiming me as a fourth. She travels into Lincoln's Inn every day from Stansted with the apparent sole intention of mothering me; the paperwork is an added hindrance, as far as she is concerned. She won't rest until she has seen me as happily married and surrounded by progeny as she is.

'Can you come in, please, Sam?' I say, having buzzed through to where she sits with four other girls on the other side of my office wall.

'Certainly, sir,' she replies sarcastically. 'Do I need to bring my pad for dictation?'

'No. I've written some poetry I want to read to you.'

'Oh, Will, I've already got a husband, remember?'

'It's not for you. It's for my new girlfriend.'

Within seconds Sam is in my office. She is wearing an orange shirt with a purple skirt, one of her trademark almost-hip colour combinations, and wiping her nose with a tissue. She is a tiny force of light with a permanent cold, a fluctuating number of dependants – depending on whether you count her husband, Keith, and me – and an unerringly positive attitude.

'Tell me, tell me, tell me,' she says.

I gesture at the framed, untidily cut picture, which is sitting on my desk.

'Not Jenny!' she exclaims. (She knows all about Jenny and me, at least she did when Jenny and me were still fiction.) 'Not Jenny!' she repeats, then demands the whole story. Her face flickers with excitement as I relay it to her.

'So what do you think?' I ask, when she has heard the whole tale.

'I'm jealous.'

'Sorry, sweetie, all those mouths to feed, no time for me.'

'I know, I'm all washed-up and dragged down by multiple motherhood. But, Will, this sounds brilliant.'

'Do you think I'm wasting my time? Will she walk all over me emotionally and leave me a crumpled, broken waste of humanity?'

'You're serious, aren't you?'

'Yup.'

'Blimey.'

'Yup!'

'Well, I think you've got to find out – but try to be a little bit fairer on yourself. I know that Jenny Joffee's a good catch but, believe it or not, so are you.'

'Pardon?'

'Well, you've got nice hair.'

'Oh, well done me. Is that all?'

'Stop it. All I'll say is this. The girl who ends up with you will be rather lucky. So there.'

'How kind.'

'So what are you going to do?'

'With your approval, I'll start by sending her a poem I wrote on the tube this morning.' I explain the setting: my flat, Sunday morning, *Starters For Starters* on TV, Jenny making lemon mousse, then Jenny leaving. 'It's called: "Naff mousse poem", by Will Tennant:

> 'Jenny, Jenny on the loose
> After making lemon mousse.
> Lovely, lovely lemon moussey
> Splendid yellow light and juicy.
> You know the mousse was underrated.
> Want to meet to celebrate it?!!!'

'Work of genius!' says Sam ironically, clapping her hands.

'I know. And they said romance was dead, eh!'

'No.'

'Should I send it, then?'

'You certainly should.'

5

Wednesday, 5.50 p.m., at least twenty-four hours post-dispatch of the poem. No response from Jenny. It's ridiculous to be anxious so soon, I know that, but it creeps up on me like a tide that never turns. And it doesn't help that Sam bounces into my office every five minutes to ask if there's any news.

Already I have in place the mental framework necessary to deal with rejection. One night with a famous person is better than no nights at all – at least, that's what I'm telling myself. In terms of nights with famous people, I am one–nil up on Alex and Jake. And I'll always be able to tell Jake proudly that the girl on the box has a small mole under her left nipple and that I have kissed it.

Back in my teens, when I was still cool and undamaged by women and I was known for my great hair rather than my great inability to find someone with whom to share a relationship, I assumed that this twitchy, anxious, on-tenterhooks behaviour was peculiar to womankind. I can't explain why I believed that but I did. I thought girls were girly and boys were not. I guess I hadn't been a boy for long enough to know otherwise. How different the world looks today.

Outside, shafts of late-afternoon spring sunshine are

still lighting up a corner of the grass on the quad below my office window, yet dark reality sits squarely in front of me. I am forced to smile and accommodate it. It is the one and only (praise the Lord: we couldn't handle two) not-seen-him-for-four-years Harvey Goode.

I doubt that Harvey has ever experienced the diverse thrills and pain of courtship to which I have been subject today. In fact, I am tempted to ask him how he strolled so easily into two marriages. What infuriates me, though, is that relationships – talking after lights out, cosy telly together, all the nice stuff – can fall twice to someone like Harvey when there are such deserving recipients as Jake, Alex and me wondering where to find it.

But that is not what Harvey has come here today to talk about. We are sitting opposite each other in high-backed chairs at a mahogany table on one side of my impressive office (hastily tidied for his visit), discussing his proposals for a second divorce as if it were just another business transaction.

'I know I'm going to take quite a hit in the wallet again, Will,' he says, a vein on the left side of his forehead bulging. 'But I won't take as big a hit as before. I'm telling you, I refuse to. You've got to lessen the blow. I know you will.'

So Harvey doesn't want to give any of his cash to his soon-to-be-ex-wife. Well, there's a surprise. I'd forgotten about his pulsating vein, but otherwise he's exactly as I remember him. Four years and another wife appear to have left barely a mark. Today, he's wearing a Savile

Row suit, smart but not trendy, those new oblong designer glasses with no metal rim around the lenses, and his all-important all-year tan. He is forty-eight but could still pass for mid-thirties, charming, dark and, most people say, good-looking. 'A touch of Hollywood sophisticate', I've heard, and even 'Gregory Peck', but I think the way his heavy eyebrows meet above his nose makes him look ludicrous. And, yes, the eyebrows are as joined up as they ever were.

Somewhere, hidden in the attic of one of the two houses he still owns, there must be a portrait of Harvey in which his hair is grey and thinning and his face is aged and diseased because that, I'm afraid, is the state of his soul. Just to make this clear – in case anyone might suspect that I could be remotely jealous of this wealthy, good-looking, twice-married man – I'll explain, in legal terms, just how bad Harvey is. Contrary to popular opinion, the law declares that adultery is largely irrelevant when settling the finances of a divorce. It doesn't matter. It's everywhere in the divorce courts and has little or no effect on the outcome. There is, however, the rare exception to the rule, bracketed 'exceptional circumstances', where the behaviour of one of the parties has been so outrageous that it is impossible to disregard. I have never handled a divorce in which this rule was invoked – and I'm well over the 250-mark now. But with Harvey's last divorce I came close to it.

It wasn't just his sister-in-law who cluttered up his first marriage, as I discovered during the proceedings

when Emma named his other women – none of whom
he had told me about. It wasn't either that he was
a greedy adulterer who couldn't help but follow his
penis into trouble – I do business with those every
week. What set his case apart from the rest was the
intricacies of deceit he employed to keep the truth away
from the homestead. He even constructed a long-term
alibi around weekend golf trips. He'd leave home and
return with his clubs in the car, yet he couldn't play
golf. Never had. And Emma didn't know. She even
bought into the conspiracy by telling people he had a
handicap.

With infidelity as hopeless as his, you cannot help but
wonder why we assume man to be monogamous. Or
why we shouldn't forget about marriage. Yet Harvey
went back for more.

'I'm sorry to see you back again so soon, Harvey,' I
say – and I mean it: I'd rather not have to see him at
all. The only consolation is the whopping great fee I'll
get to charge him.

'Yes, well, it seems I've been let down once again
by a wife.' He sighs, one hand propping up his head,
the other gesticulating in the air, as if to indicate how
hopeless wives tend to be.

'You don't seem to be doing too well with them,
do you?'

'No. And that's definitely it for me. No more.'

'I'm sure that's what you said last time, isn't it?'
I'm overstepping the mark here, I know, but I can't
resist it.

'How kind of you to remind me. Now, how do I kick this whole divorce thing off?'

'Well, the standard route, of course, is for me to consult with your wife's lawyer to check that she isn't going to contest the divorce.'

'Not contest it? She doesn't even know about it yet.'

'Ah. You hadn't made that clear.'

'I'm making it clear now.' Without a trace of remorse.

'You mean, you haven't even discussed it with her?'

'No.'

'What exactly is the state of play at home?'

'She's still under the impression that our marriage is for ever.'

'So Lauren – you did say her name was Lauren, didn't you?'

'Yes.'

'So Lauren will be quite shocked by this?'

'I'd have thought so.'

And thus we continue. It's a game I remember from last time: Harvey will play the role of wounded husband, the gap between appearance and reality will be vast, and gradually I will discover the real reasons behind his marriage failure, though I suspect I know them already. The breakdown in a marriage, I have come to learn, is almost always the fault of two people rather than one, even though neither party ever believes it. Harvey will be, once again, the exception to the rule.

'I'll have to write to your wife,' I explain. 'It's called a "letter before action".'

'Good. When will she receive it?'

'I'll write it tomorrow so she'll get it on Friday. That'll give you a chance to warn her beforehand.'

'Oh, I don't think there'll be any need for that. I'll be out of the country.'

'As you like, Harvey.' You bastard. 'Shall we leave it there, then?' I shuffle my chair backwards as if to stand up.

'No. I want to talk about the financial settlement.'

'OK. What about it?'

'I'm not going to be taken to the bloody cleaners again.' Harvey has gone all intense now: the forehead vein is really throbbing. 'This is your job, Will. I'm not paying her. Got that?'

'Well, there's no child involved this time – I think I'm right in saying that?'

'Yes.'

'That might make it considerably lighter for you.'

'Good. But I don't want to give her anything like the amount of money I'm still giving Emma. Different league altogether.'

'Of course I'll do my best for you.' I pause to let him relax a little. 'But can you tell me a bit about Mrs Goode, so I've got something to go on?'

'Sure. She's thirty-five, American, been in England for some time.'

'And what does she do? What's her financial situation?'

'She used to earn pretty well in a head-hunting company – smart little cookie – but she resigned when we got married.'

'And hasn't worked since?'

'Still does the occasional day with me, but she set up recently on her own.'

'Oh. And what is it that she did, and occasionally still does, for you?'

'Hardly anything.'

'Right. That should do it for now.' I can see that Harvey's attention is already distracted.

'Who's that girl?' he asks, pointing at my *Mail on Sunday* portrait of Jenny.

'Just some minor TV celebrity.'

'I'm sure I know her.'

'Oh, right.' That's all I need. 'Her name's Jenny Joffee, she's the presenter of *Starters For Starters*, a kids' cooking programme.'

'That's right. My daughter watches her on Saturday mornings. What on earth's she doing on your desk?'

'Ah.' I feel like a schoolboy caught with a crush – which is, maybe, exactly what I am. 'She's, er, sort of my girlfriend.'

'What? The sort whose picture you have to rip out of the newspaper?' What can you say to that? Because, when you put it like that, it *is* pretty pathetic, isn't it? 'You clever bastard,' continues Harvey, changing tack with a welcome-to-the-shagging-club wink. Then he stands up, pats my shoulder approvingly and marches out of my office, briefcase in hand, thanking me for the meeting and telling me again that I'm a clever bastard.

I know he's right. If Jenny did become a sort of girl-friend rather than just a one-night stand who'd received a lemon-mousse poem I'd written on the tube, I certainly would be a clever bastard. But it was the surprise in his voice that I am left to ponder. Surprise that I should have telly-star Jenny as a sort-of girlfriend, or that I had a sort-of girlfriend at all? I hope it wasn't the latter.

No sooner has Harvey gone than Sam is through the door. Simon, my head of department, has demanded to see me as soon as the meeting was over. This is interesting, if only because it's unusual.

Simon Henderson is a reasonable, unflappable, well-measured boss, the sort who hardly ever feels the need to call you to his office. He is a bit of a fusty public-school old boy: his hair still bears the traditional side-parting that, presumably, it acquired when his mother first brushed it, and his suits are conventional, slightly too stripy, not as understatedly fashionable as mine – and not with designer labels like Harvey's.

I find him on the phone in his office and he nods me to a seat in front of him. When he puts down the receiver, he seems pleased to see me. 'Will, old boy, how did it go?'

'How did what go?'

'The meeting with Harvey Goode, of course.' I don't understand the 'of course': he never usually asks about run-of-the-mill meetings.

'Fine. You know – er – yes, fine.'

'Good. Well, I might be pointing out the obvious but I just want to stress how important Harvey's business is. It's more important this time than last for everyone. He was a minor client last time and you were a junior working on the brief. Now almost all the company work for Intertalk is done by the eggheads in the Mellstrom Roberts commercial division and they earn a lot more money for this firm than we do. And you're being promoted to the big league because Harvey requested that you lead his case. The pressure's on you. Basically, Harvey is important to you, Will, and he's fucking important to us. What I'm saying is, don't fuck up this divorce.'

'Oh, right, thanks for the tip. I was hoping not to anyway.'

Simon smiles at my cheek. 'I know. It's just that he's a client we're pretty sensitive about. We've got to lick his arse. I thought it was only fair to tell you.'

'Thanks very much, Simon. I get all the great jobs.'

'Well, I'm not supposed to tell you this, but there's quite a lot in it for you too.'

'What do you mean?'

'I mean that you're highly rated here and, even though you're pretty young for it, you're on the verge of being made a salaried partner.'

'Blimey.'

'Blimey exactly. Remind me how old you are.'

'Thirty-two.'

'Hmm. Without checking I'd say that'd be one of the youngest salaried partners we've ever had. Keep Harvey happy and I'd be surprised if you don't make it.'

A salaried partner. Fantastic. The corridors of a solicitors' office aren't the place for leaps of joy, but mentally I am bouncing. On my return, Sam's bouncing too.

'Will, Will, look, look, look. A strange-looking package has just arrived by special delivery. Open it, open it, open it.'

A largish square parcel is sitting on my desk with my name scrawled on it in thick black pen with the words 'Important: Take Care, Please Keep This Way Up'. I don't recognise the writing.

I rip into the sellotape, string and brown paper, ensuring simultaneously not to tip the package. Inside there is a plastic Tupperware box and my heartbeat quickens as I see what has been written, in the same thick black pen, on top: 'Dear Poet, don't be a bitter lemon. Meet me outside London Zoo. Main gate, 3 p.m., Sunday.' There is no name, but the signature is inside the box: a bowl of lemon mousse.

6

What I was supposed to do if I couldn't make Sunday three p.m. at London Zoo, I've no idea, but if Jenny wants to make the rules I can just about cope. Maybe one day we could find a middle ground, neutral territory, go for a long weekend to Switzerland, something like that. But, for now, anywhere on her terms is fine and Sunday can't come fast enough. My imagination has been constantly assailed by endless dress rehearsals – first lines, cool things to do at the Zoo, new hair gel to try, all teenage, first-date stuff but I can't help it.

Now Sunday has arrived and I have an engagement with Alex and Jake to get through first. Alex wants us to see a flat he's thinking of buying on a street off Kensington High Street – or, to put it more accurately, he wants us to see the estate agent who is showing him round the place for the third time. She is called Kirsty and works for Savills and, Alex announces before we get to the 'spacious two-bedroom flat with its special show-piece mezzanine-floor lounge', she has already slept with him. Not, however, in the showpiece mezzanine lounge: that wouldn't have been professional, would it?

Little does poor Kirsty know that Alex is more inter-ested in the estate agents than their wares. And we're not just talking about Kirsty here. After her, Alex will view properties with girls from Chestertons, Barnard Marcus and Faron Sutaria. He gave up with Foxtons, he said, scrupulous to the last, because they always sent men.

This behaviour may not be politically correct but neither, in Alex's case, is it unusual. He once went to the dentist three times in a month because he fancied the hygienist, and only gave up on her when they had a row over his flossing technique. Now he is thoroughly excited.

'What do you think, guys?' he asks us, arms stretched wide, as if to indicate that he wants our opinion on the flat when everyone apart from Kirsty knows it's her we're talking about. 'Lovely or what?'

'Fantastic,' says Jake. 'Certainly too nice for you.'

'Yes,' I chime in, 'way out of your league, mate.'

Kirsty doesn't know what to make of the conversation. She flushes, looks down at her prospectus and announces that the grand tour of the flat is about to start. She is game for a laugh, and seems pretty good at coping with us. We certainly make an unlikely trio: Jake has a hole in his jeans and a rip in the sleeve of his sports jacket; I'm dressed for a date at the Zoo, and Alex is so relaxed that you'd think being shown round a flat by an estate agent he's just slept with is something that happens to him every day. I can see why he would want to bed her. But clearly she is self-conscious about the situation, which is hardly surprising. I wonder if Alex has noticed.

We finish our tour in the special lounge, which, of

course, isn't quite as showpiece as billed. 'Do you think it suits him, then?' she asks me and Jake, attempting to inject some enthusiasm into her sales pitch.

'Is it freehold or leasehold?' asks Jake, pretending to be serious.

'Ninety-three-year lease,' she replies.

'Very good question, Jake,' says Alex.

'Is it? I'm not sure what it means, but I suspect it's one of the things my mother would want me to ask about if I were to do anything as sensible as buy a flat.'

'And the location,' says Alex.

'Location, location, location,' chirps Kirsty. 'That's what we say.'

'Why do you say it three times?' says Jake, drily.

'They've not got very good memories,' says Alex, laughing. Kirsty digs him in the ribs with her elbow. They almost look sweet together.

'Do you think ninety-three years is enough for you, Alex?' I ask him, putting him on the spot. 'You never normally hang around for much longer than a couple of weeks.'

'Ooh. That's a bit harsh, mate.'

'I'd be happy to get hold of anyone, to be honest, on a freehold, a lease or anything,' says Jake, rescuing him somewhat.

'Pardon?' says Kirsty.

'Honestly.'

'Don't worry,' says Alex, protectively, to Kirsty. 'It's just banter. Bit of a funny guy, our Jake.'

'And devilishly good-looking, Kirsty – I don't know

if you've noticed,' chips in Jake. 'Come on, you must have a horde of nice single friends who'd like to meet me! I can promise them a ninety-three-year leasehold if that would make them feel more secure.'

'Oh, God, you're not all single, are you?' asks Kirsty.

'We're not sure about the answer to that at the moment, are we, Will?' says Jake. And I'm forced to explain that I've got an exciting first date in just under an hour at London Zoo.

'And he's been writing her poetry,' says Alex.

'If you can call it that,' says Jake. He and Alex laugh rather too long for my liking.

'I thought you said the poem was amusing.' I'm trying not to let my voice betray too much concern.

'It is, Will,' says Alex, 'in an unambitious sort of way.'

'If you like lemon mousse,' says Jake. More laughter from the pair of them. I know I'm not exactly Keats, and I never expected my ode to stand next to any Grecian urns in a future A-level syllabus but I didn't expect this either. 'Look, we're joking, you paranoid muppet,' says Jake reassuringly, having interpreted my silence.

'Oh, right. Very good. Just what I need when I'm forty-nine minutes away from what is possibly the most significant date in the history of romance since that couple who formed Dollar started courting.'

'Oh, what, David van Day and Thereza Bazar?' says Alex.

'I knew you'd know their names.'

'Christmas, Will, David and Thereza of Dollar! They

were pretty hot.' The sarcasm is flowing. 'You don't think you're setting your standards a bit high?'

'Well, maybe I wouldn't have if I hadn't started shitting myself about my qualifications as a poet.'

'Look, Will,' Jake replies firmly, 'the poem was funny. If she didn't understand that, then she's a TV luvvie with her head stuck a mile up her own arse and you don't want to go near her anyway.'

'I see. So my poem has now become some sort of personality test for her. Next time I'll play it safe and copy something out of a book. What do you reckon, Kirsty? I bet you get love poetry tumbling through your letterbox every day.'

'Oh, yeah,' she says, shuffling her feet. 'It gets a bit boring after a while.'

'So you think poetry's out, then?' Jake asks her.

'No, it's lovely.'

'Alex? You write nice poetry, don't you?' says Jake, provocatively.

'Shut it, Jake.'

Kirsty looks down to avoid eye-contact, embarrassed again. To change the subject, I get up to leave, jangling my car keys. Only forty-two minutes to go. 'Right, I'm off, chaps.'

'He is, Alex,' says Jake. 'And he's leaving us behind.'

'As if . . .'

'Now, are you sure your hair's looking all right?' asks Jake, who's not going to let me get away with anything today.

'Good point. Is my hair all right, Kirsty?'

'Perfect, Will.'

I knew I could rely on her. 'Good. But you promise the poem was OK, guys?'

'Oh, come on, Will.' Alex is patting my shoulder assertively, as if he's sending me into battle. 'What you're doing is so bloody cool. You're performing feats that no normal mortal would dare consider undertaking. You're Scott Tracey of *Thunderbirds*, you're a bloody hero. We wouldn't joke about it otherwise.'

'Oh, OK. So I have your complete respect, then?'

'Yes,' interjects Jake. 'We're jealous, you're the main man, we want to be you. Does that make you feel better?'

And, yes, it does, even if Jake *is* being sarcastic. I don't think the prime reason for having a celebrity girlfriend – or just a celebrity date in my case – is to elicit the envy of your mates, but I'm afraid it's undoubtedly a factor. But I don't need to share that thought with Jenny.

7

Off to Jenny, with stomach-tightening, brow-slightly-sweating first-date exhilaration. And trepidation.

I walk from the car park through Regent's Park towards the Zoo. There is a pleasant warmth in the air, sunlight and smiling daffodils: a load of splendid seasonal clichés have come out for the day. Those who write poetry more profound than mine would embrace Nature today and say that spring is with us, the season of rebirth, new hope, new life. All that stuff. And if they so chose, they could say that I'm the living embodiment of it: young man meeting new girl, a new relationship (here's hoping), new love (the pinnacle of my ambitions).

Meanwhile, I focus on the job in hand. The screech of distant primates informs me that the Zoo is near so I sit on a park bench to do some thought-gathering, some last-minute grooming and to re-remember any zoo jokes that might come in handy. This is what I normally do before a big meeting at work, except for the zoo jokes.

Last thing, of course, is my hair. I run my hands through each side of my parting to tease and tousle it up a bit. I do this a second time, then a third. I'm midway through this process when I get a tap on the shoulder. I look up and a grinning television blonde is standing in front of me. Jenny has caught me doing my hair.

'Leave it alone, you look great,' is her opening gambit, which she delivers with a chuckle.

'I can't believe you caught me like this. Can't you leave a man a bit of space when he's grooming himself?'

'Do you want me to go away and come back again?'

'Er . . .' I ponder for comic effect (I'm not sure that I've quite hit my comic vein yet) '. . . no. I think it would be nice if you stayed.'

'Right, OK,' she says, looking encouragingly sweetly into my eyes. 'What about "hello", then?'

I stand up and awkwardly attempt a kiss. Lips or cheek? God knows. Instead we both hit thin air, exchange a kissing noise and withdraw, relieved that the moment is over. And, yes, she looks fantastic. Alex and Jake would kill to see her now: more hip-looking, less children's-TV-looking than ever. She's in black jeans squeezed tightly where I like tight squeezes, black leather jacket, big-heeled black boots and a sky blue corduroy baseball cap pulled down over those scoops of vanilla hair. No makeup, no matter: there is no need for it and I rather like that.

'I hope you don't mind coming here,' she says, as we start walking to the Zoo gates.

'No, no.' As if! 'No, not at all.'

'It's just that I've got a thing about penguins. I, er, like them. I really wanted to come and say hello to them. And I hoped you might like them too.'

'Serious?'

'Yup.'

'Penguins it is.'

How brilliant to want to go and say hello to some penguins. *I* could really like penguins. Phenomenally simple: better to converse about penguins any day than, say, the funding problems facing opera or the future of digital television. Penguins don't leave me remotely out of my depth. I reckon I can swim with the best of them.

Thus, within the confines of London Zoo, past the reptile house, the meerkats and the flamingoes, I feel my early nerves dissipate. This is a good thing, particularly because London Zoo is packed with the age-group that watches Jenny on television, and although no one says hello, or asks for an autograph, excited children lose interest in the Malayan tapirs and the bearded pigs when we walk by, staring, tugging at their mothers' arms and pointing.

'God, even when I'm dressed like this they know who I am,' she says apologetically. 'I hope you don't mind.'

I don't. At least, half of me doesn't: the half of me that's on such a huge ego-trip I could claim air-miles. The other half, the half I'm struggling to suppress, still feels insecure, as if I don't belong in such elevated company. The world is no stranger to odd couples: Charles and Di, Chris Evans and Billie Piper, Michael Douglas and Catherine Zeta-Jones, Beauty and the Beast. And here is another walking through London Zoo. Me and Jenny Joffee. I know this isn't the right line of thought to pursue, I know my head should be full of positive thinking, self-belief and self-help tapes, but it's too late for amateur psychology now. Come on, I tell myself, you can do this. It'd help, perhaps, if one or two of those snotty-nosed kids came up to me and announced that they'd always admired my work as a lawyer; especially in the field of ugly divorces, and could they have my autograph? But that isn't going to happen. I am out here on my own.

I can do it, I can.

But there is so much here in my favour, and not just penguins. On most first dates you get to drown your nerves in a couple of G-and-Ts and a bottle of Chardonnay. There's no such assistance here, but London Zoo is a fantastic first-date venue: there are no awkward silences across candle-lit tables and you don't have to worry about ordering the wrong wine. At the Zoo, the conversation topics are all around you.

'Why aren't the howler monkeys howling?' asks Jenny.

'Why aren't the Capuchin monkeys making coffee?' I reply.

'Those wildebeest look pissed off,' says Jenny.

'They should count themselves lucky that they're not being pursued by lions like they always are on television.' Which is not my wittiest one-liner. The laughs would come easier if I was feeling less tense.

But Jenny – bless her – is warm and encouraging. She laughs at the right bits and she may be helping me along a little but all the irksome initial apprehension begins to dissolve. I might be gambling here, but I'd say we're having a pretty good time. And we haven't even got to the penguins yet.

'Dylan would never come to see penguins with me,' says Jenny, jutting out her bottom lip.

'The bastard! I never thought you were right for each other.'

'I was just using him to get to you!'

'Hey, listen. You told me I'd regret this,' I say, smiling at her. 'All I'm doing is helping out as your chaperone today.'

She punches my shoulder playfully. I push her away playfully. We continue playfully past a couple of pygmy hippos and, suddenly, there they are, some forty of them in a white tub as big as a medium-sized swimming-pool. The penguins.

Jenny squeals with delight, grabs my hand and drags me towards them, skipping with every four or five steps she takes. This is all rather sweet, but I'm thinking only of my hand, that it's wrapped round hers. This is physical contact, our first of the day. We hadn't even touched when we kissed. I am now as overjoyed as she and find that I am nearly skipping too.

'Hello, Penguin,' says Jenny, basking in a rosy, penguin-inspired glow. 'Hello, you, hello, you, hello, you . . .' Our hands are still entwined. Maybe that's because I'm holding hers so firmly that she couldn't let go if she wanted to, but it's fine by me for now. This smallest of gestures, whether she meant it to last so long or not, indicates so much. Our night together was no mistake, she likes me, yes, even when she's sober. This may be the most significant hand-holding of my life. At least, that's my interpretation of it.

We lean over the wall. 'Did you know,' says Jenny, without taking her eyes off them, 'that penguins are monogamous?'

'No, but good on them.'

'Yes, they pick one partner and stick with them for life.'

'They don't even go through a carefree, promiscuous stage when they hit adolescence, go to teenage discos and try to snog every other penguin in sight?'

'Oh. I'm sure they do that.' Her hand gives mine a squeeze. 'They'd be terribly dull if they didn't. They just like to settle down once they've got all that out of their system.'

'Hmm. I don't think Alex would approve.'

'I don't think it's a bad way to get by, is it?'

'No. I'd love to settle down with a penguin.' She gives my hand another short, sharp squeeze. 'But how on earth, if you're a penguin, do you know if you've picked the right partner? And what do you do if you've been married to another penguin for a couple of years and the love fizzles out? Are you trapped in your penguin relationship for life? It must be a nightmare for them, having no access to the divorce courts. And what would I do if I was a penguin? Penguin divorce lawyers must struggle to get business. I'd have to retrain in another field. Do you think penguins ever make mistakes?'

'No,' she replies, turns away from the wretched birds and looks up into my face. Her right hand is squeezing mine again, and she strokes my cheek with the left. This is a good moment, I feel certain of that, so I smile. She moves up towards me and presses her mouth to mine. I was right.

Beside the monogamous penguins, I am kissing the TV star, long and enjoyably. I am *carpe*-ing the *diem*. Today is mine, me and Jenny, the penguins, the kissing, more penguins than Dylan Dale ever saw, probably far more kissing than a B-list telly star should be doing in public, but it's brilliant. I'm a success, a collector's item of a success. Jenny was my long-shot, my dream outsider on the longest odds imaginable, and she has just come in. Kissing.

'Hello, you,' I say smoothly, fixing her in the eye when she comes up for air.

'Hi.'

'You're good at making the first move, aren't you?'

'I haven't broken the rules, have I?' she asks, apparently worried.

'Not at all,' I reply, as encouragingly as I can.

'Oh, good. It's just that it's been so long, you know, since I started something like this and I'm not sure I know how it's supposed to progress.'

'Well, it's progressing pretty well,' I say. Corny, I know, but she seems not to notice.

'I always make the first move, do I?' she asks.

'Sort of. That's the second time I've wanted to kiss you and you've beaten me to it.'

'When was the first?'

'At the wedding. Where else?'

'I know, I know. I just can't remember how it started.' She grimaces.

'You were drunk.'

'Oh dear.'

'Don't apologise,' I say, laughing. 'I think you've behaved admirably.' At which point Jenny moves forward and initiates another kiss.

A considerable amount of kissing later, we make our way to the exit. Just before the gate, we pass a wooden hut with a painted sign in front of it that reads: 'Adopt One of Our Animals Today'. Jenny grabs my hand again – which is good, I'm still a long way from getting used to it – and drags me towards the hut whooping excitedly. 'Does it mean you can get your own penguin?'

The Zoo's adoption scheme, it turns out, is a blatant but entertaining way to raise income. You can buy a percentage of a tiger, for instance, for thirty-five pounds; you can adopt a whole two-toed sloth for £175. You also get free tickets to the Zoo, a certificate with a photograph of your animal, and your name goes on a plaque on the animal's cage. This is explained in the hut by a quiet man with thinning hair, spectacles and a maroon cardigan. No sooner has he finished than Jenny asks the cost of adopting a penguin for a year. Three hundred and fifty pounds.

'Let's get a penguin together,' she suggests. And before I have a chance to say anything, she is fishing out her cheque book. 'Come on,' she says, smiling at me. 'I want a hundred and seventy-five of your hardest earned pounds.' Can I argue with that? I wouldn't know where to start.

'What do you want to call him?' I ask.

'Percy. Percy the Penguin.'

'No. That's too obvious. We don't want to palm him off with a sad alliteration for a name. Can't we call him Richard?'

'Why?'

'It's just such an unpenguin name.'

'OK, Richard he is.'

'It would be nice,' I say, turning to the man in the cardigan, 'if we could take Richard out for weekend exeats. Maybe we could drive him to Brighton to muck around on the beach.'

'I'm terribly sorry,' he replies, full of self-importance, 'your penguin will not be allowed out for weekends.'

'Not even for Christmas?' asks Jenny.

'I'm afraid to say that the animals are never allowed to leave the Zoo premises.'

We hurriedly fill in the forms, cough up three hundred and fifty pounds and exit the Zoo sharing suppressed laughter. We turn left out of the gates, walk a little way and fall, giggling, on to a strip of grass. We are now not only sharing a good joke but a penguin, a whole penguin and you don't take the responsibility of adopting a penguin lightly, do you? Our adoption contract for Richard lasts a year. This is commitment, a whole year's worth of it for just a hundred and seventy-five pounds each. I couldn't sign up to it fast enough.

My mobile phone rings. I take it out of my pocket and find that Jake is at the other end of the line.

'What the fuck do you want?' I ask objectionably. 'Can't you give me a bit of peace and quiet?'

'Sorry, Will, but something serious has happened.' And his tone suggests he means it.

'What?'

'Someone's arrived at the flat. She's fucking pissed off with you, says you've fucked up her life, says she'll wait here till you come home. It's a divorce problem.'

'What's her name?' I ask, with trepidation.

'Lauren Goode.'

'Oh, fuck. She hasn't got a knife with her, has she?'

'I hope not.'

'Right. I guess I'll see you in about half an hour, then.'

8

Our moment is ruined. Jenny says she'll come back with me, which is nice, and I drive home. We step gingerly into the flat, stop in the doorway and listen for information. There is no wailing or screaming, and the sound of machine-gun fire is absent, which is good, and I can hear Jake's voice in the sitting-room, so we know at least that his blood hasn't been splattered over the Charlie's Angels poster. Divorce – this blessed invention from which I make my healthy living – is not a jolly business. It can turn the nicest of people psychotic, and the fact that Mrs Goode has tracked down her husband's lawyer to his Shepherds Bush flat on a Sunday afternoon does not bode well for her state of mind.

The scene in the sitting-room, however, is unhomicidal. Jake and Mrs Goode are sitting on the sofa next to the Sodastream and there are bits of pink loo-roll on the floor in front of them. Jake looks up as we walk in and pulls a long face, which suggests that he could do with assistance. We cannot see Mrs Goode's face because it is buried in Jake's shoulder, where it is emitting soft sobbing noises.

'Hi, guys,' says Jake quietly. 'Um, Lauren, this is Will and Jenny.'

Mrs Goode pulls away from my flatmate. She has a drink in one hand – vodka, I suspect – and a bundle of pink loo-paper in the other, with which she dabs her right eye. She pushes her hair off her face, straightens out her purple sweatshirt and composes herself, as if about to speak. And, yes, she is certainly good-looking, but she is also what I suspect is a prototype Harvey Goode girl: shapely, made-up, shoulder-length blonde, well-groomed, bejewelled and happy to take turns with him on the sunbed. I call them conveyor-belt beauties, but that counts for nothing right now because some serious flak is evidently about to shoot my way.

'So, this is the friendly flatmate who writes such charming letters,' she says.

'I've been trying to explain,' Jake says to me, in a controlled voice, 'that you were just doing your job, only following instructions, and that underneath it all and not too far deep down, you are a splendid bloke.'

'Jake's put together a pretty decent defence of you,' says Mrs Goode, a foreign twang now coming through in words that are almost whispered but slowly and impressively delivered in a manner that suggests she is trying not to cry. 'But I'm a long way from being convinced. I can't believe you deserve a supporter as charming and sympathetic as he is. He can even make a drink using a Sodastream. My guess is you don't deserve him at all.'

'Um.' Christ. What the hell do I say to this? A Sodastream joke would hardly work, would it? There's a frigid silence as I search for a response. Mrs Goode sweeps back her hair with both hands, ensuring that I do not lose her unremitting gaze. Jake winces, and Jenny looks nervous. I have no option but to blunder on. 'You're probably right, Mrs Goode. I am extremely lucky to have a friend like Jake.' Deep breath. 'Listen, I'm really very sorry that your marriage hasn't worked out.'

'Well, it's nice of you to extend such heartfelt feelings to me, Will Tennant,' sarcasm sings in her soft voice, 'but I'm afraid that when a letter-writer of your chilling talent professes to sympathise with me, it doesn't provide much comfort.'

'No, I suppose not. I'm sorry.' Jenny shifts from one foot to the other and places her hand on my back supportively. I am dying to break the tension but haven't a clue how to do it. 'Listen, is there anything I can do? Is there a particular reason for your visit?'

There is another silence as we wait for Mrs Goode to unleash another of her killer lines. She sweeps her hair over her ears again, then launches off once more: 'Well, I've been sitting on this news and crying a lot and making stiff drinks and doing the sort of things that I suppose pending divorcees do. But I finally felt I had to lash out somewhere, and since the bastard Harvey has vanished, the source of the letter seemed a reasonable target. You weren't hard to track down, Will Tennant, although now I'm here, drinking your Sodastream and receiving sympathy from your friend Jake, the edge of my rage has been tamed and I simply feel sorry for myself again.' She turns to Jake and appears to be shedding more tears. Jake puts an arm round her, wincing apologetically at me again, and Jenny walks to the sofa, kneels down by her and tries to comfort her too.

'Listen, please don't feel too sorry for me,' she continues, surfacing once more. 'I was fucking stupid to marry him in the first place and a million and one people told me so. I've been waiting all of the last year for the goddamn thing to end. It was obvious it was coming. But like this?' And she fixes me again with those sad eyes. 'With a cold legal letter? I go through the mail one morning and there's a bank statement, a mail-order shopping catalogue, a flyer from a pizza shop and, oh, yes, what's this? A shortish note from a suit at a law firm to inform me that my marriage is over. Tell me, Will, do I ever get the chance to hit him? Do I ever get to know why this has happened? Or will you simply have me deported to the States on the next boat? My life, it seems, is in your hands. Just sentence me now because I can't stand the suspense.'

'Mrs Goode, I really am sorry.' And I am. Because she seems a hundred times the human being that the bastard Harvey is, and right now, here in my flat, in front of Jenny, she is not making me look good. 'No, of course your life is not in my hands and I'm sorry I've been so instrumental in your unhappiness. I'd also like you to try to believe that I'm not quite the insensitive monster I'm coming across as. But surely you appreciate that you should be speaking to your own lawyer not me? Harvey is my client and my job is to represent him.'

'My own lawyer? I haven't got a lawyer yet. And, yes, I get your meaning. I understand the position you're in and I know it's not the done thing for me to come here. Sorry. I ought to go.' She gets to her feet, avoiding eye-contact with anyone and straightens herself out again.

'I'll order you a cab. That's the least I can do,' I say. I have barely uttered these words before I find myself on the receiving end of scornful looks from Jenny and Jake.

'Come on, Will, that's a bit harsh, isn't it?' says Jake. 'She can stay if she likes.'

'Come on, Will,' says Jenny. Now all three are looking pleadingly at me from the sofa and it's quite clear that I've been transformed from good-guy London Zoo penguin-loving kissing machine to complete bastard. I beckon Jake and Jenny into the kitchen and, under my breath, try to state my case.

'Listen, guys, I feel awful about this woman, but you've got to understand the situation. I can't possibly have her here in my flat. I know she seems like a decent person and I'd imagine she's in the right with Harvey. I know he has the morality of an earthworm and, given the choice, which I never am, I'd represent her ahead of him any day of the week. But the fact is that I'm paid to be on his side. She is the opposition and I can't have the opposition here in my flat. What if Harvey were to find out? I hate having to be so self-centred and small-minded, but I've got no choice. I could lose my job for this.'

'Sorry,' says Jake. 'I shouldn't have let her in in the first place.'

'Never mind, you didn't have much of an alternative,

I suppose. Maybe I should just phone Harvey and tell him what's going on.' As I reach out a hand for the telephone, Jenny, who has been listening quietly and, I thought, compassionately to me, thrusts out her right hand and snatches away my wrist. Suddenly the three of us are sharing another horrible silence and exchanging awkward glances. Jenny, who has been gripping my wrist tightly, drops it as if it is diseased and looks embarrassed. 'I'm sorry, Will,' she says. 'I didn't mean to grab you like that, but you really can't ring Harvey.'

'I know.'

'We don't have to chuck her out, do we?' she asks.

'It can't be your fault if she turns up out of the blue like this, can it?' says Jake. 'She's crying out for help. Why don't we just get her another drink, help her calm down a bit, then I'll take her downstairs and get her a cab? Can you go for that, Will?'

I can – grudgingly: what choice have I? – and we file back into the sitting-room where Mrs Goode is sitting with a little makeup mirror in her hand, removing the evidence of her tears. Jake gets her a drink, and Jenny sits down next to her and puts her arm round her. I'd love to get involved too, but my list of possibilities – getting her a new loo-roll, buying her flowers, finding her a half-decent husband – is topped by my obligation to make a little speech.

'Mrs Goode—'

'Oh, call me Lauren,' she interrupts, her American accent coming through more obviously now. 'If we're going to be enemies, we might as well be enemies on first-name terms.'

'Sure, great.' I think that was humour, but you can never be sure in the divorce business. 'What I was going to say is this. I'm happy for you to stay for a drink, and if there's anything we can do for you right now please ask, because we'd like to help. But in exchange I must insist that you don't tell Harvey you've been here. Please, please don't tell him. I'm sure I don't need to explain why.'

'Good God! If I ever see him again, there'll be topics on the agenda that are a tad more life-shaping than the quality of your Sodastream. Don't worry.'

'Good.'

'Lauren,' says Jake, taking the heat off me, 'what are you doing about living? Is Harvey going to move out of your house?'

'Well, I was wondering if I could stay here. I've got my toothbrush in my handbag.' The three of us are stunned into silence. 'Joking, guys,' she says. 'Sorry, it's not easy to do comedy when your life's just been ripped apart, but at least I'm trying. In answer to your question, Jake, the bastard had the kindness to drop me a note yesterday saying that if he bought me a house, would that settle our account? He used those very words. He's clearly desperate to get shot of me. But the offer of a house can't be so bad. I think I'll go for Hampton Court.'

'So he's expecting you to move out?' asks Jake.

'It would seem so.'

'That can't be right, can it, Will?'

'Jake, you know it's not fair to ask me that. But, no, it isn't necessarily right,' I reply, compromising myself.

So here I am, giving free legal advice to the wife of the man whose divorce I'm employed to oversee. It might be suicidal, but at least it produces a warm, approving smile from Jenny. Good. So I've found the way to her heart, though it would be nice if I could do it without having to jeopardise my career.

'Come on, we'd better go,' says Jake to Lauren, seeing that my goodwill is evaporating. 'I'll walk you down the road and help you get a cab.'

I thank Jake, then Lauren thanks Jenny, and Jenny wishes her luck in the battle ahead. Finally Lauren thanks me and says, 'See you in court, nasty-letter man.' What with her accent, her tears, her soon-to-be-divorced state of mind, I'm not sure whether she's being ironic or whether she hates me. But Jenny puts her hand on my shoulder as we see them out of the flat, and that's enough for me.

9

When I'm kissing Jenny, and I cock open an eye to see what she looks like when she's kissing me back, she looks better than ever. Some girls pale a little when viewed from about an inch away, but Jenny's skin is fabulous and her eyes look so pretty and peaceful when they're half-closed and fixed on kissing me; what I particularly like is the expression in them which suggests they are really intent on some of the best kissing they've ever done.

The moment the door swung shut, separating Jake and Lauren from Jenny and me, we were kissing. All this kissing the moment the coast is clear is splendid first-date stuff, I know, and I'm not going to apologise for it, not when it's Jenny Joffee whose mouth mine is glued to.

There is some extraordinary wish-fulfilment being enacted by my front door. When couples kiss on screen, is it not always fabulous? Do they not always kiss exquisitely well, so well that you're just desperate for a taste? Clearly, they're acting – I mean, that's their job, isn't it? And, anyway, I can't believe that all film stars kiss as well as they make it look. Celia Johnson, Anna Friel, Victoria Principal (Pam Ewing was always a top telly kisser) and the rest of them all look like brilliant kissers, but there must be some dud snogs among them. I realise now, with Jenny in my arms, that I'd just assumed she would kiss as perfectly as Celia, Anna and Pam seem to. I know that's unfair and perhaps expecting too much of her – she's never, to my knowledge, done any kissing on screen in her programme. But none of that matters, because the kiss I get from her is every bit as sensational as Celia and Anna and Pam make it look.

Eventually we pull back a few inches and look, rather romantically, into each other's eyes. 'God, that wasn't very nice,' says Jenny, with a frown.

'I assume you're talking about the Lauren thing and not the kissing.'

'You assume right.' She squeezes me under the ribs, then grabs my hand and leads me into the kitchen where she opens the fridge and nods at a bottle of white wine.

'Please don't judge me on account of that,' I say.

'What? The kissing?' she jokes.

'No, Lauren. My career in matrimonial law doesn't mean that I'm a full-time professional bastard.'

'You mean you sometimes help put marriages back together?'

'Well, that's not in the job description.'

'Don't worry, I'm teasing.' She gives my arm a squeeze – she's very squeezy all of a sudden. 'You were pretty good with her. I thought you were going to throw her out callously on to the streets but, as Jake said, you're quite decent underneath it all, aren't you?'

'I wasn't aware I kept it that well hidden.'

'Oh, weren't you?' She's teasing me again. 'But it must make you wonder about the point of it all.'

'Being half decent?'

'No. Marriage.'

'Oh, that. Marriage is great. Marriages make divorces and without divorces I wouldn't have a job. But to be serious – just for a moment – I cling to an old-fashioned belief in marriage, despite the evidence on my desk every day. That incident just now was quite light in comparison with some of the stuff that goes on.'

'I know.'

'How?'

'Well, my parents did it all when I was nine years old. They fought each other, and when they were finished, they fought to become my best friend.'

'You poor thing. Who won?'

'My mum. Hands down, really. Dad moved in with someone else, who soon became his next wife, so it wasn't hard, even for a nine-year-old, to spot why the marriage had broken down. Mum convinced me that Dad was a bad man, and she was probably right. He tries to persuade me otherwise about once a year when we meet, but he hasn't managed it yet. So there you are. That's my cheery little life story. I don't know why it popped out so suddenly. I give myself three out of ten for childhood happiness. What about you?'

'Oh, um, probably the same. Yes, pretty grim, three.'

'Really? Why?'

'I was always bothered that I wasn't better at football.

I always had a weak left foot, which made my childhood quite tough. And I also thought it'd be a nice bond for us if I gave myself the same marks out of ten as you.'

'You're making it up, you bastard.' And I get another squeeze.

'Yes, I am. Sorry, but the truth is much more boring. I'd get seven out of ten for standard, uneventful warmth and cosiness.'

And thus, within minutes of our being alone together, I am sitting on my sofa with Jenny's legs draped over mine, a bottle of Chardonnay open on the floor next to the bits of pink loo-roll, and we are talking. Real talking. You know, the heart-to-heart, soul-sharing, you-and-me-babe serious stuff that boys tend to avoid unless they're sitting on sofas with girls like Jenny. It's not that I'm the classic, impenetrable male, and I'm not doing the real-talking thing with Jenny purely in the knowledge that there may be a reward for me at the end of it. That would be Alex's approach, not mine.

But Alex doesn't do real-talking with me and nor do I much with Jake, and I guess that's because we're boys. And I also think that that's a shame. We talk about leaseholds and freeholds, cute estate agents, children's cooking programmes, the love-life of the lead singers of Dollar and, on the whole, it's quite a laugh. But I can tell that Jenny doesn't want a conversation about Dollar, and if that's how she feels, it's all right by me.

I agree instantly to her suggestion that we play a favourite game of hers: we tell each other three stories about ourselves, one of which is untrue, then guess which is the lie. If the revelations are not personal enough, you have to go again.

'And it's my game,' she says, 'so you have to go first.'

'Right.' I pause for thought, then launch in. 'One: I am useless at splitting up with girls. The stress invariably produces some sort of physical side-effect. When I split up with this girl Steph, I thought I had anorexia. I didn't, of course, I just went off my food for two weeks. When I split up with another girl, I contracted eczema on my face and had to go to a Chinese herbalist to find a way of curing it.'

'Oh. Very interesting.'

'Was that all right? Personal enough?'

'Yes. Very good.'

'OK. Two: my second-worst break-up after Steph was with this lovely girl who I went out with for about five months at the end of which she explained that she was leaving to move in with the girl she had been having an affair with for, er, about five months. I know that a bisexual girlfriend is supposed to be every boy's dream but, believe me, it wasn't.'

'Very good. I like that one.'

'I didn't.'

'No, I suppose not.'

'Number three.' I pause again. The look on Jenny's face suggests I'm doing quite well so I take a breath and plunge into something more audacious. 'This is quite a hard one to explain. It's a good one, sort of, tied up in undefined thoughts and feelings, but anyway ... OK, number three: Jenny, I really like you.' She stares at me, apparently dumbfounded. 'I know it sounds crap to say it like that, doesn't it? But it's true. But the real point is, I don't say it, you know, what I've just said, very often – I mean, I'm not in the habit of telling girls I like them. In fact I often start seeing someone and decide after two weeks that I don't really like them. So what I'm saying – albeit not very well – is a nice thing about you.' Christmas! That didn't come out very well, did it? It might have helped if I'd thought it through. I look at Jenny and she, thank God, is smiling at me.

After a longish pause, she rolls her eyes. 'Very interesting,' she says. 'I've known you for a week now, so I suppose that gives me about another seven days of your company. Lucky old me.'

'No, no, no. Bugger. No. Look, OK, I'd like to officially invite you on a second-week anniversary date next Saturday. I'm going to the pub with Jake and Alex and while I doubt that that's the most glamorous invitation you've ever had, I'd be delighted if you'd join us.'

Jenny's smile is even more encouraging. 'Well, it was all fantastic stuff,' she says, applauding. 'It's such a shame that one of them has to be a lie. I hope it wasn't the last one. There was a bit too much information in that for you to be making it up. I'll go for the lesbian lover. I can't believe any girl would leave you like that.'

'You're right. Of course they wouldn't. There have been no lesbian lovers. I remain ever hopeful.'

'So does the glamorous invitation for Saturday night still stand?'

'Absolutely.'

She leans over and kisses me, and it looks as if my side of the game has been a success. 'OK, my turn,' she says, sitting back again.

'One: my first ever TV appearance was as a five-year-old, dressed as a Rice Krispie in a Kelloggs advert. There were three of us and I've never to this day been able to find a video recording to discover if I was Snap, Crackle or Pop.

'Two: I can't cook. I mean, I hate cooking and I'm a hopeless cook. Strange, isn't it, me being a TV cook and all that? But there you go. And that's a closely guarded secret, by the way. I'm confiding in you now. If you so much as mention it to anyone, you'll face a custody battle over Richard.'

'Well, I'm not prepared to put a penguin through all that. It'd be too traumatic. I'll keep quiet instead.'

'Good. OK, number three. It's really sweet of you to say that you like me. I mean, hey, that's some compliment, lucky me and all that. But please remember, Will, it's still only been ten days since I split up with Dylan. I've no idea what I'm doing here with you. It's probably madness. I've just committed to seeing you in a week's time and I'm not even sure that that's very sensible.' She narrows her eyes into an expression of earnestness and grabs my hands. Is this ominous? 'Please don't think too much about all this, the "us", the "relationship" or whatever, and don't put me on your God-forsaken two-week trial period, because I'm not even sure I want to pass the test. Can't we just have a laugh together? I do like spending time with you, and I'd love to go out with you and your mates on Saturday. But I don't want to think about where this is going. I just want to enjoy it while it's there to be enjoyed.' She looks me in the eyes again, frowning, as if she's given me some medicine and wants to check that it doesn't taste too awful. 'Does that make any sense?'

'Yes, it makes sense, but it's clearly the lie.' And I realise that's a little hopeful.

'Sorry. No, it isn't.'

'Oh, OK.'

'Honestly, Will, can't we just take each day as it comes?'

'You sound like a football manager.'

'Look, I'm being serious,' she says beseechingly. 'Do you mind?'

'No,' I reply, trying to sound upbeat. 'No problem.' I suppose I'm not being totally honest. 'Jenny, that's fine.' Which it isn't.

'Good.'

'Right,' I say breezily, because we need to change the subject. 'Well, the lie was the one about hating cooking. It had to be.'

'No.'

'You're joking.'

'I mean it. I can't cook and I do hate cooking.'

'Oh. So you were never a Rice Krispie, then?'

'Wrong again. They were all true. A bit cheeky, I

know, but it's my game so I'm allowed to break the rules. To be honest, I hadn't planned my number three until I got to it.'

'That's almost as outrageous as being a TV cook who can't cook.'

'I know, it's terrible, isn't?'

'But how can that happen?'

'I just got sucked into it. I was asked to audition, so I hammed up a recipe from a book, practised it a million times, and before I'd had a chance to think about what I was doing, I'd got the job.'

'Unbelievable.'

'I know. And now I can't get out of the loop. In fact, I'm making a pilot for another cooking show, a proper adult one, next Thursday. Do you fancy coming along to watch?'

'I'd love to.' And is it just me, or am I getting mixed messages here? She tells me to back off a bit and then she invites me out. All I'm sure of is that I started today with one date with Jenny and now I have two more. And that's a pretty good return – even if the one-year lease-hold on the penguin together looks a bit hopeful. 'Well, your cooking can't be any worse than my poetry.'

'What do you mean? Your poem exhibited an unri-valled mastery of the English language. I demand another.'

'Really?'

'It was the poem that got me here.'

'Not my lovemaking?' A bit bold and off-the-cuff, I know.

'No, sorry, sweetie.'

Now I'm wondering about the sex. Was it any good? As good as with a TV exec? Or was she just too drunk to remember? There's only one way to find out. So we go back to her flat and do it three times that night.

10

Monday morning. Today I will start trying to tear Mrs Reddin of Chobham away from the management consultant to whom she had been married for eight years when she got a call from the local police to say they'd taken him in for masturbating in the car outside the couple's house. It turned out that he'd been doing this on his return from work for several months. They hadn't had sex for three years. Oh, happy days.

My record number of divorces in a day is four. That's not from beginning to end, but completed, signed and settled. Sometimes clients send me thank-you letters: for giving me my life back, for the freedom, for removing the noose from round my neck. Funnily enough, they never fill me with the life-fulfilling glow that I suspect they're intended to inspire.

I am on the telephone to Mr Reddin's lawyer when Sam marches into my office with a cup of tea and a Post-it note instructing me to ring Alex urgently.

'Hello, lover-boy,' he says on answering. 'How's the penguin?'

'Oh, Jake told you, did he?'

'Yup, it all sounds pretty heavy. A year's adoption? Are you up to the commitment?'

'I'll try.' Alex doesn't need to know about the other part – Jenny's football-manager, taking-every-day-as-it-comes, this-isn't-necessarily-a-long-campaign part. 'But you can't adopt a penguin half-heartedly. It requires a lot of time, thought and dedication. In the meantime, I've written another poem for her, which you might like to approve. Anyway, I was told you had something important to say.'

'I do, but it'll have to wait for lunch, today. You and me. Non-negotiable.'

'Can't do it. Too busy, mate. I'll meet you for a drink, though. What's so bloody urgent?'

'Will, this wife of a client of yours, the one who pitched up at your flat. Jake told me about that too. I can't remember the name.'

'Lauren Goode.'

'That's right.'

'What on earth do you think you're doing? You need to be talked to. Seriously. Jake doesn't have a clue how damaging it could be for you if anyone found out, and there's no reason why he should. But *you* should.'

'Of course I do, and I feel pretty uneasy about it.'

'Good, so you'll meet me for a lunchtime beer, then, to talk about it?'

'But we've talked about it. What else do we need to say?'

'You'll see.'

'Oh, very cryptic. OK. Quarter past one, then, in the Angel.'

'See you.'

I get back to Mrs Reddin, who distracts me for the next few hours, until I'm sitting at a table in the pub watching Alex's portly figure weave towards me through a corridor of suits with a pint of lager in each hand. He looks good in a suit, despite the questionable waistline, but this is Alex: always well turned-out, presentable, good at whatever he turns his hand to and a little too meticulous in ensuring that this remains the case. Alex would never let himself be caught wearing a pair of Father Christmas boxer shorts, which is probably why Jake and I view him with a glimmer of envy.

He plonks the beer on the table and I pull my latest love poetry out of my inside pocket and unfold it. 'OK, Alex, listen to this. And I don't care what you think of it, because poems are the key to Jenny's heart.' And, in a slightly hushed tone, I start to read:

'Just three times a night, just three times a night,
We could have kept going until it was light.
We could have set records, we could have done more
On the bed, on the sofa, the ceiling, the floor.

The first time was magic, our union sublime,
Though admittedly that was for quite a short time.
The second was better, our passion a feast,
And this time I lasted a minute at least.

The third: I'm fantastic, a great god of love,
Compared to your hopes, I was now way above.
"Oh, Richard! Oh, Richard! Oh, Richard!" you said.

"Oh, Richard, you are the king penguin in bed."

So three times that night, just three times that night.
I would have gone on were it not for that fright.
Next time we'll be better, we'll go past the third,
Just please don't refer to that ludicrous bird.'

I look at Alex, waiting for his response, but he is drinking his pint. Eventually he puts it down. 'Are you trying to tell me that all that happened?'

'No, I'm trying to find out what you think of my poem.'

'I don't care about your rhyming fucking couplets,' he says, grinning. 'I just want to know about our sexual-deviant, penguin-loving TV star. Is all that true?'

'Pretty much. Except that the second time I kept going for an impressively large number of minutes, rather than the "one at least" that's in the poem. I just found it impossible to make it rhyme any other way. It makes me more amusing in a self-deprecating way, don't you think?'

'Sod that. What about all the "king bloody penguin" business? Is that true? She really started calling you Richard?'

'Yes. But only for a joke.'

'Oh. Why didn't you go on after the third time?'

'I fell asleep.'

'Oh, good. So you are still human, after all. When are you going to send the poem?'

'It's already gone, by email first thing this morning.'

'Amazing.'

'Still Scott Tracey, then?'

'Yup, can't deny you that.'

'Good. Now what's this intriguing thing you want to say to me?'

'Two things actually.' He pauses for gravitas. 'First, as I said to you on the phone, I think you've been far too nice for your own good by having that woman in your flat. But you don't need me to tell you that, which takes me on to the second thing. I lied about wanting to talk about mad Mrs Goode. There's something far more interesting.'

He is now going red and looking me straight in the eye. He seems both embarrassed and excited, and I don't think I've ever seen him looking bashful before. I haven't a clue what he's talking about.

'I've met someone,' he says, smiling.

'You mean you've slept with someone.'

'Yes. I suppose I do mean that. But she seems quite nice, and you know her too.'

'Oh, God. Not the lovely Kirsty? She seemed great.'

'No. After Kirsty, I had to meet Fiona from Chestertons, remember? She was quite nice but married, and then there was Trudi from Barnard Marcus, and she was quite nice too. Well, *then* I had an appointment with the girl from Faron Sutaria and there I struck gold.'

Faron Sutaria? I don't think I know any estate agents full-stop. This has never really bothered me before, in fact, if anything, it would be something I'm quite proud of. 'Sorry, Alex. No idea who you're talking about. Any more clues?'

'Yup. OK.' Alex pulls a photograph out of his jacket pocket and tosses it on to the table. It spins, then comes to a stop, leaving me with a horrible tightening sensation in my stomach. The photograph is old, with one of those white borders around it. There are two people in it. One is me, aged *circa* twenty-two, I have a flat-top haircut – which, I have to say, looks pretty good. There is a girl under my arm: Steph, complete with shoulder-length reddish-brown late-eighties hair. We are sitting on a wall in Nottingham, where she was a trainee nurse and I was in my postgraduate year doing law. Jake and Alex had graduated by then, leaving me alone to do foolish things like fall for Steph. I can even remember when that picture was taken: at the beginning of the summer term, about four weeks before I discovered she was sleeping with someone else.

'Where the hell did you get this?' I ask, more threateningly than I intended.

'You two do look rather sweet together,' says Alex. He seems to finds this amusing.

'Where did you get the photo?' I say, with an attempted chuckle.

'Where do you think?'

'*For fuck's sake, where did it come from?*'

'Steph. Your famous mystery girl from Nottingham, the one Jake and I were never allowed to meet. I'm so glad I've finally bumped into her.'

This is too much. I don't know whether to be indignant or laugh. I opt for sarcastic innuendo. 'She's still got some nice big properties, has she, Alex?'

'You could say so.'

'Oh, right. How many times have you viewed them?'

'Just once.'

'And that's it, is it?'

'I'm booked in for another viewing on Friday after work.'

'Oh, Alex.' And I'm trying to josh around here, pretend to be lighthearted – I mean, you shouldn't be overly bothered about a girlfriend of ten years past, should you? – but I can hear desperation in my voice. Stephanie Honeyfield cannot come back into my life. It's not as if she's likely to anyway: Alex's girls barely last a week, and Steph's week will be up on Saturday morning. And Alex simply wouldn't let her come between us. You don't do that sort of thing. It's there in the rules, Scouts' honour, your mates come first, all that stuff. Some girls are no-go zones and you know it instinctively. Alex knows about Steph. I've told him and Jake. He knows that Steph is a no-go zone. You just leave girls like Steph alone. It's simple. Which begs the question that blurts out of my mouth: 'What the hell were you doing with her in the first place?'

'I didn't know who she was.' He is now coming over all innocent. 'I mean, I didn't know who she was in terms of you and her. Not until yesterday morning.'

'What happened yesterday morning?'

'I saw this photograph tucked away on the mantelpiece in her bedroom.'

'Really?'

'She's still got fond memories of you.'

'I ditched all my pictures of her years ago.'

'Yes, she said she doubted that she figured in your good books.'

'She'd be right. Does she still worship Starsky and Hutch?'

'Yup.'

'Bitch. That's why you like her, then?'

'Well, it *was* an unexpected bonus to find a signed photograph of David Soul hanging in her sitting-room. She's still got her single of "Don't Give Up On Us, Baby", but it was when she put on "Let's Have A Quiet Night In" that I knew I'd pulled.'

'Alex!'

'No, Will, I'm serious. She's a great girl. I can see why you went out with her for so long.'

'*I* can't.'

'Will,' he takes a slug of his beer, apparently unperturbed by my unease, 'you spent almost a year with her. She can't be that bad.'

'She is. I promise.'

'She isn't.'

What did I do to deserve this? Over a quick pint in the Angel, Steph has become Banquo's ghost. At thirty-two, you think you have a modicum of control over your life, you think you can control who you want in it and wipe out everyone you don't. But here is Steph, back from the dead to haunt me.

'Look, Alex. I spent nine fucking months with her. You've had one fucking night.' Any attempt to remain unflustered is now past. 'Can you at least pay me an ounce of respect and trust my judgement on this? She's bad news. You know what she did to me, Alex. She fucked my friend. Surely I don't need to remind you.'

What is now weird is that Alex doesn't seem remotely surprised by my fretful overreaction. Instead he huddles over the table and talks with hushed certainty. 'Yes, but there was more to it than that, wasn't there?'

'What do you mean?'

'Come on, Will. You really, really liked her, didn't you?' And he is saying this as if he *knows*.

'What are you saying?' I ask, with the attempted innocent chuckle again.

'Will?' Alex is spreading his arms now, almost laughing. 'She told me.'

'That doesn't mean you should believe it.'

'Will, there's nothing wrong with it. It's OK.'

'What is?'

'Will, Steph told me.'

'She told you what?'

'That you proposed to her.'

Silence. I suppose it was obvious that this was what he was coming to. It was wishful thinking to assume that we would avoid my great down-on-one-knee disaster. 'Yeah, well, it's true,' I say eventually, looking vacantly at the table. I never thought that this would come back to haunt me but here it is, being brandished tauntingly at me by Alex as if it was a toy sword. 'What a fucking idiot I was.'

'Why didn't you ever tell us?'

'Because it was such an unbelievably stupid thing to do. Because it's embarrassing, humiliating. Because you don't go round proposing to people when you're twenty-two. Because I got turned down. Because it's so uncool. I don't know. All of those reasons, I suppose. What a prat I was. What a bloody idiot. Oh, God!' This is agony.

'It doesn't matter,' Alex says beseechingly.

'Well, maybe you're right. I mean, I didn't know what I was doing, I hadn't thought it through or planned it. I was naïve, stupid, impulsive and pissed. But did that mean she should go off and fuck someone else?'

'I asked her about that.'

'What? And she said we weren't officially together at the time?'

'Something like that.'

'Well, she's right, Alex.' I'm talking faster and faster now. 'OK. Christ. Look, this is it, straight, exactly what happened, because I can see I've got to explain myself.' Alex winces but I blast on. 'The sixteenth of May 1989, half past twelve at night, we've been to the pub with some friends, then a slow, meandering walk across town and we end up together in the Market Square. We're having a really good time, it's a warmish, clear night, the rest of the square is deserted. It's one of those moments when everything seems perfect – at least that's how it seemed to me. Get the picture? And I ruin it by doing the most stupid fucking thing in the world. All overcome – and I still don't know where this came from – I'm down on one knee asking her to spend the rest of her life with me. What a twat. Steph, naturally, takes fright, as anyone of that age would do. She says I'm fucking mad and then she's telling me we should maybe cool things off a bit, stop seeing each other so much, stuff like that. We have a pathetic little argument and stomp off in different directions. We don't see each other for a week. I'm regretting what I've done but presuming that we'll get back together again. She decides the opposite and goes off and fucks Danny Arnold, who played right back in the college football team. I was right midfield, for fuck's sake. I thought we had some sort of an understanding.'

I stop for a sip of beer and Alex looks embarrassed. 'So that's it. There was no legally binding agreement between us, no contract. You might think it was OK for her to go off and do what she did. She obviously does. But I don't think it's on. It really hurt.'

'I'm sorry, Will,' Alex says. 'She regrets what she did, you know.'

'Sure, but it's a bit late for all that, isn't it? You don't *really* like her, do you?'

'I'm not sure.'

'Put it like this: she is going to be just another fling, isn't she?'

'Probably. She hasn't been flung yet, though, not completely. I don't think she's quite hit the ground. Almost but not quite. She's got another set of flats for me to see on Friday, if you see what I mean.'

'You mean you want to fuck her again?'

'Well, that's one way of putting it. Do I have to get your permission?'

'No. Don't be ridiculous,' I find myself saying, meaning exactly the opposite. 'Of course you can see her again. Just lose her quickly for your own sake.'

11

Until today, I have lived under the misconception that there were only four horsemen of the apocalypse. I now realise that the Book of Revelation was wrong and that there is a fifth: Stephanie Honeyfield. A horsewoman of (quite suddenly) Biblical proportions.

As I wander gloomily from the Angel to the office, the pavements are wet, there is a cold greyness in the air and all the warmth of Saturday's spring day with Jenny seems worlds away. I don't think this is just my mood interpreting the weather. This really is a shit day even if it has – for probably the first time in my life – got me into idle contemplation about the subtext of Biblical prophecy. An American religious leader once foresaw that the apocalypse would come on 22 October 1844. Hindsight suggests that he was at least 160 years premature; maybe he'd like to plump instead for the day Steph returned to my life.

What I can't get out of my head is Alex's demeanour. He could easily have said he'd never see Steph again, but he didn't want to. He could have presented the whole story as a finished chapter but he didn't want that either.

'You don't look very happy,' says Sam, bouncily, on my return to the office.

'There's a good reason for that. I'm not.' And with that I shut myself away for the rest of the day with the divorce of Mrs Reddin who fails to compete with Stephanie Honeyfield for my wandering attention.

Just before six o'clock, though, Sam dances into my office in a whirl of excitement with a package that has arrived by recorded delivery. 'It's from Top Table Television,' she says.

I rip open the package, pretending to be less excited than Sam, which isn't hard, and out tumbles a packet of Penguin biscuits with a note: 'Dear Poet, see you Thursday, 2 p.m. at Top Table. Love from the Unqualified Cook. PS Keep yourself free for dinner afterwards.'

Brilliant.

'She takes the biscuit, Will,' says Sam, nudging me.

'She's got style, hasn't she? I could get to like her.' Even if she is unqualified, even if I do have to take each day as it comes. A packet of Penguins from Jenny and the horsemen of the apocalypse have vanished.

In celebration, I decide to work late and devote to Mrs Reddin the quality of time for which she is paying.

It is nine twenty by the time I'm wandering back down Davenport Road to my flat with a bottle of red purchased at the off-licence on the main road. I had been expecting either silence or the sound of the television when I got in, but not two voices.

One, of course, is Jake's. He is standing in front of the fireplace looking sheepish when I appear in the sitting-room doorway. The other belongs to the woman who is sitting on the sofa, also looking sheepish, in a rather soft-focus way. There are two glasses of wine, both almost finished, on the coffee-table next to the Bengal Elephant ashtray.

'Lauren, what an extraordinary surprise to find you here again,' I say, with all the sarcasm I can muster. 'You should have told me you were coming. I'd have raced home earlier.'

'Will,' says Jake, surprised at my tone, 'calm down, mate.'

'Sorry, Jake, but this can't happen. Sorry, Lauren, you're an infinitely nicer person than your bastard soon-to-be-ex-husband who I represent, but I've got no choice. What are you doing here?'

'She needs help,' says Jake protectively. And I suppose, looking at Lauren, it's easy to see why he feels that way. She looks more composed than she did on Saturday, still vulnerable but more feminine, and the lines around her eyes that betray her age make her more attractive. She certainly inspires sympathy.

'Oh, Christ, what sort of help?'

'Harvey came back last night,' she says, in her soft, educated American accent. 'It was the first time I'd seen him since your lovely letter, Will. He's already pressuring me to move out of the house. What's going on here, Will? Is he throwing his weight around to try to scare me, or will you be on the doorstep tomorrow morning waving one of your legal papers in my face and telling me it's 'bye, 'bye, Miss American Pie?'

'Lauren, it's your lawyer who can answer that, not me.'

'My lawyer? You think I've got round to that, do you?'

'Look.' I put down my briefcase and open it. 'Lauren, I can offer you a Penguin biscuit. You've had a glass of wine. But I can't give you legal advice. Do you fancy one of these biscuits? They've got great sentimental value.'

'No thanks.'

'Well, I have to ask you to leave, then. I'm really sorry.' And I am. The more I see of Lauren, the more I see what Harvey once saw in her. She isn't a conveyor-belt blonde at all. She has poise and a delicate, gentle face and that rather sweet way, using her thumb and forefinger, of tucking her hair behind her ears.

She gets up to go and Jake says he'll walk her up to the main road to get a cab. The awkward silence as she puts on her jacket is too much for me. 'Oh, look, Lauren,' I say impatiently, my back turned to her, 'this moving out thing, it's rubbish.'

'Oh, really? Well, according to my lovely husband, his lawyer has said that he can have me extricated pretty quick.'

Harvey, ever the gentleman! A response pops out before I know it: 'Lauren, he can't kick you out of your house. Harvey's pulling a fast one. He's certainly never discussed it with me. It's bollocks.'

There's another short silence. I cannot possibly say any more – I've gone too far already. I remain back-turned, to indicate that she must leave. As I wait for the front door to shut behind her, I lean against the mantelpiece, which means I am right up close to the Charlie's Angels poster, my face almost in Kelly's lap, and this is a happy circumstance because Jaclyn Smith was always my favourite.

But instead of the noise of door-shutting, I feel Lauren's lips pushed against my right cheek in a soft kiss, which is followed by a whispered, 'Thank you.' It's too hard for me to leave it at that.

'Look,' and I still don't turn round, 'Lauren, get Jake to give you his mobile number. If anything desperate happens, if you *really* need help, maybe we can work it out that way. OK?'

And I know that, suddenly, I've really compromised myself. Sometimes you have to be a little chivalrous, don't you? I'm rewarded with another kiss, and now I turn round. She is walking out of the sitting-room.

'Lauren.'

'Yes?' She lingers in the doorway.

'Did you ever do any work for Harvey?'

'Er, just a bit.' She snorts ironically. 'Let's see. I recruited half of the senior management at Intertalk, for starters. I entertained capital investors and clients. Yes, you could say I did a bit of work for him. Why?'

'I just wondered. 'Bye.'

12

Thursday morning. Another Jenny day, my fifth, if you include the mornings that have followed the nights before. It's now sixteen days since Jenny split up with Dylan Dale, and for me to have been in there on five of them isn't bad. The equation is even better if you count the days since Jenny and I met: five out of twelve is outstanding. Some married couples don't even see each other that much, especially the ones I deal with professionally. And I realise, of course, that we're only taking each day as it comes, but there have been quite a few days coming now, haven't there?

And I know you're not supposed to do this, *especially* when you're taking each day as it comes, but my mind has been wandering down ludicrous avenues and I seem powerless to stop it. I am sitting at my desk, it is 11.25 a.m., two and a half hours before I am to arrive at Table Top Television. I have a huge heap of paperwork to get through, but I can't eradicate from my mind an image of Jenny and me in a cosy wedding photograph, with a classic English country setting – except Jenny is wearing her *Starters For Starters* apron. Throwing confetti over us as we walk out of the church are Delia Smith, Jamie Oliver, Gary Rhodes and a couple of other senior TV chefs whose names I can't pinpoint. Even Dylan Dale, whom I've never met, makes an appearance – an ugly man with a low hairline, heavy caveman eyebrows, a sculpted beard and three nipples à la Scaramanga. He is scowling in defeat, barely in focus, at the back of the shot.

I know my mind is straying into unhealthy territory here, but the extent to which it seems to have worked everything out – the three-nippled Dylan particularly – is astonishing. The plan involves Jake buying me out of the Davenport Road flat, then Jenny and I moving to Hampstead or Islington, somewhere more befitting of our life in television. And there are good, respectable ground rules to our marriage: I'd still go to the Dolphin, stick by Jake and Alex, and they would understand that, on the male-bonding front, nothing between us had changed. I'd not be the sort to disappear off to early nights and healthy living, it's just that I would have a wife and Jake and Alex would not. Whether this is wishful thinking or the early onset of Alzheimer's, I've no idea. My reverie is disturbed by the phone.

'Will?' It's Sam. 'I've got Harvey Goode's PA on the phone. She says he wants a meeting with you this afternoon.'

'That's a bit late notice, isn't it?'

'That's what I said. I asked if she knew how important you are and that you didn't just jump to someone else's orders.'

'Sam, you didn't say that, did you?'

'No, of course not.'

'Well, put her through, then.'

And a posh-sounding lady called Camilla is on the line and I find myself being squeezed in for a meeting at Harvey's Canary Wharf offices at five o'clock.

'Is there anything in particular he wants to discuss?' I ask posh Camilla, without sounding too paranoid.

'His divorce settlement.' How helpful. Does he know that his wife has taken to dropping round to my place for a coffee and a cry? Can he have found out already? Is my career over at Mellstrom Roberts?

I smack the top of my desk with the open palms of both hands. This makes a loud noise and I imagine the secretaries outside raising their eyebrows and wondering what's up. Why did I talk to Lauren Goode? Why did I break all the codes of conduct? What on earth did I think I was doing?

The answer should be that my conscience took over, that I met a downtrodden beggar and couldn't walk by on the other side. And maybe that's part of it. But I also know that the situation appealed to my vanity, that this attractive, fragile lady made me feel important and powerful. And a fool.

I have to speak to Simon.

Twenty-five minutes before I'm due to leave for Table Top Television, I am informed that Simon can see me. And I'm frank with him because there's no alternative.

'Simon, I'm worried about the Harvey Goode case.'

'Why's that?' he asks, unmoved.

'White v. White.'

'Pardon?' He looks at me as if I've gone mad.

'I think the White case might apply.'

'You'd better be joking.'

But I'm not, and I explain why.

White v. White was a battle that tumbled out of the House of Lords a month ago after years in court. We all watched with interest as the case played itself out, changing the face of divorce litigation. And it looks as though it has come back to haunt me already.

Mr and Mrs White were farmers, married for thirty-three years during which they built up a business worth £4.6 million. When they divorced, Pamela White was initially treated conventionally by the divorce court and given an £800,000 lump-sum payment. Convention, then, was that the figure would reflect the woman's 'reasonable requirements' – housing, maintenance, that sort of thing – which was how the figure was arrived at. But Mrs White fought this, arguing that her contribution to the house and the business warranted a fifty-fifty split.

To my amazement, her lawyers won the day and the Law Lords declared that there should be no bias in favour of the money-earner against the home-maker and child-carer. Pamela White didn't quite get her 50 per cent, she got nearer 40, but this was way ahead of all precedent. When Harvey Goode divorced the first Mrs Goode, he parted with around 14 per cent and there was a young daughter involved.

'Mr Goode is under the impression,' I explain to Simon, 'that because there are no children in this divorce it's going to cost him a lot less.'

'Not an unreasonable assumption,' says Simon, unhelpfully.

'I know. But in the three years of this marriage, his fortune has approximately doubled, he's made another twenty million, and if it can be argued that White v. White applies, Mrs Goode has a claim to a high percentage of that.'

'Why should the White case apply?'

'The White case, as we know, is about as clear as mud. But what worries me is that Mrs Goode has worked unofficially for Intertalk. Besides simply being the home-maker – which may be enough to invoke White v. White anyway – she's been in the office at Canary Wharf working at Mr Goode's side. If it's possible for her lawyers to show that she's had a hand in building his empire, then surely she can stake a claim to a large percentage of it.'

'Was she paid by Intertalk?'

'I'm not sure. I suspect not.'

'What did she do for them?'

'I don't know.' And that's a lie, but I'm not supposed to know. 'She used to be in head-hunting, so she may well have worked on the recruitment side.'

'Shit.' Simon stands up and looks contemplatively out of the window. 'You may have a point here, Will.'

'What do you want me to do?'

'Ignore it. Pretend White v. White never happened. You may be right, Will, but until Mrs Goode's side brings up the White case, do nothing about it and certainly don't go putting old Harvey's nose out of joint by mentioning it.'

'Last question: do you still think I'm the right person for the case? This is suddenly rather less straightforward than we'd imagined.'

'Of course you're the man for the case, Will. Harvey asked for you.'

'Right, OK.' No getting off the hook for me, then.

'As I say, let's just proceed as before. Remember, Mr Goode is a charm offensive as well as a marital dispute.'

And so to Jenny at last.

I leave Simon's office and get into a cab to Table Top Television in the Docklands. I give my name on arrival and the lady on the desk responds with a murmur of recognition. 'Food of love, sir?' she says.

'That's right,' is my reply, before I recall that *Food of Love* is the title of the programme I have come to see and not some clever telly joke.

The woman hands me a plastic visitor's pass to hang round my neck. It says, 'Will Tennant, *Food of Love*, Special Access'. Within seconds, I am being shown down a corridor by Dee, a gangly girl with a clipboard in a pair of jeans with a skirt on top. I like my special treatment: my name is on a pass, I have Dee, my own personal assistant, and special access. It's not quite being back-stage after a rock concert to engage in Class-A drugs and free sex, but it'll do. I wonder if Dee has been fully briefed: watch out for Jenny's new bloke, the poet, yes, the three-times-a-night guy, coming here today, oh, my God! Yes! Three times a night! Table Top must be gasping with excitement. Or maybe not.

Dee leads me into the back of an auditorium where there are five rows of seats on a temporary raised platform. They are empty apart from six more clipboard girls and a few other hangers-on – none of whom, I notice, with a pathetic stab of pleasure, has 'special access' round their necks.

'Everyone's been a bit stressy today,' whispers Dee, once I'm settled in. 'We rehearsed this morning and it didn't go very well. Couldn't get the soufflé to rise. Bloody nightmare. It wouldn't budge an inch. I had to dash down to Sainsbury's to buy a tonne of chocolate and strawberries instead.'

'Oh. How awful.'

'I know,' she replies, my sarcasm lost as she waves her hands frantically to convey the horror of the soufflé crisis. 'And then our celebrity dinner guest dropped out.'

'Oh dear.'

'We've all been ringing round for a last-minute replacement. I nearly got one of the male nurses from *Casualty*. That would have been really cool, but no one wants to appear on a pilot show that may never see the light of day.'

'Oh, I know someone who was on *The Weakest Link*. I could give him a call.'

'Thanks, but it's too late,' she replies, missing the point again. 'Our head of programmes is going to do it instead.'

'Brilliant,' I respond. Given her track record, poor Dee hadn't a hope of picking up the irony.

Jenny had warned me there was a chance that on my visit I might encounter the head of programmes, who goes by the name of Dylan Dale, but she didn't say he might be starring opposite her. She had also warned me, with amusement, that *Food of Love* wouldn't be high-brow, that Channel Five were looking for a 'sexy cooking programme' and that Table Top's idea was to have her tart herself up in short skirts and see-through tops and whizz up some 'sexy food', with a hunky celebrity guest coming on at the end to be seduced by a candlelit dinner *à deux*.

The idea of all that doe-eyed flirting over a passion-inducing pudding had struck me as amusing then, and I had liked the idea of coming to support Jenny: she had explained that this was an important day for her – Channel Five would never commission a series if the pilot wasn't any good and it was essential the soufflé rose to her command. But now that Dylan Dale will be cooing at Jenny and encouraging her to lick the chocolate off his spoon, I'm not so keen.

But it's too late for second thoughts. The lights go down, the clipboard girls nudge each other, another girl with a headset covering just one ear shouts out the countdown – 'three, two, one' – and 'Take My Breath Away', the hopelessly over-sentimental version by Berlin, blasts in as the title music. The show has begun. And this is showbusiness. It seems to involve my Jenny wearing almost nothing. She floats on to the set in a dress that Liz Hurley would have left in the wardrobe: a triangle of shiny black material that makes no effort to cover her back and little more to cover her front. I suppose the choker and posh shoes are intended to make her look classy rather than tarty, and find myself wishing she dressed like that for me.

'Good evening and welcome,' says Jenny, in an alluring *sotto voce*, one eyebrow raised. 'As Bertoldt Brecht once said: "Food comes first, then morals," and that is certainly the rule in my kitchen. By the time I've whipped two simple courses into a peak of excitement, I don't intend to let any man find me more resistible than the banquet that comes first.' She raises a glass of wine, whispers, 'Bottoms up,' into camera three and takes a slow, seductive sip without taking her eye off the lens.

'Each week on this programme,' she continues, 'I shall be cooking dinner for two and a celebrity guest will be coming to join me. By the time he's dined, his defences should be down. My intention is to show you at home how the right ingredients, sizzled and steamed to perfection, can get the juices oozing to make a mouthwatering evening that would stir even the tenderest of loins.'

After that mouthful, Jenny embarks on preparing dinner. 'I've decided to go for asparagus drizzled with butter as my starter,' she explains, as she lights the two candles on the studio dining-table. 'Rule number one is that finger-food is fun. And asparagus is lots of fun. But we're taking finger-food to extremes this evening. In fact, we're banning cutlery altogether. After the asparagus, we'll move on to Peking duck pancakes and then, to finish – and if this doesn't work nothing will – a sort of chocolate fondue, lovely rich warm chocolate with fresh juicy strawberries to dip into it. Oh, it'll be sublime. I can hardly wait for my guest to arrive.'

I had imagined I'd feel sorry for Jenny, tarted up as a high-class prostitute and playing the role of the kitchen call-girl: I hadn't thought it would work for the big-eyed innocent face of children's TV. And this isn't the Jenny I know: this Jenny would sooner spend her days in Ann Summers than by the penguin pool at London Zoo. Nevertheless, even with four different cameras a few inches from her nose, it soon becomes apparent that the Jenny I know has the class to pull off the Ann Summers act. I also notice the clipboard girls nodding at each other approvingly. When the girl with the one-eared headset shouts, 'Cut,' there is a general hustle-bustle and a murmur circulates that things are going well.

Minutes later, we are under way again. In the break, I never got so much as a wink from my half-dressed superstar, but I can handle that: when all the cling-ons have dispersed, I'll have her to myself. First, though, Jenny has to get through a whole thesaurus-full of *double-entendres* before the celebrity guest can arrive. 'I've just got to bring the asparagus to a peak so that there are beads of juice running down the inside of the long, firm, glistening stalks,' she says, somehow maintaining a straight face. Then a doorbell chimes. Jenny turns to camera two and says breathlessly: 'Let's hope it's all worth it.'

Now, I may be somewhat biased against Dylan Dale, and I can't envisage Table Top canvassing me for my opinion, but if they did, I would tell them that the moment he came prancing through the studio front door, in black-tie and brandishing a bunch of red roses, the programme dipped. He isn't at all the hairy Neanderthal I had imagined: he is tall, wiry, with dark-rimmed designer spectacles, a pinched face and a thinning crew-cut. It seems to me that he overplays the three cheek kisses he is allowed. He goes for the lips on number three and his hands spread round Jenny's waist are a little excessive too. But so is Jenny's raised-eyebrow expression into camera one. 'Cor blimey, girls, I think I'm in there,' is her message, 'I'll just go and turn down the bed.'

'Oooh, so succulent,' says Dylan, as he withdraws his first asparagus stalk lewdly from his mouth.

'The texture is delicious on the tongue, isn't it?' replies Jenny.

'Here, let me . . .' he says, and they feed each other, the show descending further into soft-porn when Jenny runs her finger along Dylan's lower lip, apparently to remove 'a dribble of gleaming melted butter'.

I can't say I feel particularly cool about this – indeed, the idea of Jenny teasing and tempting her way through a weekly dinner date with the hunky likes of some male nurse from *Casualty* doesn't fill me with delight either. But at least I know it's me who gets to take her home. That's what counts, isn't it? And, anyway, the seduction scene is ridiculous. After just over twenty minutes preparing her three courses, Jenny is allowed less than ten to welcome her guest, consume the meal, lick ice-cream from his belly-button and shag him sense-less on the studio floor. Even the unedited version is a *Krypton Factor*-type assignment that would crush the most furious libido.

When the theme tune blasts through to signify that their time is up, Jenny and Dylan are still stuffing their faces with chocolate and strawberries and trying desperately to swallow in time to clink glasses and smile for a final-frame pose.

Some twenty-five minutes later, Dee is chatting to me about the show as we wind through the corridors towards the star's dressing-room. There she says good-bye to me as if we have become best mates and lopes off. So, now is my time.

The dressing room is less showbiz than I had expected. I had thought it would be full of Table Top executives praising Jenny and toasting a glorious future. Instead she is alone, wiping away makeup – and the odd tear.

'Jenny, you were fantastic, what a star!' I bend down to kiss her but get little response. 'What on earth's the matter?'

'No one fucking agrees with you, that's what.'

'What?'

'It's been awful, Will.'

'Why?'

'First that fucking soufflé. Why did I fucking agree to a soufflé? If you can't fucking cook, you might just about be able to kid a couple of *Bob the Builder* fans, but you've got sod-all chance of getting an erection out of a soufflé. And the recipe I used was almost an exact copy of the one in the book. If I can't plagiarise a soufflé, I should give up.'

'But the chocolate and strawberry thingy worked quite well, I thought.' Did I really say that?

'Yeah, I know. But it's more than that. I've just had Dylan and Zac, the new-projects bloke, in here telling me that we've got to re-record large chunks of it. Apparently I didn't ham it up enough. Got to be more sexy. I mean, what more can I fucking do? Oh, and they didn't like the Brecht reference either. Not right for our audience. But we rehearsed all morning and it was fine then.'

'I was impressed by it. Where on earth did it come from?'

'*The Oxford Book of Quotations*. I can't even make up my own lines. I don't think I should do this.'

'Stick with it. You were good.' I sit back against the dressing-table and pull a tissue out of the box. 'Here, let me.' I wipe away the makeup from under one of Jenny's eyes.

'Oh, you're lovely.' She seems to have simmered down somewhat. 'I'm sorry you had to watch me cavorting on set with Dylan.'

'I didn't mind.' Which is a lie.

'Good. Now, what about tonight?'

'Still on for it?'

'Yes. But can we stay in? I'm shattered.'

'Fine.' I pull out another tissue and get to work on the other eye.

'And there's no way I'm doing any more cooking today, so we'll get in a delivery. Fancy a curry?'

'Yup. No cutlery, though. It's sexier that way.'

'Excellent.' At least I've got her smiling now. 'Will you pick me up? It'd be lovely if you did.'

'What time?'

'Six forty-five.'

'I'll try, but I might struggle.'

'OK. If you can't, just come straight home instead.'

'Fine.'

'And then we'll make love four times so you can write me another poem.'

'Only if you wear that dress you were in just now.'

'Cheeky sod.'

'Speak for yourself.'

13

Harvey Goode has a don't-fuck-with-me air about him when I walk into his vast office. The entire outside wall is glass and affords a generous view of the Millennium Dome and the untidy clutter of East London beyond. But now is no time to enjoy the scenery.

'Right, Will, sit down,' he says assertively, ushering me to a black leather armchair on the opposite side of his desk. 'Let's get down to business.' No time, either, for hello, how are you, how's your nymphomaniac celebrity cook.

'Sure,' I reply. 'I haven't had a response from your wife or any solicitor representing her, so I'm not certain that we can take this thing much further yet.'

'I appreciate that. But there is the odd issue that I want to resolve here and now.' Oh, God, here we go. He opens a drawer under his desk, perhaps to get out the Magnum with which he's going to put me out of my misery.

'It's Lauren,' he says, putting on a pair of rimless glasses, which he takes straight off again and wags at me. 'I've seen her only once, very fleetingly, since she received your letter.'

'Well, that's not surprising, is it, Harvey?'

'No, I can understand she's upset. But I get the impression she's up to something.'

'I'm not sure what you mean.'

'I'm not either. I just thought you might be able to tell me.'

'Oh. Er, no.' This drawn-out feigning of ignorance is agony. Why doesn't he just finish me off here and now?

'She keeps on disappearing.'

'She probably just wants her own space right now. That wouldn't be unusual.' Is that convincing or patronisingly obvious?

'Will, she keeps on going missing.' It wasn't convincing. And, to make matters worse, Harvey's forehead vein has popped up to join us. There is, of course, a simple way out of this awkward position: I could front up with Harvey and tell the God-honest truth, that the emotional wreckage of his wife has twice washed up uninvited at my flat. Professionally, that is the only option left open to me, but I know I'm not going to take it. Could I drop Lauren in it like that? No, especially not with Harvey sitting in front of me coming over all bulgey-veined and heavy-handed.

'Maybe she's looking for somewhere else to live,' I say, attempting to turn the direction of the conversation.

'Maybe. I doubt it. I've encouraged her to find alternative accommodation and she doesn't seem keen on the idea. That's another thing I want to talk to you about.'

'Go on.'

'If I bought her somewhere to live, would that be sufficient as a marriage settlement?'

'It'd have to be a pretty decent house.'

'I was thinking of something in the region of half a million pounds.'

'I think that's a bit hopeful, Harvey.'

Harvey looks me hard in the eye, the hairs on his joined-up eyebrows turning inwards as if to suggest that my last comment didn't go down very well. He shoves back his chair, gets up and paces around threateningly. 'Will.' His voice is condescending now, as if I'm a school-boy who has said something extraordinarily stupid. 'I have two priorities in this divorce. And they are going to be delivered. I want it dealt with quickly and I don't want my bank account obliterated by it. Simple as that. I can stomach half a million, but that's the limit. The commercial arm of your law firm, to whom I bring a lot of work, have given me their word on this and I have spoken to your boss, Simon. He has also said that it can be done.'

'Right.' How kind of Simon to keep this conversation from me when I put the facts in front of him this morning. 'Harvey, I can assure you that this will be processed quickly. You want what we call a "clean-break settlement" and the status quo between you and Mrs Goode is fine for that as there are no children. A clean-break of half a million is quite a challenge but we'll see what we can do.'

Half a million is more than a challenge, it's impossible – and that's before White v. White comes into the equation. I haven't started detailing Harvey's assets yet, although this morning I had a quick trawl on the Internet. The last *Sunday Times* richest-people-in-Britain list had him at number 829 along with Nigel Mansell, Van Morrison and Ozzy and Sharon Osbourne on £40 million. And I suspect that's a conservative guestimate. I'm delighted that Van the Man has done so well for himself, but I'm certain that Harvey has done even better. If I offer half a million, Lauren's lawyer will ask us to declare his assets and sting him for far more. Now, despite having discovered that gentle Lauren is far too good for him, I find myself wishing that they could be back together again, as happy as Ozzy and Sharon.

What would be an honest middle-ground settlement? A million, maybe. Lauren's lawyer could do two things: push for more than that, then drop to it, or gamble on the White case and attempt to sting my client for considerably more. It would be interesting to see how Harvey's forehead vein took the news if he were to hear that instead of half a million, he was going to lose seven or eight. But I, of course, am duty-bound to screw Lauren out of seven-odd million quid that may be rightfully hers. So this is my moral scruple of the day. Do I (a) behave totally unprofessionally and disloyally to my employers and help the nice girl get her hands on the money she is due; or (b) save the bastard infidel a few million and get myself a promotion?

My answer, of course, is (b). I'm a lawyer, aren't I? The problem with this, though, is that (b) probably isn't possible.

If Lauren really does cash in from this, then maybe I could clear out of Mellstrom Roberts and sail off into the Caribbean sunset with her. But that's not going to happen either and, anyway, the chances are that it would probably have an adverse effect on my relationship with Jenny. And I want to keep her, even if only on a day-to-day basis.

'Will, I can see you're not too positive about this,' says Harvey, in a lighter tone, the forehead vein dormant, 'but I don't think you should worry. I think we'll be fine.'

'OK.' I am nonplussed.

'You'll be able to see it through. I suspect I know the lawyer Lauren will use and I don't think she's in your league.'

'That's kind of you. Who is it?'

'I suspect she'll use a girl called Georgina McKnight. She's an old friend of ours – well, Lauren's, really. I never got on with her, which is why I think Lauren will use her. Have you come across her?'

'Not often. I know plenty about her, though. Works for Chilton Shaw?'

'That's right. Quite impressive. She's a bit of an academic, and a bit too hot on women's rights. But I doubt she'll be particularly tough and, as I say, Will, if it ever came to it, she's not quite in your class.'

His sudden recourse to flattery is unexpected – in fact, almost as unexpected as Georgina McKnight being described as *quite* impressive, not particularly tough and not in my class. Clearly Harvey has only met her outside work. The Georgina McKnight of the law courts is seriously tough – to be honest, she scares me though this has something to do with the fact that she's going to hang me out to dry on this case, and rather more to do with her undeniable, older-woman sex appeal. A story once did the rounds that she doesn't wear knickers in court. It was probably just a rumour, or maybe it happened once, but, tellingly, no one has had the courage to ask her if it's true. I am certainly not going to be the one to do it, at least not now.

While Harvey has been stressing his desire for speed in his divorce, the grey London view has begun to darken. The newspapers today apparently reported that a staggeringly wealthy heiress had got her divorce through in ninety seconds, so why, Harvey wants to know, has it already taken me four working days? The old vein has popped back to join us. What hope have I with a client like this? And now he has made me late.

The question he leaves me with is the same one he started on. Lauren: what the fuck has she been up to? I still have no answer and I'm not sure whether he knows I'm lying. Either way, I'm going to be late for Jenny.

It is 6.05 p.m. when I leave his office. I have to get back to Lincoln's Inn to pick up my car, then down to the Docklands to collect her and, in forty rush-hour minutes, that's not possible. I ring Jenny on her mobile, but there's no answer. I go down into the Underground and there's no tube either.

14

It is 6.50 p.m. when I get back to my car and the traffic from there to Docklands is appalling. I ring Jenny's mobile again. Still no answer. I reach Table Top studios, where a middle-aged man at the front desk tells me she has already gone home.

I head for her place in Primrose Hill. Still no answer on her mobile. I would ring her at home but I haven't got the number yet and it seems she's ex-directory. I stop at a garage near Euston and buy some flowers that are above average garage-flowers standard. I'm confident that although I'm late, the superior flowers, my supportive role at the TV studios, and my hair – in fact, the whole Will Tennant package – leave me well placed to ensure that she will enjoy taking another day as it comes with me. I am buoyed up by the Beatles CD in my car, which I've programmed to play 'The Long and Winding Road' on repeat. I've done that not only because it's a good soulful sing-along but because Lennon and McCartney's road leads to 'your door' and there's no better song to pump yourself up to when you're driving alone to a front door belonging to someone of the calibre of Jenny Joffee.

I feel quite good about my telly star. I was unfazed by

my first exposure to telly life – at least, on the whole. And only twelve days after our first meeting, Jenny and I are joint loving guardians of a penguin, we've had an evening's real-talking, sex three times in one night, and now we're about to share a chicken biryani, saag aloo, two poppadoms and a naan from her local posh Indian. At least, that'll be my side of the order. The point is this: she and I are no longer just a shallow, drunken, post-wedding tumble, that took place in front of a cardboard Elvis Presley wearing a baseball cap, but a relationship steeped in depth and history, curry and sex, touched by fame and mediocre poetry.

'The Long and Winding Road' begins again as I turn right at the set of lights before the left that leads to Jenny's door. Her flat is brilliantly located: it's at the foot of Primrose Hill, within walking distance of cool Camden and touching distance of sophisticated Hampstead. Also she can walk from there to London Zoo to see Richard.

The streets are quiet, lit by those old street-lamps that lend them a Victorian charm. The houses and flats are large with high ceilings. This is classy property, the sort of thing Steph could probably sell to Alex with one flick of her flirtatious eyelids.

Jenny has half of the ground floor of an impressive-looking building and I park outside it, go through the heavy black wrought-iron gate and down a set of steps. There is no indication of life inside, so I ring the bell. The air is cool and I feel a wave of goose-pimples glance over me, but I think that's probably more to do with being on Jenny's doorstep.

There is a rattle on the other side of the door and my stomach tightens. It swings open and I find myself staring at a man with a towel round his wiry little waist. What hair he has is wet, and he is clutching a drink with a slice of lemon in it. He is looking fairly at home. There is no black tie or oblong spectacles, but this is unmistakably Dylan Dale.

My feet feel suddenly as if they are planted in concrete. This wasn't in the plan. Eventually he tilts his head, looks at me patronisingly and breaks the silence: 'Can I help you?'

'Where's Jenny?' is all I can muster.

'Still in the shower,' is the gloating reply.

'In the shower?'

'That's what I said.' And when he says this, his right eyebrow raises by half an inch. The left one stays put. I hate that right eyebrow.

'She can't be in the shower,' I say.

'Why not?'

'I don't know.'

'Well, she is.'

'Hmm.' I am horribly out of my depth. I remain glued to the spot, frozen in silence. All I can say is 'Hmm' and that isn't achieving much. None of my sharp, witty lines that were intended to bowl Jenny over had incorporated meeting a half-naked smug ex-boyfriend at the door. My long and winding road has turned out to be a cul-de-sac. I feel my shoulders slump. I could melt.

'Aren't you that penguin guy?' he asks.

'It hardly matters, does it?' And then I finally find the

right words: 'Fucking hell. Jesus. Fucking hell. Fucking, fucking hell.'

'Do you want to wait?' he asks, unruffled.

'Do I fuck.' I turn to leave.

'Can I leave a message, then?' he asks.

'You can get fucked.'

'Very nice to meet you too.'

15

So I am on my own again.

After thirty-two years bereft of any overwhelmingly significant success with womankind, and with a failed marriage proposal high on my love CV, you'd think I'd have equipped myself to deal with failure. But lying in bed the morning after the G-and-T and raised eyebrow of the night before, it's clear I haven't. My insides are twisted, I feel pressure at my temples, and I don't want to look anyone in the eye in case a tear or two dribbles out of mine. I don't want to go to work and have to explain to Sam how stupid I've been made to look, and I don't want to tell Jake, so I remain curled up in the fetal position, waiting for him to leave.

It is a quarter past ten by the time I haul myself into the office. I grunt at Sam on my way past her and keep my door shut for the morning. Before I have even sat down, I turn the photoframe of Jenny face downwards on my desk; by eleven it is in the bin. I settle to another day of broken, bitter relationships – I'm in good company – but I can't stop my mind drifting back to Jenny's doorstep, the self-satisfied post-coital TV executive raising his eyebrow and calling me 'penguin guy'. One day I'm a three-times-a-night seducer of the stars, the next an insignificant cuckold called Penguin Guy.

At lunchtime I attempt to flit off unnoticed, but fail.

'Will, darlin', come here.' Sam has been lying in wait for me. 'What's the matter with you?'

'Why d'you ask?'

'Because you've not spoken to me all day and you don't have that picture of Jenny on your desk any more.'

'Ah, yes.' I'd rather keep the Jenny business sealed hermetically inside me right now. Indeed, the last place I want to be forced to open up is in front of all the secretaries. Sam may be brimful of goodness, but she doesn't click on to the fact that I don't fancy a natter about loneliness and the horror of rejection under the noses of Theresa and Kate, two of her colleagues who have been almost as excited about Jenny as she has. 'I'm afraid it's bad news.'

'Oh, no, what's up?'

'It's kind of finished.'

'Oh, no!' Sam, Theresa and Kate respond in unison.

'Why?' asks Sam.

'I don't know.'

'You poor thing,' says Kate.

'You poor honey,' says Theresa.

'Yes. Look, er, I've got to dash.'

I retreat hastily to a corner table in a small sandwich shop where I can sit in peace with a tuna, basil and mozzarella special – my appetite hasn't gone this time –

read the *Guardian* and the *Sun* and sulk. Self-indulgent,
I know.

'Ah, Will Tennant,' says a firm female voice behind me,
just as I'm finishing my lunch, 'I believe we may soon be
seeing a bit of each other. How nice.'

I turn. The voice's owner is wearing a double-breasted
pinstripe suit, a masculine-looking designer outfit fitted
snugly round slim hips. Georgina McKnight is scarily
impressive in it. She looks down at me, and while I notice
that her black hair is cropped tight round her face, it is
her dark brown eyes that hold my gaze. She isn't pretty,
more . . . handsome, I suppose. And she has a handsome
body too. Not a squeezy, well-proportioned girly body,
but toned and muscular. Or maybe I'm just believing her
publicity. The lady is awesome – and absolutely the last
person I would want to meet in my present state of mind.

'What a pleasure,' she says. 'You don't mind, do you?'
She is already sitting down opposite me.

I don't know what to say so I watch while she sets out
her lunch – salad, cutlery, Diet Coke and a medium-sized
Galaxy bar – in front of her, as if arranging toy troops to
destroy me in battle. Then she looks up to address me.
'What on earth are you doing here, all miserable and on
your own?'

'I'm just a miserable and on-my-own sort of person,
didn't you know?'

'No, I didn't, and I'm disappointed because that means
you'll be no fun as an adversary. Come on, what is it?
Have you just split up with a girlfriend?'

'Christ, Georgina, you don't pull your punches.'

'No, I don't. Everything you hear about me is true. And I don't wear underwear in court either, do I?'

'Georgina . . .'

'So I'm right, you *have* just broken up with a girl!' She delivers this with a real sense of triumph, the can of Diet Coke raised in the air as if she's toasting my failure. I can't believe that in less than a minute she's squeezed this out of me. 'Have you got a picture of her?'

'I might.'

'Show it to me.'

And suddenly I'm fishing around in the pockets of my wallet looking for some evidence and handing it to her.

'Will,' she says quizzically, 'this is a penguin.'

'Oh, fuck. It's a pretty good-looking one, though, isn't it?'

Shaken, but still just capable of conversation, I find the picture of Jenny and replace the penguin with it. Georgina takes her time studying it. She even has a mouthful of her salad.

'Will,' she says finally, 'she looks lovely.'

'I know,' I reply, with all the sarcasm I can muster. 'A lovely, lovely ex-girlfriend. Lucky old me.'

'Oh, right. Sorry,' says Georgina, sounding less all-conquering as she hands back the picture. 'Listen, Will, you know who really is a lovely person, though, don't you?'

'Pardon?'

'Lauren Goode really is a lovely person.'

'What?'

'Lauren. She's a lovely person. And she doesn't deserve to be pushed about by that arsehole Harvey Goode who you're in the unfortunate position of having to represent.'

'What are you saying?'

'Nothing. You've got a job to do in all this, exactly like I have. I just feel sorry for you and wanted to lodge it in your mind: Lauren, lovely person, Harvey, complete shit.'

'Oh, right. Fascinating. Consider it lodged. And, for what it's worth, your character appraisal of Harvey Goode is beyond dispute.'

'I know. So you won't mind, then, when we take him for every fucking nickel and dime he's worth.' She puts down her Diet Coke with emphasis. 'I know it's unladylike, unprofessional, unlawyerlike and maybe even somewhat uncool to talk like that, Will, but I mean it. And I think we both know that Lauren could empty quite a lot out of Harvey's piggy bank. We do, don't we, Will?' She's looking into my eyes for acknowledgement.

'Georgina . . .'

'Will,' she interrupts, before I'd even worked out what I was going to say, 'I mean it.' Then she cups her right hand over my left cheek. 'I'm sorry about the girlfriend, OK?'

I want to get up and run for my life, but it's not so easy when Georgina McKnight is stroking your cheek. This is a Fleet Street sandwich-shop version of sexual assault.

When I finally get up, Georgina is brandishing a false meek smile and batting her eyelids. 'Don't worry,' is her parting shot, 'if it ever gets to court, I promise to dress appropriately.'

16

If that was a warm-up for a legal tussle with Georgina McKnight, then God only knows the damage she can inflict when she's not play-fighting. I retire bruised to my office and remain there licking my manifold wounds until long after Sam – and anyone else who might expect a serious conversation – has gone.

The next morning I'm still in full sulk mode. I get up late, watch Sky Sports, listen to some David Gray, because he's normally broken-hearted too, then stumble across a repeat of an old *Cagney and Lacey* episode on a satellite channel. Even my lovely, tormented Sharon Gless can't cheer me up. As ever, she's having relationship problems. I understand, Cagney. You and me too, eh? I always knew we were made for each other.

Jake is nowhere to be seen, which is a shame because I'm almost ready to tell him about Jenny. I'd much rather tell people on my own terms than have them laughing as the news zips round in a Monday-morning email: dear old Will, always out of his depth with her, wasn't he? And now he's back where he belongs. And they might be right.

At four o'clock, three *Cagney and Lacey*s later, I'm feeling a bit stronger and ready to go to the pub. In the space of three episodes, Cagney has found a new man and then lost him and that's pretty sad and so she then picked up a drink problem instead. And yet she always manages to lift herself for the next episode, so I feel maybe I should try a bit of that too. What I need is a good dose of Alex – Alex without Steph, that is. He will skirt round the painful truth, and won't ask questions about the troubled state of my soul. He might even get me smiling. He'll welcome me back to the land of the single man from which, it now turns out, I had only been on temporary leave.

Alex will have had his last rumble with Steph – at least, he'd better have – and he alone can sell me the theory that the land of the single man is a better place: it's more fun, populated by the carefree and out-all-night, and it's where we belong. We will be reunited, both returned from jaunts over the border.

I go for a three-hour walk, over Hammersmith Bridge, down to the towpath by the Thames, back over Putney Bridge, through Fulham, up Gloucester Road and into Hyde Park. Finally, I'm in the Dolphin, perched with a pint on a bar-stool.

I have almost finished the second when bad news comes. It is not Alex who turns up but Peter, tanned, smiling, back that morning from his honeymoon. On any other day it would have been great to see him, but when you're waiting to be enrolled back into the land of the single man, you don't want to be confronted with a pleased-as-punch newly-wed. Could the subtext be any clearer? Here I am, going backwards in my life, and here is Peter, who has just taken a massive leap forward.

'Hello, mate,' he says, in delighted-to-see-you tones, draping one chummy arm round my shoulders. He looks as if he's just cracked the meaning of life.

'Hello, married person,' I reply, with as much warmth as I can muster. I'm pleased for him, of course I am. It's just that I envy him too. And maybe I despise him. 'I'm not sure if I can talk to you. You've dropped, mate. You've now joined the other side.'

Peter laughs, not realising I meant what I said, and puts his arm round me again. 'But from what I gather, that's not quite the case. You've pulled the best girl we had on offer at our wedding.'

'Ah. Not any more.'

I am thus obliged to embark on the first explanation of the break-up. It will be by no means the last. That's the trouble with going out with a B-list celebrity: everyone wants to know why you're not with her any more. It's hard to spit the words out, even with Peter comforting me appropriately. Lovely bloke, Peter, even if he is married, and I'm sure his post-honeymoon brand of sympathy is unintentional too. 'You'll be all right,' he says. 'I really hope you meet someone soon, you deserve to . . . It's wonderful when you do . . . Don't worry . . . You'll find the right person in the end, I know you will . . .'

Peter is still banging on about how one day I will be as happy as he is when his words are suddenly sailing over my head. I am staring at the pub door in disbelief. I thought I had already located the meaning of unhappiness but an unquantifiable disaster is now taking place. Alex has walked in with his arm round a girl. She has reddish-brown hair and large breasts. She is unmistakably Steph Honeyfield.

This is a unique situation and I have no idea how to handle it. My expensive education has taught me law, a language and logarithms, and has peppered my brain with Shakespeare misquotes, odes from Keats and stretches of 'The Rime of the Ancient Mariner', but it has left me with no idea of how to behave when you have been dealt a hammer blow by one girlfriend and an ex then breezes in to finish you off for good. We never sat down at class to go though that particular textbook.

Did Alex not tell me that Steph was just a passing fancy? Did I not make it clear that I didn't want to meet her? Is this a joke? I look at Peter, then at Alex, searching for a knowing glance, some sort of sign, anything. But there is none. I scan them a second time and Alex, by now, is half-way across the pub, about fifteen yards from my stool. A hollow sensation is rising in my ribcage. What sort of a day is this? Christ.

Alex is now six yards from me, Steph just behind him. They're holding hands. Holding hands! Alex doesn't do holding-hands! There's an unusual moistness in my eyes. Surely I'm not about to cry. I have only one option. I leap from my stool and set off at breakneck speed for the loo.

It generally takes a minute or two to urinate, but now it takes well over five: about thirty seconds' pissing, then a world of time gazing into the mirror. 'Come on,' I whisper, without any conviction, to my reflection, 'come on, you're OK. You can get through this.' Can I? 'Yes, you can.' I don't *think* I'm going to cry – I've never cried in a situation like this before. But, then, thankfully these situations don't come up very often. I am weighed down by uncertainty, but somehow I tread gingerly out of the gents.

'Hi, Alex,' is the bold statement with which I open, tear ducts still intact, when I arrive at the table where they have settled.

'Hello, mate,' says Alex, with an excessively sincere, unAlex-like look on his face. 'You remember Steph, don't you?'

I turn to her and attempt to fill my face with disdain. She smiles at me with what appears to be nervousness, and fixes me with her hazel eyes. Yes, her breasts haven't changed; they're hugged by a white cropped T-shirt, which reveals her belly-button. She is still very good-looking. Her hair is longer and swept off her face, but her face has taken on a more gentle, natural beauty. Nevertheless I find it easy to detest her. When you're as punch-drunk as I am, ill-will seems to come all too easily.

I turn back to Alex and, probably for the first time in my life, say something foul to him: 'Alex, I can't believe you've brought this fucking girl here.'

'But, Will—'

'Alex, we're mates. Mates don't do this.'

'Come on, come on,' says Peter, trying to play the peace-keeper. 'Easy now, Will.'

'Peter,' I reply, almost shaking, 'this is nothing to do with you. Now, Alex, what is she doing here?'

Steph looks away

'Will,' Alex says beseechingly, 'I thought the best thing to do was confront this, for you two to bloody well meet each other again. I'm sorry, but Steph's my girlfriend.'

'Your girlfriend now, is she? And how long's that going to last?'

'I don't know. That's why I wanted you to meet. Maybe quite a while.'

'Well, tell me when it's over,' I reply, spitting the words out fiercely. 'Until then I'll be drinking at the bar on my own.'

I stalk back to my stool, leaving them stunned into silence. I'm never fiery, melodramatic and over-emotional but I have just been all three. What I cannot judge, given my state of mind, is whether I have been unreasonable too. I order another pint, seethe a bit, and stare into my drink.

Then I stare at the pub door, which I thought was a safe place to rest my eyes, but it is not. Next in through the spinning doors comes Jenny.

I see her long before she spots me. She only comes in a few steps, then scans the room. I don't think I've ever seen her looking so bad: hair untidy, no makeup, face pale, eyes tired, in jeans and a baggy grey sweatshirt. Then she walks slowly towards me, her eyes on the floor. I feel numb now: the whole room seems to be moving and talking in slow motion and I remain glued to my little barside perch. She stops about two feet short of me, and since I have no idea what to say, I say nothing. Jenny says nothing either. We stare unswervingly at each other as if we are children playing a no-blinking game.

'Well?' she says eventually. At least someone's thought of something to say.

'Well what?'

'I didn't have your home number,' she's talking quietly, almost under her breath, 'and I couldn't get through to you on your mobile.'

'I turned it off.'

'I left messages.'

'I know.'

'Will, I left messages!'

'I know. I ignored them.'

'Jesus Christ, Will!' She screws up her eyes, looking into my face as if for explanation. 'Finally I had to come here.'

'Congratulations. You've found me.'

Jenny shoots me a different look that I can't fathom but suggests desperation. Either way, it is not filled with joy and happiness. 'Look,' she says, much more loudly now, 'maybe the way you and your friends behave is alien to me, I don't know. But the way I understand things is that when someone has done what you've just done, the very least they can do is to give a fucking explanation.' Jenny snaps out the expletive powerfully.

'I can't believe this,' I say, and I can't. 'I can't believe this at all. Yes, Telly Queen, we obviously are alien. Because I was under the impression, the completely fucking wrong impression, that you and I had something decent going. I know it was only a taking-every-day-as-it-comes casual sort of thing – I managed to work *that* out – but it was still a thing, wasn't it? Something, anything – but not nothing.'

'Of course it was fucking something.'

'Listen, I know what you're doing.' I'm almost shouting now, and people are turning to stare at us. 'Don't for a moment think you can give me a hard time, because I *know*.'

'What the fuck are you talking about?'

'About Dylan.'

'What?'

'You and Dylan.'

'What?'

'You and Dylan.'

'Yes, you just said that.'

'Yes, well, you know what I'm talking about, then. You and fucking Dylan Dale.'

'No, I *don't* know what you're talking about.'

'God! I'll spell it out, then. You had Dylan round at your place on Thursday night. I know because I called round, didn't I? But instead you surprised me by sending Dylan out with a towel round his waist, looking all post-fucking-coital and pleased with himself and celebrating with a gin and tonic. OK? That's it. The end.'

Tears well up in Jenny's eyes, she shakes her head, and, almost in a whisper, calls me 'a stupid fucking idiot'. Me? 'You stupid fucking idiot,' she says, a second time. Then she draws a succession of deep breaths.

'OK. Yes, you stupid, stupid idiot' – she's talking slowly as if she is, indeed, conversing with a stupid, stupid idiot – 'yes, Dylan was round at my place. No, I'm not seeing him or sleeping with him or doing any of the things with him that you clearly concluded I was. He was there because he'd just dropped me off from work. I'd had a big day – remember? Full of tension – remember? And at the end of it, he was pretty decent to me. He told me to forget all the shit from the studio session, and he was nice. It was pretty much the first time we'd talked to each other since we broke up. And, yes, he had a shower and, no, I wasn't in it with him. He showered because he was exhausted, about to go out for dinner and didn't have time to get home first.'

'But didn't he tell you I'd called round?'

'Obviously not. I don't know why. I guess the bottom line is that he's still a bit of a twat.'

There is then silence.

The storm has passed.

'I don't believe it,' I say, shaking my head slightly. 'You've got no idea. I've just been through two days of hell.'

'Hang on a sec, I've got every idea.'

'Ah.' I see the hurt in her eyes, and that the reason they look tired is because she's been crying. 'So you haven't had a very nice time either?'

'No,' she says quietly, the confidence of the confrontation gone from her voice and tears in her eyes again. 'I haven't had a very nice time at all.'

I wonder what to do next. 'I know it's a bit late,' I say, 'but can I give you a hug?'

Jenny nods forlornly, so I wrap an arm round her, draw her in towards me and squeeze her hard. She responds, squeezes me tightly too, and rubs her hand up and down my back. Then she pulls back, looks me in the face and runs her hand through my hair. Now that I'm confident that a happy ending is in sight, I decide to see if she'll kiss me. She does.

Part Two

17

In my bed, Saturday morning, two and a half months on, 28 June. My eyes are getting used to the morning light. There is no Jenny next to me. That isn't entirely bad news, though, because I am now focusing on why I've woken up.

Jenny is framed in my bedroom doorway, completely naked. Magnificent. Actually, she has a New York Rangers baseball cap on her head, and on her face a grin, partly because she is holding what appears to be a breakfast tray but primarily because she is evidently enjoying giving me this treat.

'Room service, sir?' she says coquettishly.

'From the Naked Chef. The one who can't cook, that is. What an intriguing prospect. I suppose you've burned the toast?'

'No.' She puts the tray on the bed and squeaks with delight as she slips back under the duvet. 'You have a lovely machine called a toaster, which seems to prevent any such disaster. I must recommend them on my programme.'

'You're mad. Did Jake enjoy the sight of you prancing round the kitchen with no clothes on?'

'No. He doesn't appear to be here.'

'Again? Very interesting. And is there any particular reason why you're being all housewifely this morning?'

'No. And don't think you can start getting used to it. I just got bored of your snoring and I decided to surprise you.'

'So it's nothing to do with the fact that it's our anniversary today?'

'What anniversary's that?'

'Three months. A quarter of a year since your lucky number came up and you met me.'

'Is it really? Gosh, I'm lucky to have lasted this long, aren't I?' She wriggles up next to me and her hand slides seductively down my torso. 'Do I get a prize?'

'Funnily enough . . .'

'Oh, Will, I hope it's really expensive.'

'You might be disappointed, then. It was free.' I lean over to my side of the bed and pull out a sheet of paper from a book. 'Here it is.' I unfold it. 'Your quarter-of-a-year anniversary poem.'

Jenny squeals like a delighted schoolgirl. I hope she likes it. She seems to have enjoyed my previous efforts and had asked recently why the poetry had dried up. I, of course, insisted that it hadn't. After the Dylan Dale incident I had set our relationship back on course with a steal from Wordsworth, which began:

> I wandered lonely as a cloud
> That's blown and battered in a gale,
> Because at once I saw a towel
> Around the waist of Dylan Dale.

I was pleased with that, and Jenny loved it. A couple of weeks later I had persuaded her that she was now my girlfriend, officially, and that I was her boyfriend, officially, and that we were no longer taking each day as it came. She agreed to this without any reluctance. Indeed, she seemed rather sweetly pleased and told me how much she was looking forward to publishing my first book of love poetry.

This, however, came back to haunt me: as week followed week, I delivered nothing, not even a dodgy limerick, and Jenny told me that my writer's block meant either that our honeymoon period was over or that I didn't love her any more.

So here we are, a quarter of a year old together, and Jenny is wriggling under the duvet in expectation at last, of another poem. I clear my throat.

'Never before, never before
Has a girlfriend of mine had an underwear drawer.
They've left the odd item around on the floor,
But never before had their own place for more.

You came with a name and with oodles of fame
But the rules of the game were exactly the same.
If a chap like me loses control, it's a shame,
So to keep foreign garments away was my aim.

But here's your surprise, yes, for you, a surprise:
Your very own clothes drawer that no money buys.
There's meaning to this which I cannot disguise.
An underwear drawer, Jen! Be proud of your prize!'

Before I've finished, I can tell from the squirming that it's going down well. My little bed-friend ends up on top of me and kisses me, then rolls over, laughing. 'Will, brilliant! You're very funny.'

'Oh, it was nothing,' I reply, with false modesty.

'Are you serious about the underwear drawer?'

'Absolutely.'

'You're going to give me my very own?'

'Certainly am.'

'Wow. Well, aren't I just the luckiest girl alive?' she says, in a cutesy American accent. 'I mean, a three-month relationship with the great Will Tennant, capped by getting my very own drawer! What more could a girl ask for?'

By now my mind is lost in the post, which was so expertly delivered on my breakfast tray. 'Look at this.' There's a skiing catalogue, a flyer from a local cleaning company and a handwritten letter, which I have opened and am now holding between thumb and forefinger as if it were a dead toad. 'It's a letter from Steph.' I haven't received one from her for eight years.

Sitting up in bed together, like a grown-up couple, we read:

Dear Will,

I'm writing to you to ask you and Jenny if you would come to Alex's birthday party on Wednesday week (8.30 p.m.-ish). It's just dinner, very informal, round at our place.

It may seem a bit ridiculous to be writing to you like

this, but I wanted to put everything I had to say into words and I wanted there to be a reasonable chance of you taking them all on board. Given that I've only seen you twice since our rather unsuccessful reunion in the Dolphin back in April, and that one of those occasions was in a crowded room and the other brief, I think it's fair to say that it's not been easy to talk. I know that I've found it all quite awkward and I don't think that's at all surprising. As ever, you manage to make it look as if it's no problem for you, but I can't believe that's really the case. I appreciate that I'm probably the last person you'd have wanted to march back into your life, but don't you think we owe it to ourselves to sort this out? Don't we owe it to Alex even more?

It would certainly make Alex unbelievably happy if you and Jenny came to his birthday bash. I know that whenever you see him for drinks after work, you remind him that I'm a disaster and that one day I'll end up causing him irreparable damage and he'll regret me for ever. And I can just see you saying it in your disarmingly charming, don't-take-me-seriously manner. And I can see him laughing it off, too.

But you might be surprised to hear that Alex isn't as tough and Yorkshire and unflappable about all this as he may seem. After that awful Dolphin disaster, he was devastated, really cut up. He never ever thought you'd react like that and he wouldn't have brought me to the pub that day if he'd known you would. Afterwards he felt guilty, really worried that he'd let you down.

And now, when Alex comes home having seen you, he always reminds me proudly that you're his best mate. He really respects you, you know, so it's become even more important to him that you and I get on. I tell him that my estimation of you could hardly be higher – and that's still pretty much the case even if we're not quite able to speak to each other any more – but the thing is that he needs approval from you too.

So, with his birthday approaching, I thought now might be a reasonable moment to do some hatchet-burying. With Alex and me now living together, there's no point in you and I just avoiding each other any more. Can we just have a go?

I would love it if you and Jenny could come on Wednesday week. But I was wondering also whether you and I could perhaps meet for a drink sometime beforehand to try to clear some of the crap that stands between us. I'll be in Horatio's bar at the top of Ken Church Street, 9 p.m., on Thursday night. Ring me if you can't or won't do it. Otherwise I'll be there hoping to see you.

Before that, though, I'd like to get in some sort of an explanation regarding Nottingham all those years ago. I know I owe it to you and hopefully it'll make things easier for us if you read what I have to say, which is really quite simple: I am deeply sorry for what happened and for causing you so much hurt. I never intended to hurt you. What happened with Danny Arnold was bloody stupid, thoughtless, meaningless and impulsive and I regret it intensely.

I really, really did like you, Will, and I hope that one day soon, hopefully by Wednesday week, you will find a way to forgive me.
With fondest hopes,
Stephanie

Convincing stuff. Annoyingly good.
'What do you think?' I ask Jenny.
'She's amazingly nice about you, isn't she?' she says cheerily, squeezing me affectionately under the ribs. 'Is there something I haven't spotted yet?'
'Do you have any more serious thoughts than that?'
'Yes, I do. I'm thinking about you and how happy – or unhappy – you are about all this. I mean, she's right. You haven't being seeing that much of Alex, have you?'
'I've seen a fair bit of him.'
'Yes, but not with Steph. That's the point, isn't it?'
'I suppose so. Fucking ex-girlfriends. I hope you're not going to come back and haunt me like this.'
'I wasn't aware that I was an ex-girlfriend yet. Not so soon after being awarded my own underwear drawer.'
'You're not. There's plenty of life left in you.'
'Oh, lucky me,' she says. Then we share a silence. I lie back with my head half on the pillow and half in her lap, thinking about Jenny and longevity and that all would be smooth for me right now had not Steph sent these ripples to disturb the water. I really do hope there's plenty of life left in my TV star and me. Maybe even enough to get to the finishing line.

'Well?' she says.

'Well what?'

'What do you think of the letter?'

'I think the handwriting's prone to lose its shape, but grammatically it's not bad.'

'Come on, Will.' Jenny is speaking softly, and I might as well be on a psychiatrist's couch. 'Do you think you should see Steph? Is it worth it, as a show of solidarity with Alex? Or will it hurt too much?'

'You sound as if you think I *should* see her.' I swivel round to face her, surprised.

'The others think you should.'

'It hasn't turned into that big an issue, has it, that everyone else has an opinion? I mean, I know it's been a bit frosty between me and Steph, but it'll sort itself out.'

'Yes, but Alex would clearly like it sorted out a bit quicker. And Jake hasn't been dropping the most subtle of hints.'

'So that's good enough for you, is it?'

Jenny sits up. 'I'm not saying I agree with them.'

'Well, what *are* you saying? I could do with you being on my side here.'

'It's just that because you don't really like talking about it, I'm not sure I really understand why you're so against Steph. I know you're embarrassed about her, or, more to the point, the proposal thing.'

'Yes, partly.'

'But there's nothing to be ashamed of, Will. It's sweet and romantic – and you were only twenty-two. I don't think you should be embarrassed. It's Steph who should be embarrassed. You did nothing wrong, but it's you, not Steph, who has the mental block.'

'I haven't got a mental block.'

'You should go for this drink with her, then.'

'God! You're really pinning your colours to the mast, aren't you? Does everyone think I'm being an idiot about her?'

'No one thinks you're being an idiot. In fact, it's you everyone seems to be looking out for here. People have great affection for you, and they don't like to see you all wounded. 'But come on, this isn't just about you, you know. Look, here I am, your girlfriend, trying to persuade you to see your ex-girlfriend. That doesn't make sense, does it? Of course I'd rather you didn't go. Ex-girlfriends are a pain in the arse, everyone knows that. And ex-girlfriends who leave so much emotional baggage behind are even worse. Personally, I wish Steph had never existed. But she does.' And Jenny voices these last words with a look you never see when you watch her on telly. It indicates frustration and that a certain mark has been overstepped. By me.

'Oh, fuck.' I didn't mean it to go quite this far. 'Sorry. I know, I know, I know. Let's forget about this for the moment. Why don't we go and watch you being all lovely on telly?'

'No. I want to talk to you about this, to understand it a bit better.'

'OK. I'll go for that drink with her on Thursday. I

promise. It's not a problem, it's fine. You're right. Of course it's time to sort all this out.'

'So do you want to talk about her?' She is speaking calmly again now.

'Not really.'

'That wouldn't help?'

'No.'

'Wouldn't it help me understand what this is all about?'

'Listen, she hurt me. Is that enough?' I hope so, but while it might evoke some temporary sympathy, I know it isn't. The fact that our silence is suddenly so awkward is a giveaway.

The sound of a key in the front door provides welcome respite. 'Where have you been, you dirty rat?' I yell at Jake from my bed.

'The usual,' he says, as he appears in the doorway of my bedroom, still in yesterday's work suit. 'Kinky sex with two girls at the same time, a bit of leather, some role-playing, with a horse and a couple of farmyard animals thrown in for good measure.'

'What were their names?' asks Jenny, laughing.

'Oh. Er. Matt and Lawrence, two guys from work, actually. We got pissed last night and I crashed at Matt's place on the spare bed. Now, moving on quickly, do you fancy some more breakfast?'

'I wouldn't mind eggs benedict. My breakfast's been rather average.' I receive an elbow in the ribs from Jenny.

'Well, come and join me and the lovely Mrs Goode, then.'

'Pardon?'

'She rang me again late yesterday. Says she wants to talk. Is that all right?'

'It's all right for you.'

'There's something she wants to tell you about her business. She said she wasn't sure if you'd be allowed to see her, though.'

'Oh, well, I'm not. Where are you meeting?'

'Bar Blue – you know, it's ten minutes' walk into Chiswick. Come on, I'm going to be late.'

'I shouldn't.'

'I know. Just come for a short while, then.'

'D'you fancy it, Jen?' I ask.

'No, but you go. I've got to go home anyway.'

'OK. I'll just pop in for a few minutes, Jake, but that's the most I should do, OK?'

Twenty-five minutes later, Jake and I are pushing open the door of Bar Blue. It has heavy wooden tables, saw-dust on the floor and hung-over couples sifting through weekend newspaper supplements. Lauren Goode is look-ing up at us in a rather vulnerable way, indicating that she's had enough of sitting on her own.

Jake stoops to kiss her cheek, sits down next to her and rubs her back in a gesture of moral support. I remain standing in front of them with my hands in my pockets to show I'm feeling compromised, but thinking how different Lauren looks from those two tear-soaked invasions of our flat three months ago. I have seen her just once, very fleetingly since then, and even that was suicidal. That was eight weeks ago and I have only dared to communicate with her since through Jake, suggesting he call her every three weeks or so to check that Harvey isn't bullying her too much.

Even from such a distance, though, I have become drawn hopelessly and – yes – foolishly towards her, not only because she is attractive in the frail way that makes you want to protect her, but because she *needs* protection. Because, as Jake has explained to me, Harvey is trying to break her.

Some nine months ago poor Lauren set up her own head-hunting company and there was no lack of ambition in the way she did it. There was a big launch party, glossy brochures, a PR campaign and three staff in decent West End offices, which, Jake told me, had required a five-year guarantee at £90,000 per year. This all necessitated a large bank loan, secured with a personal guarantee from Harvey, out of which he has now wriggled. And the bank is now wondering who will guarantee the loan instead or, alternatively, when Lauren is going to return its cash. It is no surprise that if she is not already at her wit's end, she is getting close. What had started for me as a fleeting, flirting brush with a calculated risk has developed into an association with an intriguingly striking businesswoman whom I'm helping to make insolvent.

Dangerous, I know, but here, with Lauren sitting in front of me in Bar Blue, I find myself pleased – guiltily so – that I had dared to try to look after her. I feel guilty too that I'm happy at the idea that Harvey is freeing her to be a single woman again.

Because her natural beauty is blooming. Any trace of the old Barbie doll look has vanished. Her hair, I see, was never naturally blonde because now it is sandy brown, and she has become a makeup-free zone too. It works, as if a picture restorer has wiped away a fake to reveal a masterpiece beneath it. Or maybe I'm getting carried away. But if this is what divorce does for you, then we should all have one.

'How are you?' I ask.

'OK. It quickly gets better the more time I spend away from your client. Won't you sit down for five minutes?'

'You do understand that I shouldn't?' I lower myself meekly into a chair on the other side of the table. 'I just wanted to check that you were getting by all right and were being looked after.'

'You're very sweet, Will. I really appreciate it. I understand you're seeing my Miss McKnight on Monday.'

'That's right. A formidable piece of work, McKnight, you've done well to get her.'

'Good. I don't want you to have too easy a time. But, Will, can I ask you something?'

I knew it wasn't small-talk she had in mind. 'You can ask, but I can't promise to answer.'

'I know. Thanks. Well, listen, I know it's a liberty and I apologise for that, but I just wanted to say this. I moved out of the house, as you know. I hung up the white flag pretty quickly on that one – it was an act of self-preservation. But what he's doing to my business – I'm not prepared to stand by and take it.'

'Lauren, that's got nothing to do with me.' Which I've told her before. 'And you've got a handy lawyer of your own, you know.'

'I know, I know. But I think you can help. You see, it's got desperate. I'm starting to do some quite good business but that's probably irrelevant because I'm practically bankrupt. I've paid off one member of staff and it looks likely that poor old Jill, who's got an unemployed husband and a kid, will have to go too. Oh, God, it breaks my heart. Far more than Harvey ever did.' She laughs in an unconvincing attempt to mock her own misfortune. 'My real trouble is the office. The rent is costing me so much that I've got to get out of there. That means sacrificing the fifty-thousand-pound deposit and saying goodbye to three months' advance rent. It sounds crazy, but if I'm going to stay afloat I've got no choice. Meanwhile the bank's asking how I'm going to give them their cash back. It's almost a day-to-day thing now.'

'I'm sorry, Lauren.' I really am. 'I didn't have a clue it had come to this.'

'Of course you didn't, and it's not your business anyway. But look, all I ask of you is this. Can you please settle the divorce quickly? I need money fast. That's my single priority. Quick divorce, quick money. Harvey's going to fight tooth and nail for everything, and I know you've got to do that for him. But I just want out fast. I need the whole thing finished so I can take a cheque to the bank manager. Otherwise it's all over for me, my business goes, my staff go and I'm declared bankrupt.' She laughs again in that self-mocking tone. 'Do you see what I mean?'

'Lauren, I do.' And I know I'm being stupid, but I find myself promising to do my best to make it quick. And it pays off because she rewards me with a warm smile, then stands up, lays her left hand on my right cheek and kisses the other.

18

Georgina McKnight strides forcefully into the meeting room at Chilton Shaw, where I have been waiting, and fills it with her usual cocktail of terror and sex. Today she is dressed in a black skirt that doesn't quite cover her knees and a stretchy black velvet shirt. A pendant cross hangs tantalisingly from her neck, one moment in front of her shirt, the next tumbling inside it to dangle, presumably, between her breasts. When she unclicks her briefcase, I half expect her to bring out a whip rather than a file of legal correspondence.

Today I'm supposed to run legal rings round her. I'm supposed to be so dominating that she'll kneel down and beg for mercy. The end result, apparently, will be that Harvey Goode can keep far more money than any court would allow if it ever got that far.

'So, how's that broken heart of yours, Will?' she asks, as she lays out her mobile phone, a pen and three tidy piles of papers, exactly as she did in the sandwich bar, as if she is drawing up her forces for battle.

'Fine, thanks,' I reply, straightening out my limited resources of a lone biro and a single pile of papers. 'She came running back to me.'

'Which one? The girl or the penguin?'

'The girl.' I swallow nervously. Georgina isn't at her most gentle today.

'Right,' she says. 'I think we both know where this settlement has got to go for there to be a resolution, don't we?'

Here we go. She starts talking about housing needs, capitalised maintenance and the cost of forfeited career development, and I am hypnotised by her cross as I wait for her to get to the point and tell me that if Harvey really believes that all he is going to give Lauren in a clean-break settlement is £650,000, then he's going to have to think again.

'Come on, Will,' she says, readjusting the angle of her mobile phone so that she could shoot me with it, 'if your client really believes that all he's going to give Mrs Goode in a clean-break settlement is £650,000, then he's going to have to think again. We both know that, don't we?'

Luckily, I'm reasonably handy at this sort of negotiation and, furthermore, I don't think I'm too bad at covering up how in awe I am of the woman with whom I'm negotiating. But I'm also on a losing wicket.

This is how the sums stack up. We have declared that Harvey is worth just under £41 million; I have good reason to believe that a further three million is well hidden in clandestine accounts and foreign investments, but since Harvey didn't mention it when I asked him, I don't intend to mention it either. Under the old rules, which held before the White case came along, I've worked out that Lauren could expect a pay-out from this of £840,000. Somehow I had persuaded Harvey that £750,000 was a reasonable settlement; that way, I figured, he wouldn't explode too terrifyingly if it went a little higher. He and I agreed then to offer Lauren £650,000. Like that, we had something to give when Georgina got heavy-handed.

But there are two flaws in my thinking. The first is my disclosure of the value of his assets. If Georgina challenges that, which she will, and we have to come clean about the hidden extras, all the figures rise and Harvey may end up parting with a fair bit more. I doubt he'd like that.

Even worse is the White v. White issue. If Georgina cites the case, Harvey's fortune might be decimated, in which case Lauren's business will be safe for the next decade. Indeed, she'll be in with a sporting chance of retiring to a life where her most taxing challenge will be deciding which cocktail to order beside a pool in Mustique. And that's before I've had the temerity to ask him to pay my legal fees.

Nevertheless I give Georgina my best calm-voiced, detached, in-control, looking-out-of-the-window-a-lot comeback. I realise while I'm talking what it is that makes her so untouchable. Georgina is like one of the senior girls at school whom you deify when you're four years their junior, who have fully developed breasts and are sexually active, everything a fourteen-year-old boy dreams of but knows he will never even get to talk to. And here am I talking to one.

'You are aware,' I tell her, 'that there are no children

involved, that the marriage has been short, and that Mrs Goode has a high earning capacity?'

'Yes, thank you. Though her earning capacity right now certainly isn't as high as you imply.' As I am all too aware, Georgina. 'What is your point?'

'That Mrs Goode's business could soon make her no worse off than she is now, so her requirements in housing and maintenance are pretty low.'

'Interesting point, Will, but it isn't based on fact. Even if it were, it would have little or no bearing on the outcome of this settlement.'

'We shall see.'

'I'm sure we shall. And you're aware, Will, I'm sure, that Mrs Goode is also American.'

'Yes.' I pick up my biro and rotate it around my index finger.

'And therefore you're also aware that this divorce could be settled instead in the United States where Mrs Goode would be likely to get a considerably better deal.'

'That's arguable.'

'It is indeed, Will, and it would probably be rather dull, but nevertheless I would willingly take part in such an argument because I feel confident that I would win it. Easily.'

'I'm sure that would give you great pleasure, Georgina,' I replace the biro carefully, so it is pointing straight at her to return fire, 'but we both know it's irrelevant because the divorce papers were served here in the United Kingdom so it is under the jurisdiction of the United Kingdom that the divorce is carried out.'

'Not bad, Will. Not bad at all.' Her condescension is brilliant. 'Now that we've shared a nice early skirmish, shall we move on? Whether Mrs Goode was born in New England or New Malden, she is still a British citizen and is entitled to a decent settlement. A settlement more decent than the one she is being offered. If your offer remains so low, we'll end up contesting it when we meet in court, and everything will be slow and tedious. I'd like to reach an agreement before then. I forget when it is – what is the date we've been set?'

'The ninth of September.'

'That's right. Reach an agreement before the ninth of September, have the settlement ratified then, and it's over. Neither you nor I will have to associate with the man you represent any longer.'

'Until his next divorce.'

'Well, maybe,' she replies. Disappointingly, she doesn't seem too hot on jokes. 'Right. The London house. Origins of ownership. An evaluation? Any documentation?'

Our meeting regresses into dull minutiae and I have to stop myself tracing the movement of Georgina's cross and concentrate on the calculated movement of her argument. And, although I feel as if I'm close to the jaws of a lion, I don't think I'm given a complete mauling. Georgina likes being on top and, in my limited experience, when you are with a woman of such calibre, it is best to accede to her demands. She is welcome to go on top, and she can whip me and chain me and dish out whatever punishment she feels necessary, just so long as it keeps her away from the two key issues: Harvey's hidden millions and the White case.

Indeed, I make her feel so satisfied that she strays near neither subject. And I know that she has climaxed when she starts to tidy away the forcefield of stationery and mobile phone.

'So, you're happy to change your offer?' she asks.

'Not happy, but if you were to send us a proposal near to the figure we've offered, then we would consider it.'

'How very decent of you.' Condescending to the end. 'I'll speak to my client and we'll be back to you in writing. You'll have heard from me by the end of next week with an offer and a request for further details.'

'Fine.'

'And don't be so careless as to let that poor girlfriend of yours fall through your hands again.'

I suspect, however, that it is Georgina who has been careless today. Of course, she may be seducing me into some fantastically clever trap. I'm so keen to avoid that that I stop for a coffee on the way back to my office, pull out my Goode case papers and scan them. I still can't see any loophole. Her letter will reveal all. And I think I might be able to help Harvey save his money. How hollow a victory is that?

19

Thursday afternoon. Divorce of the day is McCann v. McCann.

Brian McCann, my client, thirty-four, introverted landscape gardener from Maidstone, informs me that he doesn't want to be married to Mrs McCann any more. She, it seems, has recently disclosed that he may not be the father of the boy he has loved and called his son for the five years since his birth. This seems to me reasonable grounds for not wanting to spend the rest of his life with his wife.

But while Brian McCann's life sounds unbearably awful, I'm finding it hard to concentrate because I can't stop thinking about the amicable drink I'm supposed to be having with Steph this evening. An email has just arrived from Jenny, diverting me further: 'Will, you are doing a really good thing. I hope the drink goes well. Love Jenny. PS When I say I hope it goes well, I also want you to remember that this is a one-off, you don't have to go for a drink with her every week. I like you too much for that.' How sweet.

Sam pokes her head round my door. 'The boss wants to see you.'

'Simon?'

'Yes, the posh guy with the side parting – remember him?'

'What does he want?'

'He didn't have the time or inclination to discuss that.'

'Oh. When does he want to see me?'

'He said now, as in "right now".'

'Ah, Will.'

Simon barely acknowledges my arrival and continues to stare out of the window with his back to me. Eventually, without so much as a glance in my direction, he gestures me to sit down. Then he turns round and tosses an A3-sized express-delivery envelope at me, with some force.

'Everything going well with the Goode case?' he asks, looking away again.

'Yes, thanks, Simon.'

'Good, good.' Then there is silence. Simon continues to gaze out of the window, and suddenly waves of paranoia are crashing over me. 'Nothing else to add in particular?'

'I'm not sure what you mean.' But I know exactly what he means and I'm quite scared.

'We've got some nice pictures of Mrs Goode, here,' he says matter-of-factly. 'They were taken by a private detective hired by Harvey Goode.'

And still he gazes out of the window, letting me stew a little longer. 'Go on. Have a look at them,' he says, pushing me towards my fate. 'I believe you might recognise her.'

I slide my right forefinger under the lip of the envelope, replaying in my mind the events in Bar Blue on Saturday morning. I have been monumentally stupid. I can feel Simon staring at me through the back of his head. Surely he can see nothing but arrogance, naïvety and folly.

But how public was that kiss? I slide the photos out of the envelope and turn them over to find out.

The first is encouraging. It is Jake and Lauren. I am nowhere to be seen. The quality of the pictures is not good – they're grainy, probably taken through a long fat lens. But still, no matter how grainy the image, I'm invisible.

The second is similar. Just Jake and Lauren, laughing together. No me, although in terms of my professional standing, I'm still dancing with death. My flatmate pictured with the wife of my client? It looks like a fairly unforgivable lapse in professional conduct, and that is why Simon is doing his melodramatic angry boss act. I guess I've blown the partnership.

The third and the fourth photos are of Jake and Lauren walking down a street, but the street-lights are on. This isn't Saturday morning. I look up at Simon for information and now he's staring at me.

I turn over the photographs with increasing speed. No sign of me, just Jake and Lauren, Jake and Lauren. Then Jake and Lauren holding hands in another street, which looks very much like Davenport Road; Jake and Lauren swinging their linked arms in the air like a pair of skipping children; Jake and Lauren with Jake putting a key into the door of the building that contains my flat; then, grainier still, Jake and Lauren in the flat in front of the kitchen window, then Jake and Lauren entwined in an embrace, kissing, then kissing again.

I rewind through the last three. Jake is still kissing Lauren. Lauren, the fragile beauty who held my head in her hands and tenderly kissed *me*. And Jake? Nice guy Jake who's never had a proper girlfriend?

I look up at Simon, who has clearly been studying my face for a reaction but he cannot fathom the mental mess I'm trying to unravel. I don't know what to say and I am overwhelmed by trepidation.

'Oh,' he says gaily. 'Here's one other photo that came in the same batch.' It spins across the desk and comes to rest upside-down. I turn it over and am confronted with a picture of Jenny and me. Jenny is looking tired and I'm putting a key into the same door as Jake. I see. This is how they connected me with him: the incriminating evidence against me.

'What the hell is going on, Will?' Simon is getting going now. An upper-class accent like his, combined with a cold, unflustered delivery, can be an impressive agent of malice. 'I've had Mr Goode on the phone already today spitting fury. He commissioned these – I'm surprised you didn't know – and had them sent round this morning. He is incandescent with rage, as I hope you'd imagine. You shouldn't need me to tell you this, but since you appear to have lost all powers of judgement, I will anyway. This looks bad. Very bad. What on earth have you been playing at?'

'Is there any point in telling you that I didn't have a clue this was going on?' I reply.

I'm furious with Jake, for dumping me in it like this and for his staggering deceit. And I don't want to lose my job. But there is more going on here, and it's dawning on me that this is all about my own vanity. I look long at the pictures again. Who risked so much to help her? Me. Who did she kiss so tenderly in Bar Blue? Me. Not him. And, pathetically, I liked it. I wasn't just being gallant, daring or flirtatious, I was day-dreaming that I might one day be saving her for myself.

'But if I'm not mistaken this is your flatmate,' says Simon.

'Three months ago, Mrs Goode appeared at our flat,' I reply, pulling myself together fast. 'Twice. She tracked me down, I think, because she wanted someone to shout at. I tried to be reasonably civil, but I also said that she shouldn't come back. On both occasions I asked my flatmate Jake, who is starring alongside her in these pictures, to show her out. I thought we'd never see her again.'

'So, you're telling me that you've not seen her since?'

'Never.' My calf muscles tighten as I deliver the lie.

'Even though they appear to come and go to and from your flat as they please?'

'Yes.'

'You didn't see them there on Friday night?'

'No. They'd left by the time I was pictured arriving home.'

'And is Jake a good friend?'

'Yes, surprisingly so.'

'But perhaps not such a good friend as you'd thought.' Simon is roasting me now, his hands on the desk, his voice composed and killing. I thought I'd left behind confrontations like this at school. But here I am feeling guilty and cheated on, and unable to respond to the mother of all bollockings.

'Well, I'm shocked.' What else can I say?

'And you expect me to believe that? Or, more to the point, you expect a hard-nosed insensitive bastard like Mr Goode to believe it?'

'I know it doesn't look good—'

'Good? Will, it looks fucking terrible.' Simon's back is turned again and he is emphasising every word. 'Will, Mr Goode brings all his company business to us – you know that. Our litigation and company-business departments make half a million pounds off him in a quiet year. This fucking divorce is just a tiddly bit of icing on the fucking cake. Have you any idea what the other partners of this firm would do if they knew we were about to blow all that because we can't handle his private life? There should never be the remotest question over our allegiances, Will. You don't need me to tell you that. They should never be called into question. Particularly when it comes to Harvey Goode.'

'But it's true.' I've raised my voice in response and I'm quite impressed with my own feistiness. 'Simon, I'm sorry. Jake is one of my best friends. I've lived with him for five years. He is thoughtful, decent, respectful. He is a great guy and, yes, you're right, he has let me down

and I can't work out how he can have done this to me.'
I may have been the agent of my own destruction too,
but it's probably not worth adding that.

'I don't think your hurt feelings will be much consolation to Mr Goode.' Simon pauses. He doesn't have
a clue how hurt my feelings are right now. Then he
grimaces. 'We'll certainly have to pass his brief on to
someone else. The firm's reputation is so much at stake.
I'll probably have to get my hands dirty and take it on
myself.'

'No, Simon, you can't.'

'Why not?'

'You said yourself that there was a lot riding on it
for me.'

'There was, Will. There was. Note the use of the
past tense.'

'Look, Simon, I can't tell you how well I was doing
with it.'

'What do you mean?'

'I am doing really well on the brief. Harvey's personally worth in the region of forty million and he says he's
only prepared to part with £750,000. You and I both
know that that is bloody ridiculous. But he's insisted on
it. I've tried to lower his sights, tell him that he'll never
get away with a settlement like that, but he's refused,
so I've gone in with all my guns blazing, expecting to
be shot down in flames. And that's without White v.
White coming into it. But the amazing thing is that I'm
winning the battle. White v. White hasn't even had a
look-in. And you know who's representing Mrs Goode?

It's only Georgina McKnight from Chilton Shaw, and we both know how good she is. I have to say that I think she's got Mrs Goode pretty much on the point of accepting Mr Goode's terms. That's what I mean.' It's hard to make a point when the man you're speaking to is so determinedly turning his back on you, but I press on. 'Please, Simon, give me a chance to complete it. The fact that we now have evidence that Mrs Goode has another partner, albeit a partner who lives in my flat, can't damage our argument, can it?'

'What do you mean?'

'Well, we now have Mrs Goode apparently committing adultery.'

'You know as well as I do that in a court of law one ill-considered fuck at this stage of the game won't make any difference to the settlement.' Simon is talking slowly, thinking. He puts his hands into his pockets and sits down on the desk. He looks like he might be acquiescing.

'Will, you have to realise that this is extremely poor. I'll accept your explanation, but I also have to tell you that your job is on the line. You're hanging by a thread, a fucking thin one. I don't know what you're going to do about this Jake you claim is your friend, but it had better be pretty tidy and it had better impress Mr Goode. This firm is not in the habit of losing the sort of business that he brings in. And goodness knows how many more divorce settlements he's worth to us.' Simon chuckles, then resumes his serious tone. 'If we lose Mr Goode, I don't think it will augur well for your future with us.

That's an understatement. However, if you're doing as well with his case as you say you are, then I'm prepared – with Mr Goode's permission, of course – to give you the chance to salvage it.'

'Fantastic. Thank you very much.'

'I would suggest that your first job is to lunch Mr Goode as lavishly as you possibly can.'

'Sure.' But I am already formulating a far better plan.

20

Back in the office. Brian McCann will have to remain attached to his dreadful wife for a few hours more. I'll sort that mess out tomorrow.

I have to ring Jake. No answer. The bastard. I ring Harvey. In a meeting. I leave a message for him to call back. I ring Jenny. Not available. Hell.

I ring Jake again. His colleague picks up the phone. He is out all afternoon apparently. I try his mobile. No answer. How could he do this to me? The most mild-mannered, considerate, unconfrontational and ineffective womaniser in the world waltzes off into the sunset with the good-looking, soon-to-be-ex-wife of a multi-millionaire, getting his jealous best friend fired in the process? It'd be hilarious if I wasn't the one left picking up the pieces. And what a lot of pieces. I thought Brian McCann had problems.

Flustered, I yell for Sam, 'Sam, it's all gone wrong.'

'Oh. So you don't want to hear how many people have called, then?'

'Not unless their names are Harvey Goode, Jenny Joffee or Jake Buckland. Any of those?'

'No, just the usual handful of miserable divorcees. And someone called Stephanie Honeyfield.'

'What the hell did she want?'

'She didn't say. What did Simon want?'

'Oh, just to say that I'll probably be looking for another job by the end of the week. It's really bad, Sam. And if I go I'm taking you with me.'

'You mean you're taking me on the dole with you?'

'Yup.'

'How could I refuse?'

'I don't know. But until then you could try to save me by ringing these numbers.' I scribble two phone numbers on a yellow Post-it. 'This one's Jenny's number at her TV studio. The other is Jake's mobile. Ring them alternately until you've got hold of them. Drop everything else.'

'What the hell's going on?'

'Everything.'

'Right.' Sam disappears, leaving me to curse in peace.

Since I can't get hold of anyone else, I ring Alex. At least he answers.

'Alex, hi, Will here. The world's gone mad. Did you know about Jake?'

'What do you mean?'

'Did you know that Jake might have a girlfriend in tow?'

'Ah, I thought maybe that's what you meant.'

'So you did know.'

'Sort of. I've been telling him for two months to tell you. He's been building up to it. He said he thought you'd be professionally compromised if you knew, which you would. But he knows he's got to tell you.'

'Fucking hell! I don't believe it! How many other people are in on this?'

'Just Jake, Lauren, Steph and myself.'

'Oh, very bloody cosy. You, Jake, the woman whose money I'm trying to take and the ex-girlfriend from hell, who I'm supposed to be having a drink with in four hours, all in on this little joke and I'm ignorant as hell and about to lose my job over it.'

'That's what I told Jake.'

'The bastard! Alex, I've got a call waiting. Hang on a second.' It's Harvey Goode. 'Alex, got to go. It's the husband of Jake's girlfriend on the line. Tricky, eh? I can't believe you could all do this to me.'

'Will, it's not like that.' And Alex embarks on an explanation about how the cosy foursome have spent hours talking about 'the situation', wondering what to do and how to protect me. It seems like they wasted their time.

'Sorry, Alex,' I interrupt, 'I've really got to go.'

I pause for half a second, take a deep breath, then connect Harvey.

'Harvey, hi.' Do I sound unflustered? I don't think I'm doing too badly.

'Will, your boss assures me you're innocent. I don't believe it. Not for a moment. What do you say?'

'That my boss is right.'

'Your boss also says I should make you grovel so low in the dirt that any residue of self-respect you've hung on to so far is wiped clean from your account. What do you say now?'

'That you should let me take you out to dinner to let me explain.'

'I don't want to have dinner with you. I just want you to get me a divorce.'

'The invitation isn't just with me, it's with Jenny Joffee too.'

'Jenny Joffee?'

'The TV chef you so admire.'

'Instead of going out, why doesn't she cook for us?'

'No reason.' Except that she can't cook.

'Right, well, now you're talking.' Sam marches into the room with another yellow Post-it: Jenny is waiting on the other line. 'But why should Jenny Joffee want me round for dinner?'

'Because she loves me.'

'Ah, big talk. But, Will, I need to know: are you on my side or my wife's in this? Answer me that.'

'Yours, of course, Harvey.' It's just that I'm two-timing you emotionally.

'You're going to have to persuade me.'

'So you'll come, then?'

'Yup. Friday week do you?'

'Er, hang on a second. Harvey, can you hold the line? I'm very sorry. I'll just get rid of this other call.'

I connect Jenny. 'Hi, sweetie.'

'Hi, I've really enjoyed being kept holding like this. It'd better be good.'

'It is. Sort of. Oh, Jenny, am I glad to speak to you! I'm suddenly so deep in the shit that I think it's going to be impossible to extricate myself. Macbeth said something like that once, but probably a little less poetically.'

'What are you talking about?'

'You remember Lauren Goode? The wife a client of mine is divorcing? The one who pitched up at my flat that day?'

'Yes.'

'Jake's having an affair with her.'

'Who is?'

'Jake.'

'Oh, well done him.'

'It's not quite as simple as that.'

'I suppose not.'

'What are you doing on Friday week?'

'Going to a restaurant opening.'

'If I came up with an infinitely better offer, would you forget it?'

'Might do. What is it?'

'I'll tell you in a minute. Hang on a sec, I'm sorry but I've got to put you on hold again.'

I connect Harvey. 'Harvey, hi, sorry about that. Yes, Friday week looks fine.'

'She'd better be worth it, Will. Your life depends on it.'

'Sure, right, Harvey. I'll be in touch with your secretary about the arrangements. 'Bye.'

She'd better be worth it? What sort of statement is that? Into what realm of twisted thinking do those four words take us? No time for that. Back to Jenny.

'Sorry about that.'

'That's all right. I've been using my time productively

to compile a list of the "infinitely better offers" than my restaurant opening that you could come up with. Do you want to hear what's on my list?'

'Oh dear. Not really.'

'Well, I'll give you a taster. First is the classic standard but unbeatable weekend in Paris. In second place I've lumped together two other foreign destinations: Amalfi and Seville. Never been to either but I've heard they're great. Third – and I'd be amazed if this was what you had in mind but I'll tell you because it's cheaper and I'd like to do it anyway – is camping. Just you and me and a tent. We wouldn't even need to go abroad. It'd be lovely. You could be all big and strong and carry the tent on your back and I could burn our toast over the campfire. Go on, tell me that's what we're doing. Go on, go on.' She is chuckling to herself.

'How do you fancy hosting a dinner party?'

'In Amalfi or Seville?'

'More like your place. Primrose Hill.'

'If I could cook I might be half interested. So unless you've got some outstanding guests coming and they don't mind eating a take-away, I think I'll stick to the restaurant opening.'

'I can see I'm going to have to work on you.'

'You give me a weekend in Amalfi, I'll give you a dinner party.'

'Done.'

'But, Will,' her tone changes, 'are you all right? You sound rather flustered.'

'I *am* flustered.'

21

Still no sign of Jake and now no sign of Steph. Having spent the last three months avoiding her, I am not enjoying the irony of her playing hard to get. I'm waiting for her in the venue of her choice, Horatio's: modern, minimalist, silver and not very pleasant.

A gaggle of pleased-with-themselves late-twentysomething lads in suits is standing at the bar drinking designer bottled lager. I wonder whether any of them would hang around for an ex-girlfriend they despise who is twenty-five minutes late for a date. Probably not. And especially not if they'd rather be driving round town to track down a devious, duplicitous, love-rat flatmate who has disappeared with their professional career in his hands.

I failed all afternoon to track down Jake. The voicemail facility on his mobile phone is now full, though that is largely due to my abusive messages. The bastard. At least he's provided me with a distraction: I'd have been fretting all afternoon about this showdown drink with Steph were it not for the minor side-issue of finding that my whole career was on the line. Praise the Lord.

The lads at the bar are just ordering another round when the door behind them swings open to reveal Steph.

I watch her scan the room until her eyes alight on me. She gives me a smile – warm, peaceful and long – that I recognise immediately.

She looks annoyingly good again; I guess I'm going to have to get used to this. Her hair looks great, held back fashionably by hairclips, and I'm not sure if it's the lighting in the bar but there might be flecks of purple with the reds and the browns. She's even more petite than Jenny and has bigger breasts. I know I shouldn't compare them but it's hard not to. Well done, Alex.

She winks at me and, with a combination of nods and hand movements, we agree that she's sorry she's late and that she's going to buy herself a drink then come over and sit down. When she joins me, I stand up, kiss her left cheek and tell her it's nice to see her. She tells me it's nice to see me too and then, as we sit looking at each other, unsure how to begin, I wonder if she really finds this as 'nice' as I do or if she means it.

'Thank you for coming,' she says, breaking the silence. 'I wasn't sure that you would.'

'How could I miss a lovely opportunity like this?' I reply, surprised to be given an opening so quickly.

'Oh, Will, it isn't going to be like that, is it?'

'I don't know. I've not worked out how it's going to be. What do you reckon?'

'I reckon we have a couple of beers and try to put the past behind us.'

'Yeah, let's just forget everything that's happened,' I say drily, 'and have a bit of a laugh.'

'Will!' Steph looks disappointed.

'Sorry, sorry!' I stick up my arms as if she has pointed a gun at me.

'Oh, come on.'

'OK. OK.'

'Why did you bother coming otherwise? Let's just try, shall we?'

'Try! Yes, let's all try really hard.' I'm in full sarcasm mode again, trying hard to be hurtful. 'Then we can all be friends again and it'll be lovely.'

'We *could* work it out.'

'Oh, I know *you*'ve got it all nicely worked out. Who knows? If it works out well enough, by the end of the evening you might even get another proposal out of me.'

Steph is stoically enduring my pathetic sarcasm without responding.

'What?' I ask her, as if her thoughts weren't obvious anyway.

'Nothing. I can't say anything, can I, if this is how you're going to be?'

I hadn't intended to be like this – I hadn't planned anything. I certainly hadn't lined up my guns to mount an offensive. I guess I'm just happy to lash out at the first target. And Steph makes a good one.

But when I look into her eyes, I remember how futile it always was when I tried to do battle with her all those years ago. She just took it on the chin as she is now, and looked at me as if slightly hurt and ever so slightly amused, as you would at a little boy whose temper you are waiting to assuage.

'Sorry,' I say. I am.

'That's OK.'

'As I think you probably know, it's been quite a day.'

'I've heard. Are you OK?'

'Oh, yeah, never better.'

'Sorry, stupid question.'

'No, I'm sorry. That wasn't aimed at you. I'm being nice now.'

'OK. Is there anything I can do?'

We are talking calmly and Steph is wearing another familiar expression, the one that makes her look like the most caring, thoughtful person in the world, the one that breaks down male barriers – it had mine tumbling down anyway – and makes you feel that she's a person it's OK to get close to.

'There is one thing you could do,' I reply drily. 'You could leave Alex.'

'Will!' She knows not to take me too seriously. 'That's not going to happen.'

'Of course not. Look, Steph, it's OK. You can go out with Alex.' And I say this as sincerely as I can because I've no alternative. 'I can't sit around being childish and grumpy. I can't form a picket line outside your front door. Do it. Honestly. I'm already getting used to it.'

'Oh, Will, thank you.'

I shrug. 'You obviously quite like each other.'

'You could put it like that.'

'I don't need the details!'

'Well, we do.'

'But what gets me is that this is a serious thing, not a fling. I know what Alex is like – is it really so special that you have to write me letters and meet me for a drink to declare peace in our time?'

'Let me tell you a story. Alex would probably rather I didn't share it with you, but here it is anyway. Last Thursday night, a week ago today, we'd been out together and we both had our cars because we'd come from different places and I was going to follow him home. Anyway, before we got into them, Alex told me to watch his rear windscreen-wiper. He said that if he turned it on, it meant that he liked me, and if he left it on for a long time, it meant he loved me. Anyway, as soon as my car was behind his, his rear wiper started going. And it only stopped once on the entire journey home.'

'Why was that?'

'A police car stopped him to ask why he had his wiper on on a dry night. It didn't stop again until he turned his engine off.'

'*Alex?*'

'I know, I know. He tells me that all this would be bad for his image if it ever got out, but honestly, Will, he means it. It's lovely.'

I shake my head in disbelief. 'If Alex has gone all soft and mushy on us I'm amazed. You'd better be nice to him, Steph. You promise you won't go off with Danny Arnold this time?' Steph just gives me that same look of resignation, as if to let me know that that was another blow she'd take on the chin. 'Sorry again. I just had to get it out of my system.'

'Do you feel better for it?'

'Yeah. But I think my ammunition's pretty much spent now.'

'Good. I hear your Jenny's very nice.'

'She is. And she's got her own underwear drawer.'

'Wow! She must be very special.'

'She's not bad. Do you beat Alex at table-tennis?'

'Yup.'

'He's not very good, is he?'

'No.'

'Crap defence. Always crumbles on the big points.'

She laughs, because she understands I've brought the serious part of the conversation to an end. I don't want to talk about Danny Arnold or the intricate ten-year-old details of an ill-judged ending to a happy relationship; the time for that, it is now apparent, has long gone. And it doesn't seem I'm going to achieve much by flinging barbed comments at her either. In fact, I haven't any option but to toe the line, be a good boy, smile and accept the avalanche of bad news under which my supposed close friends seem intent on burying me.

I've never been partial to ex-girlfriends, never seen the point of them. Relationships, it seems to me, end either unhappily or in marriage. The ones that end unhappily – mine – aren't worth salvaging. I don't mind sharing an empty promise to stay in touch, but, Lord, don't hold me to it. There are too many feelings out there standing up innocently in polite queues waiting to be hurt.

Alex's attitude to ex-girlfriends is different. He goes back and sleeps with them again – at least, that's what he

did until Steph came along. And there are rare sightings –
though I've never witnessed one – of a parting by mutual
consent where no one gets hurt, though I suspect those
are just PR jobs dressed up to protect wounded egos.
But for me there's never a happy ending. In my fragile
belief system, happy endings are reserved for Hollywood
blockbusters and German World Cup campaigns (if
you're German, of course). Yet now I'm confronted
with the need to venture into the realms of 'just good
friends'. That's why I have to make jokes about Alex
being useless at table-tennis: I have no option.

'So, what happened to being a nurse?' I ask, moving
into small-talk mode.

'Nurses don't get paid much. I qualified and did it for
five years, but that was enough. It's a shame because I've
wandered aimlessly around the job market ever since.'

'Maybe you'll help me find a new job.'

'It's not got to that, has it?'

'Not yet, but I think it's going to be quite a fight to
hang in there.'

'Hang well, then.'

'But, Steph, what I really can't believe,' I sit forward
in my chair, 'is that Jake would do this with Lauren.'

'I know you can't. Of course you can't. Look, Lauren's
great, really she is. I'd like to say more but that's all for
Jake to explain.'

'It'll take quite a lot of explaining.'

'And Jake – I've not known him long but he seems as
good-natured and genuine a person as you'll find. And
although he doesn't seem so right now, he's a great

friend to you, Will.' She says this, as if she's amazed that friendship could ever be so strong and true. 'He's distraught. He's desperate not to hurt you.'

'Too late for that.'

'I know. But don't give up on him, baby.'

'As your old mate David Soul would say.'

'Exactly.'

'I can't believe you still like that shit.'

'I don't, but I can hardly renege on it now, I'm with Alex, remember?'

We laugh together, genuinely – although I can't help distrusting the way Steph catches my eye and laughs a little too long, as if she's trying to say, 'Hey, look at us laughing, just like old times, we can be buddies, after all.' I'm still not convinced of that, not even when we go our separate ways on the pavement outside the bar almost an hour later. We part with a kiss, I put her into a taxi and walk for a while before I can get another taxi to stop for me.

But buddies? When you've been waging a silent war on someone for as long as I have, it's hard to admit that maybe the enemy wasn't so bad after all.

22

Jake is at the flat. The lights are on and the comparative mess in which I left the place this morning has been dramatically reduced. Nevertheless, all is quiet.

So, this is it. Ever since those photographs spilled into my lap this morning, I've been thinking about what to say to him. Now that I have a chance to say it, I have no idea what will come out. It's only when a friendship is tested that you realise how much it means to you.

Jake isn't in the sitting-room so I nudge open his bedroom door. He's sitting on the edge of the bed, his elbows on his knees, chin on his hands, eyes raised meekly to me, as though he has been awaiting me. His fresh face looks careworn and his silence suggests that he has been there for hours. Then I look round the room and find it loaded with messages: the bedding has been stripped from his bed, the door to one of his wardrobes is open and it is bare inside. In the corner of the room, there are two large suitcases, clearly packed and ready to go.

I guess I'd have had to ask him to move out anyway, but that he has done it of his own accord changes everything. What has happened to all the anger I'd thought I was going to unleash?

'What on earth's going on, mate?' I say to him quietly.

'Sit down, Will. I've got a bit of explaining to do, haven't I?' I sit on the bed next to him. 'I'm moving out.'

'You're not going to take the Sodastream, are you?'

'The Sodastream?' He looks nonplussed.

'Well, you've probably lost me my job, so to lose the Sodastream on top, all in one day, that'd be a real killer blow.'

'Shit! You haven't lost your job, have you?'

'I don't know. Possibly. There's a chance I can hang on to it.'

'Is there anything I can do?'

'Well, you're doing it already, really,' I say, jerking a thumb at the suitcases. 'But where have you been all day? I've been trying desperately to get hold of you.'

'I've been at Lauren's lawyers, looking through a packet of photographs they received today. I expect you've seen them too.'

'They were my mid-afternoon surprise.'

'So you know the story, then.'

'Apart from why you never told me.' I still can't raise my voice. This isn't going to be a falling-out, just sad parting. 'How long's it been going on?'

'Since she came knocking on our door back in April. You know the second time she came round? Well, we'd been here for about an hour before you got home, just talking. And she was in bits again, and I was trying to mop up the tears, and we seemed to get on quite well. And then you got back and she had to go, and you asked me to give her my mobile number. So I did. I gave her my card actually. And I swear I had no intention of doing anything with her – it hadn't even crossed my mind. I just felt sorry for her and I liked her, and I said if she wanted to talk again she should call me. I never thought she would. I never imagined anything would come of it. But she did and it went on from there.'

He stops and all I can do is ask him to continue. So Jake tells me about Lauren phoning him, then phoning him again, and a few times more until they started meeting. If I hadn't been so heavily involved, I'd probably have found it touching.

'She was so emotionally bruised,' he says. 'The whole thing was very peaceful. I didn't chat her up, I never had to invite her out to dinner, all that courtship stuff I'm so crap at. And I can't say I didn't find her attractive, but because of her circumstances I never thought it might go somewhere. If I'd tried to do it, I'm sure I'd have fucked it up ages ago. But we just started talking about her business disaster and her worries about having to close down, and then we went beyond that bit by bit and eventually we ended up miles away, in a place we'd never considered going.'

'I can see that, and I can see you didn't chase after her. But that's it, isn't it? I mean, you're not expecting it to go any further, are you?'

'Yes. I am.' His voice expresses a quiet certainty.

'Jake! I'm not talking about my job here. Forget about that for a moment. I mean, you and Lauren, there's surely no way it can work out, is there?'

'Listen.' Jake stands up and is now looking down on me. 'This is the whole fucking thing. It's massive. I think I'm in love with her. I know that sounds strange coming from me of all people, I know I'm the amusing, useless guy with the overpowering mother who never gets a girlfriend, so how should I know what I'm talking about? But it's true. It feels weird to stand here and say it to you. It felt weird when I first said it to her. But she says it back to me and it's brilliant. I feel it, I really *feel* it.' And he shows it by clenching his fists and clutching them to his chest. 'I know it. It's unavoidable, it's just there all the time. And it's scary too. And that's the whole point. Every day I've been on the point of breaking it off. Every day I've thought, I've got to get out of this, this is stupid, it's suicide, she's in the middle of a divorce from Mr Fucking Big and I'm going to get eaten alive. And that's just the minor issue – because even if I don't get eaten alive, it might backfire on you and your job.'

'Which it has.'

Jake presses his hands to his face. 'I know. But every day it just seemed too damned good to let it go. I'd say to myself: "Just one more day and then I'll finish it and I'll tell Will and we can get back to before." Will, I know this thing's suddenly landed on your doorstep and I've been completely crap and I apologise, but Lauren and I have talked about you endlessly, I've been unable to sleep thinking about it, what to do, how to protect you . . .'

'And you ended up doing nothing.'

Jake shrugs and for a moment there is silence. He puts his hands on his hips and shakes his head. 'But, Will,' he's looking imploringly at me now, 'this is it. My chance. I'm sitting around talking to Lauren about how we should split up, yet I'm in love with her. What do I do? This is the only girl I've ever liked, and she likes me back. She *loves* me back. I know I sound naïve but it's true. I've been so torn. I've experienced a happiness that I thought was going to pass me by, and I've been overwhelmed with guilt about it. Was I supposed to give in to guilt and dump the happiness?'

I don't know what to say to that. Jake is looking down at me with tears in his eyes and there is silence again.

'I'm flabbergasted,' I say. 'I had no idea. I was so far in the dark about all this that I actually thought it was me Lauren liked. How ridiculous is that!' I manage a chuckle.

Jake raises his eyebrows in apparent amusement but says nothing.

'So, what are you going to do now?' I ask. My own vanity, I realise, is irrelevant. 'Where will you go?'

'I've got a short lease on a new flat. Steph sorted it out for me this afternoon when all this stuff started happening. I was pretty lucky, I suppose – something had just come in. That's why she was late for your drink. She was handing over the keys.'

'I suppose Jenny knows all this too, does she?'

'No, why should she?'

'Because everyone but me seems to be in on it.'

'You're pissed off about that, are you?'

'Yes, I'm pissed off about everything, even though I suppose I can understand it.' I'm tempted again to vent my frustration, but I see the honesty on Jake's face and any sense of displeasure is assuaged. 'And I can't blame you, can I? It sounds great what you two have got. I just hate the idea of you two, Alex and Steph all in on some cosy secret with me on the outside. I suppose you're all friends, are you?'

'Not really.'

'Have you been out as a cosy four?'

'Just once.'

'Exactly, you bastards.' I attempt to sound vaguely lighthearted.

'We still spent most of the time talking over what we were going to do about you. That's one of the reasons why it's so good that you're coming to Alex's birthday party.'

'That's "Welcome Back, Will" night, is it?'

'No, but it's important we do something like this with just the six of us.'

'So Lauren's going to be there too. Oh, God! How stupid of me not to realise. Now it all makes sense. So you lot get me to agree to go to this dinner, thinking that Steph is the problem I've got to deal with. And now you're telling me that actually it's Lauren.'

'Will, it should be a good evening.'

'Except that if I have dinner with Lauren and anyone finds out I'm buggered.'

'You'll still come, won't you?'

'Well, I've been trying to commit professional suicide and failed so far. I might as well do it properly.' I'm being sarcastic now and it's clear that Jake doesn't know what to do with himself.

'Do you fancy a glass of wine?' I say, in a bid to lighten the atmosphere.

'Yeah.'

So we do. It's just before midnight and we lie back on the sofa in the sitting-room with the Charlie's Angels poster on our right and I think Jake feels like I do: that we're doing our chummy-flatmates thing for the last time. I know I'm going to miss him and his self-deprecating humour, those Saturday mornings watching an innocent-looking blonde on TV, and those long phone calls from his mother. But now that he's seeing an American almost-divorcee and I'm going out with the girl on the telly, our frames of reference have changed.

I savour this – Charlie's Angels on one side of me and Jake on the other – and realise, for the second time that day, that I'll have to give a friend my blessing for getting into a relationship that could hardly cause me more damage.

'I'll miss you, mate,' I tell him, and pat his knee.

'I'll miss you too,' he replies, and pats my shoulder. For two friends as tactile as we are, this is the equivalent of wrapping each other in a bear-hug and soaking the sofa with tears.

After I've helped Jake down the stairs with his suitcases, I return to Charlie's Angels and the sofa, the remains of the bottle of wine and a Paul Weller CD. I sit up on my own until half past one and, although this might be a bit melodramatic, I feel I owe it to myself: over the last twenty-four hours, a vast amount of information has dropped on to me and I need to sift through it.

Amazingly, the fact that my career is in jeopardy barely seems to register on my personal Richter scale. I hate the way the Cosy Four have been so bloody cosy and left me on the outside – although the knowledge that I've been central to their every thought makes up for it to some extent.

But as I stare into my wine glass I realise what has disturbed me most and it is simple and rather selfish: Jake loves Lauren and Alex loves Steph. What about me?

I always thought I'd be happy when Jake found someone. He deserves it. He's the loveliest of lovely guys. But I never considered the possibility of him finding this sort of happiness before me. Right now, I don't even mind losing my job for him: there's nobility in that – it reflects well on me, doesn't it? But seeing him in love? It comes back to *me*. Why am I not in love too?

I have never told Jake that I love Jenny, and the reason for that is that I don't know if I do or not. Jake, however, is so convinced that he is in love that he has just stood in front of me and told me so. What struck me was that I barely knew what he was talking about. I've spent most of my last few years wondering what it's like to feel how he feels but now I'm not sure I've even been close.

I was under the assumption that I loved Steph, but I was only twenty-two. I told her I loved her, and I believed I did, but I sometimes wondered whether saying, 'I love you,' was like giving her a present, like an extra big bunch of flowers. Did I love her like Jake loves Lauren? I don't think so. I always felt that, to be absolutely 100 per cent convinced, I'd need to receive a certificate through the post saying: 'Yes, it's official, you're there, you've made it, it's love'. And, they don't do those, do they?

What I'm certain of is that Jenny and I are nowhere near it. And that bothers me: Jake loves Lauren, Alex loves Steph, and I have been left behind.

We'd started off level, all three of us single and going nowhere, but now the status quo has changed. Only a few weeks ago I was ahead: I got Jenny and stormed to the front in a cloud of vanity and self-satisfaction; I was the one with the love life, the brilliant blonde TV star, and I loved it. Then, in a flash, Alex and Steph and Jake and Lauren happened, and they've raced past me.

At least, that's how I see it. Maybe I deserve to come last.

23

Friday morning. In a daze, I wander into Jake's room – Jake's old room – sit on his bare bed and stare at the empty walls. Yesterday this room was full of vibrant mess and personality; now it is clinically clean, there is even evidence to suggest that a Hoover has been inside it. After five years in this bedroom, the only memento he has left is a magazine cut-out picture of Sharon Gless on the wall. That's his way of leaving on a joke, though it doesn't have the intended effect.

I want company to share all this with. I'd like to see Jake and Alex, but at the same time I'd rather not. They're somewhere else now, in every sense. They're moving in with their partners, decorating together, getting smudges of paint on their noses, deciding who sleeps on which side of the bed and whether to share an underwear drawer or go separate. And, yes, Jenny has an underwear drawer, but she doesn't quite have my heart. Which is why I don't want to see her either.

This is a shame for two reasons. One, I am seeing her tonight anyway, at the launch party for *Food of Love*; and two, because I need no convincing that Jenny is utterly splendid, a vibrant, warm, entertaining character. And I fancy her. And she's on the telly. As far as the box-ticking goes, she's got pretty much every box ticked. Naturally several questions follow. One: if Jenny is so splendid, why am I reassessing her? Two: does this suggest that something greater than utter splendidness, something that Jake and Alex have stumbled upon, has become my *raison d'être* for having a girlfriend? Three: isn't that a bit bloody sad? Four: even if that is the case – and I'm not saying it is – does it matter if I haven't moved in, smudged paint on my nose and shared an underwear drawer with the indecent haste of Jake and Lauren or Alex and Steph? Can't love move in a mysterious way, its wonders to perform, and, in my case, slightly slower than theirs?

I feel as if I should discuss the matter with someone, but Dylan Dale is not the person I would select, yet he is the first I meet when I arrive, purposely late, at Channel Five's launch party for *Food of Love*. We are in the Lounge, a dark, not entirely tasteful nightclub down a set of stairs off Leicester Square. The way Dylan has positioned himself as a sort of one-man reception committee at the foot of the stairs makes him impossible to avoid.

'Hello, I don't believe we've met,' he says, quite genuinely.

'I think we have, actually.'

'Oh, really, when?'

'You were wearing a towel.'

'Oh, yes, yes,' he replies, rather jocularly. 'The penguin boy. I've read some of your poetry. "Juicy moussey" something or other. Very interesting.'

He turns to the next guest on the stairs. I feel as if his rapier wit has just sliced me in two. Very good, Dylan. What a fantastic first impression I've made on my first celebrity bash. I'll have to go away and think of something sharp and clever to say in our next brief encounter.

Anyway, I step gingerly into the Lounge and assess what to do next, but the decision is taken for me by Dee – my studio-assistant friend – who appears delighted to see me.

'Hi, how are you doing?' we ask each other simultaneously.

'Fine, fine, thanks,' we reply.

We then smile and pause simultaneously and then neither of us says anything. I mustn't be dismissive of Dee because, second to Jenny, she is my best chum at Table Top, but as the boyfriend of the star of the show I'd thought I might get a somewhat better reception. Maybe Jenny just wants to keep her private and public lives separate – that would be a good celeb-type attitude. I can see her on the other side of the room, holding court to a small throng who have bags over their arms and are scribbling in notepads, the finest representatives of Her Majesty's Press available for an early-Friday-evening Channel Five programme launch. Not once does she point in my direction and giggle, or indicate that the room has brightened since I walked into it.

My conversation with Dee is helped along by the arrival of a girl with a drinks tray and another with a plate of heart-shaped canapés. Dee fascinates me with the hot news from Table Top: she has just been promoted to assistant studio manager. 'Does that mean you get to wear one of those headsets that covers only one ear?' I ask, just checking that nothing had changed on the humour awareness front.

'Yeah,' she says, providing me with the expected answer. 'It's quite cool, really.'

Then, thank goodness, we are stirred from the depths of this conversation by a speech from a senior-sounding suit who says how delighted everyone is with *Food of Love*. 'Let me show you why,' he suggests confidently. I find myself watching a five-minute video clip of Jenny, half-dressed in a series of smutty outfits, hand-feeding food of love into the mouths of a sequence of B-list celebrity men. I note Dee's little gasp of pleasure when the male nurse from *Casualty* makes it through Jenny's studio front door. I also recognise a former international rugby player and a comedian who appears on quiz shows, but the identities of the other two are lost on me and, in fact, I can't recall any of their names.

Nevertheless I join in the less-than-raucous applause at the end, then continue to watch Jenny dealing with the line of people wishing to court her. This isn't much fun, and Dee gets bored with me and slopes off, so I'm left to use up the time-wasting occupations still available to me. After I've been to the loo twice, the bar twice and once for a quick walk outside, all that is left for me to do is recede into the background until I can see the star of the show coming to acknowledge me.

'Hi, sweetie,' she says, and rolls her eyes. 'What a fucking nightmare all this stuff is.'

'You seemed to be enjoying it.'

'Oh, it's not that bad, I suppose, but I don't know if I can go through with it.'

'What do you mean?'

Jenny glances around, then presses up close to me to whisper: 'I can't do this programme, Will.'

'Of course you can.'

'I'm not sure.'

'Well, you didn't seem to be having any trouble in the clips they showed.'

'It's a fucking fraud.' She takes a sip of her wine. 'I hate cooking. I don't want to be a TV chef. People like those journalists keep asking questions and I keep on thinking they all know I'm a fraud. And if they don't now, they will one day. What should I do?'

'Why don't you give some more interviews? Or maybe hand-feed some more love-tucker to your hangers-on?' This sounds more bitter than I'd intended.

'Will!' She frowns at me. 'You're not interested, are you?'

'Well, funnily enough, I haven't noticed you being very interested in me either.'

'Don't be so unreasonable! I've had quite a lot to deal with, you could see that.'

'Jenny, I've had quite a lot to deal with too. Except you wouldn't know because you never stopped to ask.'

'Will, why are we having an argument?'

'I don't know.' Though I half suspect that I came here

looking for one. Jake and Lauren and Alex and Steph won't be arguing, will they? They'll be sploshing paint on each other's noses.

'Do you want to leave?' she asks.

'Yes, I'd love to.'

'Right, come on.' Jenny grabs my hand and her coat and, with barely a goodbye to the party, leads me out on to the street. Within minutes we are sitting elsewhere, perched on high bar-stools, ordering drinks. Jenny leans forward, puts her hands on my thighs and looks into my eyes. 'Come on,' she says soothingly. 'What's this all about?'

There are two answers to her question and I don't know which to give. Because the utterly splendid Jenny Joffee is being thoughtful and caring. She is searching my face with her beautiful eyes in a way that makes it clear that she really wants to know what my cry for attention is all about, and I can't possibly tell her the truth – that I'm confused about paint-sploshing and I don't understand why. Instead I tell her about yesterday, about the photographs, my head being on the block, Jake, Lauren and Steph, and how my little world was rearranged in one head-spinning afternoon.

'Jesus, that's amazing,' she says, puffing out her cheeks. 'How do you feel about it all?'

'I'm not sure. I feel let down by Jake and everyone, even though I understand how it's all happened. The situation at work is extraordinary, and I'm surprised I'm not out of a job already. Next week is going to be fucking weird. On Wednesday, we're going to a dinner party with Lauren Goode, and on Friday we're having Harvey Goode for dinner at your place.'

'That's the one I'm having to host, is it?'

''Fraid so. It could save me my job.'

'I suppose it might just be worthwhile,' she says, grinning, which takes some of the heat out of the moment. Then, without looking, she takes my right hand in both of hers and squeezes it.

'I hope so.'

'Well, there's always that weekend in Amalfi at the end of it, isn't there?' Another squeeze. 'You're not getting out of that.'

'Amalfi will be great, if I'm still alive by the end of next week.'

'Don't worry, sweetie. I'll help you.' And she searches my eyes again with that same, unswervingly thoughtful expression. And this is all hopelessly illogical, because how can I genuinely be questioning Jenny when she is like this?

24

Most years, Alex's birthday is a humdrum skinful in the Dolphin sort of affair, although his twenty-first was celebrated with a skinful in several Nottingham pubs. In the thirteen years I've known him, I've never seen so much effort put into his big day and, let's face it, thirty-three isn't the one you'd single out to shout from the rooftops. Alex, who likes to be in control of his image, is understandably a bit bashful about it.

He greets us at the door and takes us up the stairs in the direction of the small-talk and Blondie. There is a mini-landing just before the top where a tray rests on a small table with two glasses of champagne. Alex isn't a champagne-on-a-tray-in-the-lobby kind of guy.

'Blimey, Alex,' I say. 'This is pretty impressive.'

'I know,' he replies. 'And don't mention how clean the place is, how the furniture has changed or anything else that might draw attention to the fact that a woman may have moved in.'

We go into the main room and I find myself grabbing Jenny's hand. If the others are going to be all soft-focus and warmed by the sunlight of love, I don't want to give anyone the impression that we're not. I find myself giving Jenny's hand a squeeze as we go in.

I'm pleased to see that Jake is wearing his favourite old sports jacket or, rather, that he remains a fashion-free zone and that there's still a rip in the sleeve. Lauren hasn't got round to mending it. Jake and Lauren immediately get up from the sofa where they are sitting, the first time Jake has ever stood up for me. Like us, they're holding hands – another first: I don't think I've seen him hold hands with a girl before. The way their fingers are entwined is exactly like ours too, so I guess it's one-all on the hand-holding front. Lauren looks as glowing as she did in Bar Blue (which, of course, makes sense now) and she welcomes me with one of those smiles that seem to say, 'You'd never have believed this, would you?'

'Hi! Hi! Hi! Hi!' we all shriek with apparent enthusiasm. And we kiss and shake hands, and Lauren gives me that look again.

'Hello again, nasty-letter man,' she says warmly. 'We need to make some new rules.'

'OK.'

'Right. No mention of the divorce. Or that I'm a sad, washed-up bankrupt. We're here as friends. You're not my husband's lawyer and I'm not the bastard's wife.' She stops and raises her eyebrows. I nod, and she continues: 'No one outside this group need know about this evening – or, indeed, any time we meet, and I don't think the bastard's going to bother with his long-distance photography any more. I certainly won't tell my lawyer this has happened, and you won't tell Harvey. We're just friends. How does that sound?'

'It sounds like you've got it all worked out.'

'Good. I also need to apologise for landing you in a whole heap of shit. Right?'

'No. Forget it.' How charitable can I get?

Now, having straightened out the evening, Lauren does something that causes me to wobble again: she wraps her left hand, the one not holding Jake's, round Jake's left arm. This means she is now cuddling his arm and their hand-holding is suddenly infinitely more significant and meaningful than ours. On hand-holding they have now beaten us hands down.

The room combines kitchen, dining and sitting areas in one big open-plan space and Steph breezes down from the kitchen end, walking theatrically in step to the beat of the Blondie song whose title I can't remember, drying her hands on a tea-towel.

'Hel-lo,' she says, all-embracingly. 'Great. How nice to meet you, Jenny.' They kiss politely, then Steph greets me with a more knowing 'Hi', a straight-mouth smile and a nod that seems to say, 'I told you this would be all right.' Then she wraps herself round Alex from behind, her arms round his waist and her head resting on his right shoulder. Now those two look pretty happily united too.

'Two questions, Alex,' I ask, trying to ignore the enthusiastic coupling before me. 'Are we going to have to listen to your ancient music all night?'

'Yes, I'm the birthday boy, remember?'

'I thought as much. Second, I can't remember the name of the song.'

'"Atomic".'

'Oh, God, yes.'

'Four weeks at number one in 1980. Tragically sad year.'

'Really?'

'Yup. John Lennon and JR both got shot.'

'They don't come much worse than that.' You have to buy into Alex's retro world, otherwise you simply remain on another planet.

'Well, 1985 was worse.'

'Really?'

'Charlene Tilton was slung out of *Dallas* for being too fat. And, yes, she was even fatter than me.'

Thus I steer us towards a level of banter where we know – we boys, that is – we can operate. Jenny's and my hands are still stuck together like bits of wood and the other two couples remain draped over each other as if they can't wait for the party to be over and done with so that they can disappear upstairs to bed to trip the light fantastic. Jenny, the sweetie, can do good small-talk too. Not our sort, not 'whatever happened to Thereza Bazar from Dollar', but she has an endearing habit of displaying an apparently genuine respect for any job outside her field ('So you're an estate agent? How amazing to meet so many different people. And you're a professional divorcee? How wonderful. That must be such fun!') Lauren and Steph warm to her delicious charm.

This way, at least, the heavy-petting competition, in which I'm coming a distant last, becomes less of a feature. I notice that although the girls smile warmly at all of us, attempting to give the impression that this is wonderful fun, we split into two groups: the boys to discuss the respective charms of Charlene Tilton and Alex's adipose layers, and the girls to talk about the alterations that Steph has made to Alex's flat. This is fine until we have finished with Tilton's tummy, when Alex and Jake ask me if I'm OK.

Of course I'm not OK. How could I be? But the worst thing when you are being not-OK is having people ask if you are when they obviously think you're not. And although I understand perfectly well that there is some pressure for the evening to go well, and that the other guests may feel slightly tense in case I make my feelings known to (a) my ex-girlfriend, (b) the bloke who brought her back into my life, (c) the wife of my client, or (d) her devious boyfriend who may have cost me my career, it's still a crying shame. Because the dynamics of our friendship – mine, Jake and Alex's – have changed. Three months ago we were all just boys and now we're boys-with-girls. And it's not just that Jake is holding hands with someone and Alex has changed some of the furniture in his flat.

'Yes, of course I'm OK. Why shouldn't I be?' I reply, smiling.

'I can't imagine,' says Jake, ironically.

The best solution, as ever, is to attack the wine, which we all do with relish. Alex does the rounds with the champagne and we are going well on bottle number three and have replaced Blondie with 10CC when it is time to eat.

'You do the table plan,' says Steph to Alex.

'No, you do it,' he replies.

'Oh, come on, honey.'

'I'll do it,' he replies, playfully as a puppy, 'if I can sit next to you.'

'You're not allowed to, gorgeous,' she says, and kisses him full on the mouth.

'It *is* my birthday,' he replies, ignoring the fact that the rest of us are witnessing every cringe-making moment of this charade.

'It doesn't matter.' She kisses him again.

'But I'm thirty-three. It's pretty special.'

I can take no more of this. I have to remove myself from the whole ludicrous spectacle. I come up with the premise that 10CC has to go and that someone with taste is required to select the music. And I don't care if Alex believes that thirty-three is special or not. All I know is that I've never seen him pulling this lover-boy, hopeless-puppy act before.

So I manage to take an exceedingly long time over my temporary role as DJ, and by the time I have scoured Alex's CD collection for a glimpse of something from the current decade, the meal is being served and – thank God – so is the red wine.

'Right,' says Steph, holding her glass aloft, when her plate is finished. 'I'd like to propose a toast.'

'Cheers!' we respond in unison, as the party atmosphere warms.

'To Alex.'

'Boo!'

'To Alex, for allowing me to clean up his flat and being very big and brave and not making too much fuss.'

'Steph!' Alex responds censorially. 'You can't say that, it's bad for my reputation.'

'It's too late for that, mate,' I say, managing to disguise the seriousness in my voice before Jake takes the floor.

'OK, OK,' he says. 'My turn.' More applause. 'Um, I'd like to make a toast to a very special person. And I know that sounds as if I'm Barry White and about to burst into song, but I'm not and I really mean this.' He does, indeed, sound serious. Quite drunk too. 'So come on, sensible moment, everyone. I'd like to toast Will, because he's been a brilliant friend to me recently and I think he's been a brilliant friend to all of us when he could just as well have told us to get fucked. I really mean this, Will, and I know we don't often say things like this to each other, but the friendship and understanding you've demonstrated show what a great bloke you are.'

'But he works for my husband!' blurts out Lauren.

'Can someone silence the drunken American woman?' Jake smiles at her, then turns back to me. 'Will, I'm really sorry you've had to put up with so much shit. Thank you for sticking with us.'

There is general light applause and loud murmurs of agreement, and I know everyone's eyes are on me, looking for a reaction, so I turn coyly to Jenny for support. She gives it in the form of a reassuring wink.

'But he still works for my husband!' blurts out Lauren, raising her glass in my direction and generating laughter all round. 'Oops, sorry, Will! I've broken the rules. I love you too.'

'My turn,' shouts Jenny, raising her glass and saving me from the spotlight. 'To the cook. Steph, that was fantastic.'

'Oh, go on, Mrs TV Chef!' Steph replies modestly.

'I swear I could never have cooked that dinner.' Jenny catches my eye.

Now Alex gets gingerly to his feet and stands silently, milking the moment, awaiting quiet from his audience. 'Right,' he says, 'well, I've got something quite interesting to say, and I'd like to start by sharing with you my thoughts on Meatloaf.'

'Please!' shouts Jake, raucously. 'Anything but Meatloaf!'

But Alex continues unabashed: 'I've been thinking a lot about Meatloaf recently and discovering how much I can relate to him.' He allows us to chuckle, then clears his throat. 'Well, you see, old Meat's a bit of a fat, ugly guy, but in almost every half-decent song he sings – and there are a few of those, let there be no doubt – he heroically overcomes impossible odds and gets his girl. Sometimes, in "Paradise By The Dashboard Lights" for instance, his charm is so great that the girl throws herself at him. But on the whole, Meatloaf's is an epic romantic life story about how the fat guy gets the nice thin girl.'

The rest of us are now wondering where this speech is going and glance from Alex to Steph, who is smiling up at him self-consciously.

'Well,' continues our host, 'Steph and I were away

together on a dirty weekend on the Dorset coast and we were in bed listening to the sea crashing on the rocks outside—'

'Did it make you want to pee?'

'Shut it, Jake,' snaps Alex. 'Anyway, I'm lying there thinking about all this and how I'm the fat bastard Meatloaf—'

'You're much uglier than Meatloaf.'

'Jake, put a sock in it! Anyway, as I was saying, I'm thinking about all this and about how I'm the reincarnation of Meatloaf because I've done pretty well for myself by getting the top babe, who is Steph. And this line from a Meatloaf song keeps rolling through my head, about how he had some moonlit night with this bird of his and how it struck him that he couldn't afford to waste a single moment with her. And so I decided not to waste a moment myself.'

'Oh, my God,' says Lauren, voicing what the rest of us are thinking. We are united in silence, awaiting Alex's next line.

'And so I'm delighted to share with you guys what happened next. I didn't waste another moment. I got out of bed, stark-bollock-naked and asked Steph if she'd marry me. At first she thought I was joking, but when I'd asked her about fifteen times she realised I was being serious and said yes!'

'Oh, my God!' we respond as one, shrieking and cheering. 'I can't believe it!'

'How fantastic!'

'You dirty old dog! Stark-bollock-naked!'

'Can I be a bridesmaid?' That's Jake.

'When are you going to do it?'

'Does this mean you'll be grown-ups now?'

'Can I go wedding-dress shopping with you, Steph?' Jake, again.

'How completely wonderful!'

Then we find ourselves getting to our feet as if Alex has just scored the winning goal in a World Cup final and he raises his arms aloft in triumph. Lauren wraps Steph in a hug. Steph starts crying. Jenny goes to congratulate Steph too. Lauren is jump-started into crying. Jake moves round the table to Alex with his arms outstretched, and I guess that that's probably what I should be doing too so I copy him. Steph breaks off, runs to the kitchen and comes back with a box of Kleenex, which she shares with Lauren. Jake and Alex shake hands long and hard, and I wait for my turn, taking in the scene of undiluted joy.

'Alex! That's fucking amazing. Well done,' I say, as meaningfully as I can.

'What do you think?' he asks.

'I can't believe you can just run off heartlessly into the sunset leaving me and Jake behind. It's unbelievable!'

'But it's great, Will, honestly,' he says. 'I'm so happy.'

'I know you are, Alex, and I'm really pleased for you.'

I dive back into the merry-go-round of hugging and shrieking and queue up for Steph. When it's my turn, she sinks into me, putting her arms round my neck, and I can feel her tears on my cheek. 'You see, Will?' she says, half laughing and half sobbing into my ear, 'I told you it was right, didn't I?'

'Yes, you did.'

'And I'm just so glad that you're here to enjoy it with us.' She pulls back and wipes her face with the Kleenex, laughing at herself.

'More champagne, wife!' Alex barks commandingly at her, and she disappears dutifully to the fridge. Alex fiddles through his CDs and sticks on 'Celebration' by Kool and the Gang – what else? – and we find ourselves dancing, shrieking with delight and trundling round on the congratulations merry-go-round again.

Eventually I have to get off it because I know I'm not on board as wholeheartedly as the others. I step back a bit, clutching my champagne, and wishing that I could be as all-embracingly a part of it as I hope I am appearing to be. It should be a happy day when someone who you care about as much as I care for Alex announces their engagement, but my generosity of spirit doesn't seem to extend that far. And I don't feel proud of myself for it.

'You OK?' asks Jake, who has wandered over to join me.

'Sure, just soaking it all up, mate. It's amazing.'

'I know.'

'It's just you and me left now, Jake, you know.'

'Yeah, yeah. And who'd have thought Alex, of all people, would get to the altar first?'

'I know. Dirty bastard. And I know we always say

this when someone gets engaged or married but I still can't imagine feeling ready to take that plunge. Can you?'

Jake fixes me with a knowing grin and says nothing.

'Jake?' I ask, concerned.

'Hmmm?' he responds vaguely, as if he's forgotten my question.

'Don't tell me you're thinking of doing this too.'

'I've just moved in with Lauren, haven't I?'

'Are you telling me you're going to be the next to drop?'

'No! I can't get married anyway, can I? Lauren's still married to someone else.' And with that he turns away and shuffles back towards the whirling group of celebrants, leaving me even deeper in thought.

Alex, engaged. But Jake, too? Jake to wed! Or contemplating it – even for the thought to have flittered in one ear and settled there without departing through the other! And me left to watch from the touchline. Whatever happened to that unwritten pact we had? Were we not the last men standing? Were we not standing strong together?

'Are you all right, sweetie?' asks Jenny, who I know has been keeping an eye on me.

'Why does everyone keep bloody asking if I'm OK?'

'Because they care about you.'

'Sorry, Jenny. I didn't mean to sound like that.' I drape my arm round her shoulders and squeeze a kiss into the top of her head. We share a moment's silence while we watch Alex dirty-dancing with Steph and Jake and

Lauren moving gently together, their arms round each other, looking into each other's eyes.

'So, are you OK?' she asks again.

'Er, yes. It's quite a big thing to take on board, though.'

'I know.'

'The thing is, Jenny, they might be getting married, but they haven't got a penguin, have they?'

'What's that supposed to mean?'

'I dunno.' And I don't. But, for some reason, it seems important.

It suddenly seems important, too, that Jenny is twenty-five, significantly younger than Steph (who is thirty-one) and Lauren (a comparative pensioner at thirty-five). That's another point to me, and no small amount of kudos with it. Alex might have his all-hugs-and-kisses fiancée and Jake might have his marital future in the bag, but I've got the pert, fresh-faced, seven-years-younger-than-me (which is almost scandalously cool), three-times-a-night youngster. And Jenny is a celebrity and they're not. And Jenny was once a Rice Krispie. And Jenny has that nice nose. And Jenny is gorgeous. In fact, if you tot it all up, my girlfriend comes out way ahead of Alex's and Jake's. Put them in a head-to-head. Put Steph being good at table-tennis against Jenny having bullshitted her way to her own TV show – Jenny wins. Put Lauren's delicate, fragile beauty against younger-looking, bigger and brighter-eyed Jenny – Jenny wins. If you surveyed the man on the street – 'Which of the three would you like to take home?' – it'd be a no-contest:

Jenny would win hands down. However you look at it, she's ahead. So, if I've got Jenny, why do I envy what Jake and Alex have got?

'Will,' says Alex, who is quite pissed, 'come over here.'

'What is it, mate?'

Alex ushers me away to the television-and-sofa-end of the room. 'Are you OK?' he asks.

'How thoughtful of you to ask.' The sarcasm, thankfully, is lost on him. 'Yup, I'm fine, just a little blown away by all this, I suppose. It's amazing, Alex.'

'I know. It feels good too.'

'So it should. You deserve it.'

'Listen, Will, there's something I've got to ask you.'

'Go on, then.'

'Are you ready?'

'Yup.'

'I'd like you to be my best man.'

'You want me to be your best man?'

'Yup.'

'Oh, Alex, I'm really touched.' And I mean it.

'So?'

'Of course I will.'

'Fantastic.' He puts his arm round me and pats my shoulder in a man-to-man, male-bonding sort of way and then we hug awkwardly and pat shoulders again, and I find myself contemplating the irony of being best man at the wedding of the girl I once proposed to.

'What a lovely thing to be asked to do,' I say, giving him another pat. 'I'll be proud to.'

'Great. I'll be proud to have you at my side.'

'What about Jake? Is he likely to mind?'

'No, he's cool about it. We've already discussed it.'

'Brilliant. Let's drink to that, then.'

And we do. We drink to that and to a lot else, and it is 2.15 a.m. when we decide we've had enough. We exchange big hugs and kisses, further expressions of amazement that Alex and Steph are getting married and general acknowledgement that it has been one hell of a night. And I realise now that I have almost drunk enough to buy completely into the act of celebration.

Jenny puts her arm through mine and we wander down the road, hoping to find a taxi to take us back to my flat. There is an element of slalom in our progress, but the way Jenny straightens us out suggests that the swerving is largely mine.

'Well!' she says. 'What about all that, then?'

'It's pretty big, isn't it?'

'Do you mind them getting married?'

'I mind that Steph is the woman Alex is marrying, but I'll just have to get used to it, I suppose. I'm pleased for him, though.'

We walk on with just the sound of our footsteps to break the silence.

'Doesn't it scare you a bit,' she says, 'one of your best mates going off and getting hitched like this?'

'No.'

'Really?'

'Yup.'

We walk on, in silence again.

'But I thought you seemed a bit funny in there.'

'No.'

'Come on, Will, it doesn't matter.'

'I was fine!'

'Will!' She unlinks her arm from mine and spreads her hands in a gesture of dismay. 'It was fucking obvious that you weren't fine.'

We continue in silence, but I feel I have to explain to myself. 'I guess, Jenny, it was just the sight of those two couples together. I mean, they spent most of the evening practically shagging each other. They just looked so fucking sorted.'

'You mean they looked happy.'

A taxi comes into view and Jenny coaxes it to a standstill. A welcome arrival. I open the door, stumble inside and slump into the corner while Jenny talks to the driver through his side-window. She fiddles in her handbag and gives the driver a ten-pound note. Then she slams the door. She's still on the pavement. That wasn't the plan.

'See you tomorrow,' she shouts, through the glass. And then, before I can answer, I'm being whisked away, alone.

25

Oh God. I've got a head that hurts and a space next to me in my bed. That's enough to engage total recall.

Why did Jenny disappear like that? I ask myself the question all the way to work and ring her as soon as I get there.

'Well? What happened to you, then?'

'More to the point, how are you feeling today?'

'Not great. Why? I didn't misbehave, did I?'

'No.'

'Why did you run off?'

'Sorry. I . . .' There's a pause at the other end of the line. 'I suddenly felt I wanted to. Needed a bit of space. Something like that. Don't worry about it.'

'It was nothing I did, was it?'

'No.'

'Promise?'

'Yup.'

'You're sounding a bit evasive.'

'Sorry. There's a lot going on here right now. That's all.' The line goes quiet again. Jenny isn't keen to pursue last night as a topic of debate so I let it drop and we get down to more mundane business: tomorrow night, dinner with Harvey, and what my deficient TV chef is going to cook. I doodle on the pad in front of me. Surely Jenny and I haven't gone mundane. Even with this hangover, I can't let our conversation end like this. 'Just one other thing, Jenny. You were great last night.'

'Really?'

'Until the end, that is.'

'Sorry. But I enjoyed it too. Nice ex-girlfriend, Will.'

'Thanks. She's really something to boast about, eh?'

When I hang up, I'm distracted by a letter in my in-tray. It has the Chilton Shaw logo on the back.

Dear Will
Re: Harvey Goode versus Lauren Goode, financial set-tlement thereof.
I write to confirm that, after discussing the matter with my client, Mrs Goode, we are not prepared to accept the financial settlement of £650,000 initially offered by Mr Goode . . .

Ah, well, no surprise there. I scan the three pages of the letter. Georgina isn't prepared to accept the settlement because we have failed to declare among Harvey's assets the value of a small subset division of Intertalk called Inter2talk. OK, we can do that, no problem. She also needs proof of Harvey's shareholding in Inter2talk. No problem. Still needs a copy of the deeds of the Chiswick house, still needs an evaluation, OK no problem again, she's really keen on the minutiae of that wretched house. Blah, blah . . . And then, concluding at the end, the figure that she and Lauren are demanding.

I blink in amazement: £745,000. The concluding statement reads:

Our estimation is that Mr Goode's assets of Inter2talk are in the region of £450,000, and we herewith demand accounts of Inter2talk and documentation of Mr Goode's shareholding therein. When documentation is in place to confirm the above evaluation, and notwithstanding the requirement to renegotiate in the event of the said evaluation being shown to be inaccurate, Mrs Goode would consider a settlement figure of £745,000.

Yes, £745,000. I find myself saying this out loud. 'Really? Only seven hundred and forty-five bloody thousand pounds. Georgina McKnight! You make barely any enquiry into Harvey's undeclared fortune. And not even the faintest whiff of the White case. Harvey, we're home and dry. Mellstrom Roberts, I'm here to stay. You won't be seeing the back of me now. Only seven hundred and forty-five thousand pounds!'

And that is as good a conversation as I've had with anyone, let alone myself, for a long time. When I've sat down again, however, finished pummelling my desk with childish excitement, reread the letter and paused for thought, my spirits drop. I don't mind this, I can accept it, and I'm still extremely happy and hugely relieved, but there can be only one reason why Georgina McKnight would ask to settle at £745,000. I ring Jake.

'Jake, hi, it's Will.'

'Hello, mate, how are you feeling after last night?'

'I was feeling rather sorry for myself until just now.'

'Why, what happened?'

'I just got a rather significant letter from Georgina McKnight.'

'Oh, really?'

'Yes, so I wanted to thank you and say that this is about as generous a thing as anyone could do for a mate.'

'What do you mean?' He sounds bewildered.

'Come on, Jake, you know what I'm talking about.'

'Er, not really.'

'Maybe it's just Lauren, then. I'd have thought you'd at least have talked about it, though.'

'Sorry, you'll have to explain.'

Georgina, I explain, is as sharp as they come. She doesn't mess up. Yet Lauren is agreeing to settle at a figure that's significantly lower than would be expected. There has to be a reason for this, and there is only one I can think of. My career is on the line because of this case and, because Lauren has put it on the line, she has taken it upon herself to save it. Lauren's asked Georgina to come in with a settlement that's favourable to my client, not out of compassion to him but to protect me.

'Do you see what I mean?' I say. 'She's saved me my job.'

'She's a great girl.'

'She certainly is.'

'Hang on a sec.' Jake goes quiet. 'You might be being a bit kind to her here. Hasn't she done this purely to speed up the whole process? As she said the other day in Bar Blue, speed is what counts to her. She needs a big chunk of money quickly. That's surely why this has happened, to get it all done and dusted fast.'

'Georgina, her lawyer, wouldn't operate like that. We go to court on the ninth of September and we've got until then to agree on a settlement figure. It's only if we can't agree that the whole process drags on acrimoniously. She wouldn't make compromises until much nearer the time. There's no need to rush to a hasty one at this stage. I promise you, Jake, it must be, as I said, that she's under instruction from Lauren.'

Jake is quiet again. 'But I'm still confused,' he says eventually.

'Why?'

'Well, I'm not involved in this divorce, and in fact I'd rather not be – not least because you're acting for the opposition. But Lauren's given me no indication of what you're talking about. And if she *has* done this to help you, as you say, she might have wanted to do it on the quiet, without a fuss, without me or anyone else having to know, because she feels guilty about you and because that's the sort of kindness she's capable of. But there's something I'm confused about.'

'Go on.'

'Her business. She needs a lot of money. She not only needs it fast but she needs a large amount. Because of what Harvey's done, she's got to pay off the bank loan, the interest on it, a number of other debts and a deposit on the rental of a new office. You'll never believe what she needs.'

'Four hundred thousand?'

'Try doubling it.'

'No way.' I didn't have an inkling that this was the scale of the debt she was dealing in. I had presumed that even if we squeezed her a little in the divorce proceedings, she would still emerge with sufficient to buy a home, but whatever she gets from Harvey is going to be poured straight into a black hole of his making. No house, no maintenance, no new launchpad.

'Who's paying the rent on your and Lauren's flat?' I ask.

'Me.'

'She doesn't contribute?'

'She can't.'

'Christ.' We share another silence during which Jake allows me to fester on the enormity of Lauren's problems. 'I don't understand it. Why on earth would she have given us this cut-price deal, then?'

'If you don't understand it, what bloody chance have I got?'

'But this is shit legal advice, Jake. Lauren's paying for someone to lose her money. Unless she's doing it for me.'

'Maybe she is, after all.'

I ponder again. 'What do you think I should do?'

'Nothing, Will. Don't concern yourself with it. Just do your job.'

'What about Lauren?'

'I don't know.' He sighs heavily. 'Look, Will, I don't want to know the figures, but let me just ask one question: what sort of a percentage is she losing out on here?'

'About thirteen per cent, I'd say, quite possibly more.'

'Right. As far as I'm concerned, that's not worth getting involved with. Let's leave it, forget about it. She's going to make more money than I make in ten years, right?'

'I suppose so.'

'Well, that's fine. That's it. Consider the matter closed.'

We close it, and for the first time in eight days I feel I can see the way ahead rather than the complications that obscure it. All I need is to sweet-talk Harvey over dinner tomorrow and persuade him not to take his business away from me – and now, finally, I have some evidence to convince him with.

But I feel guilty too. Harvey and I are successfully taking nearly a hundred thousand pounds from Lauren, money that is rightfully and legally hers. And as it's my job to ensure that she doesn't get it, I'll have to live with it. More significant is the guilt arising from Jake's question: what percentage is Lauren losing out on? About 13 per cent, as I said, possibly more. But it's the more that's the problem: the more that relates to the White case. The more could be a big more, and I didn't get round to telling him that.

26

'How much are you shitting yourself?' asks Jenny, half teasing, half serious.

'On a shitting-myself scale of one to ten, I'd say I was on seven.'

'Seven? I didn't think it'd be quite that high. Is he really going to announce tonight whether or not he's getting rid of you?'

'He might well.'

'I'm surprised you're only on seven, then. We'd better have another drink before the cantankerous old git arrives.'

She leads me from her sitting-room into the kitchen where she pours me another glass of champagne with a drop of cassis.

The kitchen looks like a cross between a Marks and Spencer food hall and a war zone. There are smart plastic food containers spread liberally across two worktops and flowing on to the table in the middle. Every one is open, with food tumbling over one side.

This was how Jenny had risen to the occasion of entertaining Harvey Goode: with wholehearted enthusiasm and no aspiration to do anything other than cheat. And if anyone knows how to cheat in the kitchen, it is she.

'If we're going to entertain this all-important bastard in style,' she declared, 'we'll have to order in the best ready-made food we can find.' This was easy and all executed in a couple of minutes on the Internet. And Jenny knew exactly where to find what she wanted because she had been there almost every time she had entertained before. She placed an order and late this afternoon a man had arrived on a moped bearing an uncooked three-course meal in an airtight cooler bag. All we had to do was take the three courses out of their various plastic containers and follow such basic instructions that even Jenny was confident that nothing could go wrong. There was no toffee that wouldn't set, no soufflé that wouldn't rise, just a pan to be greased, an oven to be heated, some waiting and then – supposedly – hey presto.

'Do you think I ought to give it a stir?' asks Jenny, cheekily, peering through the oven window at the dish inside.

'No, I think you should stay as far away from it as possible.'

'That's what you should have said to Jake when Lauren first called round. It would have saved us a lot of trouble and we might have been sipping aperitifs under the stars in Amalfi already.'

'You're not going to forget about Amalfi, are you?'

'Certainly not.'

'Good.' And I mean that. We clink glasses and, as I chuckle to myself, I realise I'm amused less by my gorgeous, big-eyed Jenny than by myself. Was I *seriously* reassessing this wonderful creature? Can I not recognise a good thing when I see it? Is it not time to reassess my reassessment?

Harvey isn't as painful as I'd expected him to be. At least, that's my impression of him on arrival; he even shakes Jenny's hand.

My plan was to take him by storm: I've held back yesterday's encouraging news from Chilton Shaw, intending to impress him with it tonight and start the evening on a good footing. However, when I take out the letter from my inside pocket with a flourish, he shrugs it away. Indeed, he refuses to discuss business until after dinner.

He enjoys his wine – I knew there could be no holding back on the budget there – and after we sit down to eat, it becomes clear that he likes Jenny too. This, of course, is no surprise. Jenny has been briefed: no one was under any illusion as to the star attraction of the evening. She had wondered whether to wear one of her take-me-I'm-yours outfits from *Food of Love* but had decided that subtlety and class would suit the occasion better. She is wearing a classic knee-length black number, showing a bit of back and a bit of front, so Harvey gets a taste of what *Food of Love* viewers gorge themselves on every week. When she appears in the kitchen doorway with the main course, he rolls his eyes at me in a kind of boys' appreciation society.

'Now, what have we got here, hostess?' he asks,

beaming admiringly at his plate. 'This looks fantastic.'

'Sea trout baked in banana leaves, with a spicy ginger,
coriander, lemon grass, mango and coconut sauce,' she
replies.

'Fantastic,' says Harvey, his mouth full, a shred of sea
trout clinging to the underside of his lower lip. 'This fish
is outstanding.'

'I get it from a special place.'

'Where's that, then?'

'It's a gem I've discovered. A new fish market in East
London. I try to get down there not much after seven
in the morning when the latest catch comes in. It's the
best way I know of getting the freshest fish available
in town.'

'Fantastic! Will,' he says, directing the conversation
at me for almost the first time since his arrival, 'I
don't think you appreciate what you've got in this
girl.'

'I certainly—'

'Does he satisfy you, Jenny?' he interrupts.

'Pardon?' replies Jenny, alluringly.

'Are you satisfied that he fully appreciates you?' says
Harvey, laughing conspiratorially at her, as if I'm no
longer in the room. I notice that his forehead vein has
popped up like a little erection. No surprise there, then.
The Jenny Joffee effect is working.

'He's not bad,' replies Jenny, flirtatiously.

'I hope he's better at looking after you than he is his
clients.'

'Harvey,' that's a comment for me to handle, 'I was hoping we could have a quiet moment for me to explain all—'

'What do you think, Jenny?' says Harvey, cutting me out of the conversation again. 'Do you think he's on my side or the opposition's?'

'Well, it's not my business but I know he's working hard for you.' Jenny looks at me, uncertain of the direction in which the conversation is turning. I wink at her. I'm not enjoying this either, but it's the end product of the evening that's important, not how we get there.

'So, Jenny,' continues Harvey, 'do you know this Jake fellow who's now living with my wife?'

'I've met him a couple of times. He's a good guy.'

'Is he? He doesn't sound like it if he can piss on his friendship with Will like that. It can't make Will feel very good.'

'I think everyone has handled it quite maturely,' she replies tentatively, flashing me another look of uncertainty.

'Harvey,' I try to cut in again, 'I thought we were going to discuss this—'

'The point is, Jenny,' Harvey brushes me off like a fly, 'do you think Will can do a good job for me? Is he going to stop my wife stealing my money or does he have second thoughts for her and this self-seeking Jake boy who purports to be his friend?'

'Harvey, more wine?' asks Jenny, strictness in her voice. 'As I say, I'm not involved in all this, but I do know that Will has done his utmost to keep his friendship with Jake separate from your divorce.' Which isn't true, but it sounds good to me. 'All I can tell you is that Will is an honourable guy, about as honourable as I've ever met.'

'That's a pretty firm answer,' says Harvey, sitting back in his chair. 'Will, you must be delighted with it.'

'I—'

'And I think, Harvey,' says Jenny, also cutting me out, 'that that is the last we should say about this until you and Will can discuss it privately.'

'Fantastic!' says Harvey, slapping his thigh to applaud Jenny's plucky performance. 'You have my word, Jenny, you have my word.'

'Good.'

'And this is the *most* exquisite meal. You're a little genius, Miss Joffee. I've eaten in most of the finest fish restaurants in the world and this delightful sea trout compares with any of them.'

Dinner then proceeds more gently. Harvey becomes more inebriated, his flirtation with Jenny less subtle. His forehead vein shines as though it might glow in the dark, his face reddens and he even has to dab away the first signs of perspiration from his hairline. Jenny handles him wonderfully, and though I am reduced largely to the role of wallflower, I know my time will come and that the longer Jenny keeps Harvey happy, the better it is likely to be.

Eventually Harvey announces that it is time he and

I went through for cigars. This is a twofold problem: I have no cigars, and while Jenny's flat is tasteful, it is also rather small. There is no room to go through to. Jenny excuses herself and vanishes into the kitchen, and I make up for the absence of cigars by pouring Harvey a malt whisky. Now that he and I are ready to talk business I feel a nervous shiver pass up my spine.

'What's that letter you said you wanted me to see?' he asks, and slouches back in Jenny's sofa.

'Here.' I produce the missive from Georgina McKnight.

'She's a damned nice little thing, that Jenny of yours,' he says. 'I've half a mind to boot you into touch, Will, and run off with her.'

'I'm sure she'd find that delightful.' But my comment is lost on Harvey, who's trying to make sense of Georgina's letter. 'Turn to the last page, Harvey, and you'll see the figure you're after.'

Harvey's eyebrows rise when he reads it, but that's all. Not a comment, not even a double-somersault. He folds the letter and hands it back to me, still ominously quiet. I feel like I'm waiting for the headmaster to deliver a punishment.

'I thought,' he says, chillingly soberly, 'that seven hundred and fifty thousand was as good as we could hope for.'

'It was more of a figure to aim for, I thought.'

'That's what you thought, is it, Will, something to aim for?'

'Yup.'

'OK.' He's silent again, his whisky glass hovering beneath his nose as if the fumes aid his contemplation. 'Do you think I should be pleased with the offer? I mean, if that's what they're offering, maybe we should be looking at rather less.'

'I think it's a good offer.'

'You think it's a good offer.'

'Yes.' Why does he keep repeating what I say?

'Do you think I should retain you as my lawyer?'

'Absolutely.' What sort of question is that? 'Especially now we've got this far. To start again would set you back some time, and it's questionable that you'd find a mutual settlement so close to the figure you were hoping for.'

'You think you've done well for me, don't you?'

'Yes. And I'd like the chance to show you the Jake-Lauren thing from my angle.'

'I don't want to hear another word about those two,' he says, rising to his feet with an air of finality. 'Will, I might be making a mistake here, but I hope not. I'm going to continue using your services. Others might disagree, but I think you're doing a reasonable job and you should see it through. OK?'

'Certainly. Thank you very much.' And never before have I seen the lovely Harvey Goode in such a good light. How I have misunderstood him. To think that beneath that thick, unscrupulous skin of his, there may be the odd decent sentiment struggling to get out! I never had so much as an inkling.

Harvey disappears into the kitchen briefly to say goodbye to Jenny. When he returns, I see him out.

Once the front door is shut behind him long enough for him to be out of earshot, I find that my fists are clenched and I'm filling Jenny's flat with a long, loud shout: 'Yes!'

27

'Yes! Yes! Yes! We've done it.' I march into the kitchen with my arms aloft. 'Jenny, you were superb, you were brilliant. Thank you so much. You are wonderful. Fan-fucking-tastic. That is so totally fan-fucking-unbelievably-tastic . . . Oh . . . Are you all right, Jenny?'

Jenny is perched on a stool at the kitchen table, looking longingly into the distance, not exactly sharing my elation.

'Are you all right, Jenny?'

'Do you know what Harvey just said to me?' she asks weakly. 'He just said that if I ever fancied having dinner with him, alone, I should get in touch. He gave me his card too, and a great big wink. What a tosser.'

'I'm sorry, sweetie. He's an idiot, I know. But he's just said he's going to let me see the case through.'

'I guessed as much.'

'It's brilliant, isn't it? Let's get that other bottle of champagne.'

'Will, don't open it.'

'Why?' Jenny looks serious. 'Are you all right?'

'Not really. I'm sad, actually. Will, sit down, please.' She is talking even more quietly now.

'What is it?'

'I don't know how to say this.' She sighs. Her head drops into her hands and she rakes her fingers through her blonde hair. She has suddenly turned down the temperature of the evening so that it has become tangibly icy. Something fairly significant is about to come. I sit down.

Jenny takes a long breath. 'Will, I'm sorry. I'm really, really sorry.' She lifts her face slowly from her hands. 'I don't want to go out with you any more.'

I don't know what to say. It was obvious that something was coming, but I was hoping it wasn't this. Maybe someone could have died, or had a bad illness, or her programme had been ditched, but not this. I feel a wave of exhaustion crash over me and I still say nothing, I can only stare into Jenny's face and wonder why the rug has been whipped away from under my feet. Not this! I thought I was playing a pretty good game this time round. And I thought we'd just been a brilliant double act with Harvey. But the way Jenny's eyes are scanning mine, the first tears forming in them, shows how far off the mark I've been. And, Christ, how I detest the familiarity of the feeling I'm experiencing, the awful dawning of a new reality, a chain reaction of the body parts all reacting in their own horribly familiar way. I can feel myself melting on this stool, my insides twisting, stomach tightening, temples being sucked inwards, the nagging itch in the corners of my eyes.

'Well, go on, then.' I break the silence. 'Surely I'm allowed to know why.'

'I don't know how to explain it. You haven't done

anything wrong. I love your poems . . . But, Will, you and me, we're just in different places right now. And I didn't know how far apart we were until Wednesday night.'

'Was that why you went off after the party?'

'I suppose so. I was just really frustrated and I've been spending the two days since thinking of almost nothing else. You – and that bloody mango sauce to go with the sea trout. Mainly you, though, a little bit of sea trout, but nothing else.'

'I still don't understand what this is all about. If we're in different places, I could always move.'

'Will . . .' She turns away from me. A half-decent one-liner isn't likely to resolve the dispute.

'And I've avoided any marriage proposals this time. It can't be that bad.'

'Please don't be funny now.'

'And if it's because I'm having a not-particularly-great hair day, I'm happy to try a new gel.'

'Will!' Make her laugh and make her change her mind? Some chance.

'Well, explain to me what's going on.'

'OK.' She looks at me again with that sad, resigned expression. 'I was pretty upset after Wednesday. I was upset that you couldn't be honest with me. It was so obvious that Alex and Steph getting engaged had thrown you – and you had every right to be thrown. God, who wouldn't be? But it was the way you denied it to me that I didn't like. And you probably won't remember the last thing you said about the others, Jake and Lauren and

Alex and Steph, the thing that convinced me I wasn't going home with you that night.'

'No, I can't, I'm afraid.'

'You screwed up your face and said, "They're so fucking sorted."'

'Oh.'

'And the more I thought about it, it just seemed that that wasn't so much a statement about them but about us, you and me. They're so fucking sorted, meaning, we're so fucking not.' She pauses, as if to let this sink in, watching me take on board the sentence she is meting out to me. It sinks heavily to the pit of my gut.

'And then I was thinking about our relationship,' she continues, with that quiet, unwavering certainty, 'and why I haven't been as happy as I should be with a bloke who I really, really like, who writes poems and likes penguins. And this was what it came down to. I feel pressure with you, Will, and that's because I'm not right for you.'

'Yes, you are.'

'No, I'm not. You want us to be sorted like the others, you want our relationship to be going somewhere, heading in the right direction. And I don't. I don't want to think about whether we're sorted or not. I just wanted to have fun with you, it's simple as that. I guess this might just be a twenty-five-year-old's attitude, but it's not really a good match for a thirty-two-year-old's.'

'I could cool it off a bit if that's what you mean. I don't think that would be too hard.'

'But it is, Will. I think it's impossible. That's why I'm

so sure of this.' And thus I feel I am being dispatched from her life without the right to argue. My opinion doesn't count. My approach to the relationship, she informs me, is so bound up in its long-term prospects that I don't even realise it. 'We get a penguin,' she tells me, 'and you don't see it as just a penguin, you see it as a statement that we'll be together for a year. You write me a lovely, witty, three-month anniversary poem about an underwear drawer, but it's not really about an underwear drawer, is it? It's a sort of congratulations certificate for having reached a certain status in our relationship. Do you see what I mean?'

'Sort of, but I still don't think it's as cataclysmic as you're making it out to be.'

'Will, come here.' Jenny takes my hands in hers, and continues to deliver her resignation speech in the gentlest, most sensitive tones. 'What is it that particularly scares you about Alex and Steph and Jake and Lauren?'

'The whole thing, I suppose, the enormity of what they're doing.'

'Is that really it?' She squeezes my hands and shakes them, as if trying to cajole me into seeing it her way.

'*You* clearly don't think so. Tell me what you think it is.'

'It's not what they're doing that scares you, it's more that you're not doing it yourself, that you're getting left behind. Does that make any sense?'

'Yep.' I sigh. 'I can't deny there's a bit of that.'

'That's why I'm not right for you, Will.' She lets my

hands drop. 'I don't want to catch up the others. I'm happy where I am. I don't want a relationship I'm in right now to be judged against somebody else's life-plan.'

'OK, OK. But I still think I can chill out and we can find a way of making it work.'

'I'm sorry, Will, but I don't think you can change an attitude that's ingrained in your whole being. We were in week one of this thing and you were talking about week two, week three, six months down the line. Some time you've got to stop planning for the future and start enjoying the present – at least, that's what I want. Think of it as a holiday. If we went on holiday, I'd want to go to the beach, be together, enjoy having a holiday. But you wouldn't. You'd spend the week in the travel agent's planning the next holiday. You'd never get to the beach. I'm sorry, but I just want to be on the beach a bit.

'And I've thought quite a lot about going on holiday with you, Will. If I succeeded in stopping you spending your whole time planning the next one, I think we'd have a good time. But the fact is, I've not wanted to suggest it because that might scare you. You might construe it as me taking it too fast. You might think I was trying to trap you into another guaranteed six months in the relationship. You've got your foot so precisely on the pedal here – you don't want us to go too fast or too slow. You want to know where we're going and how we're getting there. You want to sit in the cockpit, checking every dial, that we've got the right amount of fuel, that we're flying at the right height and that we've got the right number of in-flight meals on board. I don't want that.'

Jenny slips off her stool and faces away from me out of the kitchen window. She is speaking even more quietly now, with even more emphasis on every word that is fired, like an arrow, in my direction. 'I'm different,' she says. 'I don't want a set pace. I don't even want to think about how fast we're going and at what stage we should arrive at the other end, wherever that might be.'

'You've thought this one through, haven't you?' Jenny nods at me. 'What about all that talk about Amalfi?' I ask. Jenny nods again. 'And you presumably had this planned throughout the evening, you've just been holding it back. Is that right?' The same response. 'So you really only went through with this dinner for my sake?' And again.

'Will, there are a million things I'd do for your sake, you've got to know that,' the stifled tears are now cutting a path down her cheeks, 'apart from be your girlfriend. I'm so sorry.'

Silence returns to hang over us. I had barely noticed the clock above Jenny's stove until now, but in these circumstances the volume of its ticking has increased dramatically. I hate this awkward intensity, the rush of emotions that accompany sudden rejection, the coldness that invades like an icy mist to replace warmth, familiarity, security and all their lovely spin-offs, like lemon mousse, penguins, breakfast in bed, the catalogue that started with a couple of in-jokes and personal moments and became so thick it turned into a relationship. We were quite good, I thought. But I was wrong.

'So,' I break the silence again, 'it's one of those you're-a-lovely-bloke-but-I-still-don't-want-you rejections, is it?'

'I—'

'Because I always like to go away with the consolation prize, the knowledge that I'm rated as a lovely bloke.'

'Will, please.'

'Sorry, Jenny, but funnily enough, I'm really pissed off.' And I'm sounding it now too. 'I'm hurt, I'm really hurt. Twenty minutes ago you were my girlfriend and now, apparently, you're not. Just like that! And I don't even get a say in the matter! I just have to accept it with nothing but a lovely-bloke consolation prize to tell my mates about.'

'Will, please.' Jenny's tears are flowing faster now and she's talking in barely a whisper.

'I'm sorry.' I sigh. 'Christ, I don't know why I'm apologising, but I am. I'd better go.' I get up. 'I don't want to say anything hurtful I'll regret later.'

'OK.'

'Can I order a cab? Or have you got one waiting outside for me? You probably ordered it yesterday with the sea trout.'

'Will!'

'Sorry, sorry, sorry!' I raise my hands in an admission of guilt. 'I told you I'd do something like that. Sorry, Jenny, really I am.'

Silence again. Both of us sit down, exhausted, as if the bell has rung after another round of sparring. Jenny sighs, takes my hands in hers again and puts her face into them. 'It's not your fault,' she says. 'It's mine, I'm afraid.'

'And is this your final answer?' I ask, somehow dredging up the voice of a gameshow host in a flailing semblance of humour. 'You definitely want to go for spurning the handsome lawyer rather than living with him happily ever after?'

'Yes,' she replies.

'Oh, fuck. Absolutely sure? Final answer?'

'Yes.'

'You can still ask the audience or phone a friend?'

Jenny manages a chuckle, wipes her cheeks, then closes her eyes tight as if she's thinking hard. 'Sorry, Will, but . . .' she pauses, '. . . but you could still stay tonight, if you want. I know that's crap of me but I'd really like it.'

'You mean a sort of farewell fuck?' Jenny winces. 'A chance for me to go out on top?'

'If that's how you want to put it.'

I weigh this one up and, actually, it's easy. 'No, Jenny.' I'm serious now. 'I don't feel very good about myself right now. I'm going to feel like shit tomorrow, shit the day after that and shit the day after that too. But I'd feel even worse if I was persuaded to hang around for one last dance.'

I push back my stool and stand up. This conversation has run its length and both of us know that I'm going. All that is left for me is to collect my jacket, which I put on at the front door.

'You don't want me to order you a cab?' she asks.

'No, I'd quite like a walk. It might clear my head.'

'Can I at least give you a hug?'

I manage a half-smile and we sort of sink into each other. Jenny holds me tight, much tighter than I'm holding her. I can feel the sobs rippling through her. She wants to hold the hug longer than I do but I need to leave.

'Come on, Jenny,' I whisper. 'I ought to go.'

28

It's a clear, warm night. There are stars and a moon, stillness and calm, and if I looked a bit harder I could probably find countless other symbols of peace and stability to contrast with the tide of emotion sweeping through me. I turn left from Jenny's front door and wander slowly in no particular direction. There isn't a glimmer of life on the street; every other soul in this town is tucked away cosily in their home and I'm outside on my own.

I pull out my mobile phone and toy with the idea of ringing Jake. I start punching in the numbers but stop half-way. Sympathy from Jake? Sympathy from Alex, perhaps? I put the phone back in my pocket.

In the space of one evening I've climbed back into bed with Harvey and been kicked out by Jenny. My future as a divorce lawyer appears to have been secured and my self-esteem has been shot to pieces. Does that put me ahead on the night? Would I have settled for this outcome at the start of the evening? I certainly don't feel as if I'm tap-dancing light-footed down the street, filled with *joie de vivre*, and singing West End show tunes in full voice. So the answer is probably no.

If I was Sharon Gless in *Cagney and Lacey* I'd go to

some dark bar right now and do this whole morose thing properly: get drunk, get on the nerves of the other losers who are drinking alone, and get thrown out. But I'm not Sharon, and the pubs are long shut. And I can't match Sharon: she'd put the episode behind her and march on bravely to her next disaster. And me? As I said to Jenny, I'll feel like shit tomorrow, shit next week and shit next month too. How long is it until you stop feeling all cluttered and heavy and crap inside? Jenny asked me that on the night we met. I don't know the answer, but the heaviness is already with me.

I come to a crossroads. Which way to turn? The metaphors are out to get me again.

I stop and lean against a lamp-post. I'll stay here until I get some direction in my life. In the meantime, I'll compile a list: the top five personal disasters to have befallen Will Tennant in the last eight days. Me nearly being fired from my job? Me being fired by Jenny? Alex getting engaged to Steph? Jake doing the dirty on me? Jake taking Lauren and my career (nearly) with him? Jake suggesting he'd be getting married too? Jake leaving my flat? Me being left behind on my own? That's eight. There's even competition to make it on to the list.

In my ranking, Jake doing the dirty comes pretty high. Me being left behind on my own? That's number one, according to Jenny. And she's probably right. Astute, cold-blooded, gorgeous Jenny. I don't want to get eczema again or go off my food or suffer any of my other post-relationship physical reactions, but after being treated like this . . .

I elect to head straight on over the crossroads towards a main road. I wanted Jenny, then I wasn't sure I wanted her, now I want her again and I can't have her. A pilot in control? I hardly think so. Vacillating, I have crashed and burned. And now, as Jenny so astutely informed me, I am left with the ultimate horror of being on my own.

Part Three

29

In bed, Sunday morning, two and a bit months on, 5 September, alone.

The bed still feels rather large, even though it's been some time since anyone was in it with me. Towards the end of July I had a phase of sleeping on the right, as if I was saving the left for someone else. When that didn't work I moved to the left for most of the middle of August to give other people an opportunity to occupy the right. For the last three weeks or so I've been trying a new tack, a less specific, scatter-gun approach, spreading myself everywhere and kicking out a leg from time to time in the vague hope of colliding with one belonging to someone else. But they've been air shots every time.

I guess you could say that since I made my bed I've got to sleep in it. But I'd take issue with that. For a start, I've not been making it much recently anyway. I did initially, thinking wishfully that Jenny might come rushing back to me – and for a while, it seemed worth being ready for her with cleanish sheets.

And furthermore, I didn't want any of this anyway. I didn't ask to be jettisoned, sentenced to life imprisonment on my own in a bed that's too big for one.

Ooh. Sudden pain across the top of my head. Not

surprising, really, given the familiar dryness that starts at my tongue and stretches down my throat. Vestiges of last night. Which reminds me: I was supposed to have someone in my bed this morning, wasn't I? That was the plan. Alex had briefed me. Lovely girl, single, a friend of Steph's from her nursing days, I was going to like her. Blonde, vivacious, an entertaining drunk, just up my street. Apparently I couldn't fail, which wasn't Alex saying that she was a peroxide tart but an attempt to fill me with confidence and get me back on the road with everyone else. And I didn't really fail either.

Alex and Steph have been hugely supportive, trying their hardest to help me reach their level of happiness. That's why they introduced me to Nicky, who is doubly useful to them: not only is she Steph's bridesmaid, she is single and might therefore be able to help Alex's best man out of his predicament. Thus it was Nicky the nurse and me at dinner with Alex and Steph, Pete and Di and another couple, who had to leave in the middle of pudding because their baby-sitter rang to say that the baby had coughed a couple of times in its sleep. Or something drastic like that. They looked grey and shaken when they bustled out leaving half a caramelised baked banana behind them.

At least Alex's cooking is still predictable. Always caramelises those bananas when he's entertaining. I thought Steph might have phased them out by now, but Alex is hanging on to them with grim determination. I'd rather just go out to the pub with him and get pissed, but Alex says it's important to see a lot of people before the wedding and, since I'm best man, he wants me to get to know a few too. That's why I've met Nicky the nurse, Vicky the violinist (she's not really a violinist, but her father is) and Sarah the surgeon (that's not true either, but I can't remember what she did). It's always a couple of couples plus me and A. N. Other single girl. Alex isn't so immersed in his version of true love and lifelong bliss that he hasn't noticed this pattern has come to look like a statement rather than a coincidence, but he says it's not like that at all. There's no 'us' and 'them', he explained last week, when I was lauding him for sticking so valiantly by the odd inadequate single like me. That's just the way it seems from my side, apparently. That's how it seemed to him when he was stuck on my side too, he said encouragingly. Except he didn't use the word 'stuck'.

Anyway, I almost solved the problem last night by getting unstuck with Nicky the nurse, who wasn't miles away from Alex's description. We got on well, she laughed at my jokes and my hair was looking pretty good. Almost all the boxes were ticked. Right through to the end of the evening we couldn't be separated. We left the dinner party together and joked about how delighted Alex and Steph would be at their apparent match-making coup. But then it came to working out whether we had genuinely left together or whether we'd just walked out of their front door simultaneously. Nicky the nurse turned to me, looking shy, uncertain and available, and if Vicky the violinist's father had been there, it would have been a perfect time for him to strike up a rhapsody. As it was, I weighed up what was clearly there for the taking and decided that that night I wasn't as entertaining a drunk as she.

It's not that I'm looking for an exact Jenny replacement, but Nicky has never been on television and, the way she was going, she's never likely to be. She isn't as genuinely blonde either or as petite; indeed, if Nicky ever got to underwear-drawer status, she'd not be able to squeeze in half as many items as Jenny did. That last thought shot through my mind as I was standing on the pavement in front of her and, puerile though it is, it didn't strike me as an ideal platform for starting off on the road to eternal happiness.

How hung up am I on Jenny? Initially I asked myself that question every day as I checked for the onset of eczema. Now I find myself pondering it about once a week. Maybe that suggests a natural recovery rate, but the fact that I'm still not happy suggests the opposite. Jenny called me a couple of times soon after our split, but when I had ascertained that these were just-good-friends calls and not to say 'I miss you and I can't live without you', I insisted on a blackout. All I have seen of her, then, is a *Food of Love* episode, the one with the male nurse from *Casualty*, during which I felt amused, nostalgic and jealous all at the same time.

I got in touch with her once thereafter, but I was drunk so it was utterly regrettable. The day had involved a big lunch in the City and more drinks afterwards. We dispersed at well after eight o'clock and while everyone else went back to a home where a nice partner was waiting for them, I was left on my own. I went back to the office to pick up some papers I needed the following day, sat down at my computer to check my emails and fired off a quick verse – off the top of my head, and impressively so, I thought, after a day's drinking – to Jenny.

> Jenny, Jenny, you were my light,
> For we made love three times a night,
> With you I thought my life was right,
> You shat on me from a great height.

Well done, Jenny. You took aim, fired and hit bullseye.
Yours, seriously wounded, Will.

Funnily enough, Jenny didn't email back. I wasn't proud of myself when I read the missive again two days later. I showed it to Sam and she gave me a terrible scolding. But at least it put a defined end to Jenny's and my affair. There wasn't much uncertainty as to where we stood thereafter.

But even the knowledge that I had eradicated any chance – any hope – of Jenny coming back didn't help my recovery. I continue to flounder.

Some people – almost everyone else, it seems, these days – understand themselves so well that they know for sure they want to marry a particular person, yet I'm struggling even to work out if I genuinely miss Jenny or if I just hate being on my own. I feel like a doctor looking for the cause of long-standing pain, but the only diagnosis I can come up with is that something hurts.

I'm crossing off the possible causes of pain. Initially I felt bruised and slighted, as if I'd been toppled from a great height: that was a vanity thing – I no longer had the trophy girlfriend. I got over that.

The loneliness has been harder to deal with and it's got to the stage when I've started going to the office on empty Sunday afternoons. There, I can at least feel I'm pushing on with the career part of my life, and sitting there executing divorces diverts me from the reality check of a lonely weekend afternoon. But at least I've begun to eke out some warmth in the tent I've pitched in the campsite reserved for single men. The being on my own I can handle, what's harder is the knowledge that there's a better place elsewhere and the others have wrapped up their tarpaulins and gone there. Alex and Jake are miles down the road and I haven't even pulled out the tent pegs.

And it hurts not being with Jenny. I cannot quantify exactly how much, nor can I pinpoint what I miss. I keep picturing her the way she was that first morning in my flat, wearing my shirt from the night before. Occasionally this vision infuriates me, but more often than not it surprises me that she's still in the forefront of my mind, bare-legged, rumpled, asking how to get the shower to work.

Sundays always seem darkest. And today is Sunday. Alex and Steph, Pete and Di and the couple who didn't finish their bananas will be cosily wrapped in their splendid little units. I could spend the day with Alex, I suppose, but that would mean seeing Steph, and, anyway, I don't want to become an appendage to them. I could see Jake, but that's beginning to feel awkward too. Jake and Lauren have gone in the opposite direction to Alex and Steph. Alex and Steph are so overwhelming in their desire to embrace me in the warmth of their world that I feel like a charity case. Jake and Lauren are so wrapped up in each other that I hardly ever hear from them.

I never thought it could come to this, but now I actually find myself looking forward to seeing Harvey Goode. I've got a big week coming up with the old pantomime villain, and it begins with a briefing at a lunch meeting tomorrow before his divorce goes to its hearing in court – hopefully to be rubber-stamped – two days later. Harvey will be as challenging a diversion as ever and, being a serial adulterer who wants out of marriage, he will provide a welcome respite from everyone else around me who wants in.

It isn't hard to see the amusing side of this sad state of affairs. I've even wondered whether I'd be happier if I was a girl. On the odd occasion that I sit down with Alex or Jake, it doesn't take long for us to find our way back into familiar territory and start talking about David and Thereza from Dollar or the weight problems of Charlene Tilton. The only item on the agenda that has altered is marriage. Now that Alex has dropped (and Jake's dropping seems imminent), we no longer talk reassuringly about 'us three'. With Alex's wedding only six days away, we barely talk about the big day either. I tried to encourage it a couple of times last night

– he must surely be brimful with the excitement of it – but I got nothing. I don't know if that's because he feels awkward about moving ahead in his life or about me being left behind. Instead, we talk our usual brand of nonsense and, yes, I'll always love that.

But the point is that if I was a girl, and my best friends were girls, we'd talk about real things, personal issues. We'd stroll into territory where Alex, Jake and I rarely tread. It probably wouldn't be half as much fun with the girls, but it would be deeper, and I would connect in a way that doesn't happen in a trivial giggle with the boys. It is these infinitely superior communication skills that I envy. It must be easier being single when you're a girl because you're only single in that you don't have a boyfriend, not in the sense that you're lonely. I guess girls must just feel permanently warm, supported and connected. It sounds great.

Is this why we men want to settle down with them? Is this why I'm missing a TV star who is out of my league? Do we want to buy into all that cosy conversation and share our souls because it makes us feel good? Or because we're scared of loneliness? It makes sense from our point of view.

But from theirs? Why on earth would they settle down with us? There's a simple answer to that from my perspective: they don't.

30

The private dining rooms at Intertalk are impressive. I arrive at 1.50 p.m., marginally early, and am met by a girl who introduces herself as Clare, shows me down a corridor of frosted glass and into a grand reception area with beautiful leather furniture. Three doors lead out of here, each of which opens into a separate dining room. It is in one of these that I find Harvey.

He is sitting at the head of a long table, the *Financial Times* folded in front of him, a mobile phone clamped to his right ear. He is drumming his fingers and doesn't look up for over half a minute. His conversation is peppered with dissatisfied grunts. When he eventually acknowledges me, his face brightens surprisingly. It is almost a double-take of joy. And when he concludes his conversation, he even stands up to shake my hand.

'Ah, Will, old fellow. Good to see you. Sit down. Now, tell Clare what you want to eat and she'll see to it.'

I ask Clare for a coffee and sit down, overwhelmed. I understand that Harvey is only two days away from his release from the ties of marriage, but I hadn't thought that would make me such a close chum that I'm deemed worthy of a handshake and a hot meal.

'What have you got to tell me?' he asks, rubbing his hands in anticipation.

'It's all pretty simple. Wednesday's court hearing will be standard. It's called a financial-dispute resolution hearing – an FDR – but because we've agreed the financial settlement with the other side there's no dispute to be resolved. It should be quick and easy, just rubber-stamping the agreement. They'll set aside an hour for us, but I doubt we'll need even half of that.'

'Do you think I should attend?'

'No need,' I reply, 'not when everything's agreed. I have to go, but you don't. Clients often don't when it's so clear-cut. You didn't attend last time, did you?'

'No.'

'Well, it's your shout. Do you want to go?'

'Probably. Yes, actually. I want to be there to make sure.' He is nodding with real enthusiasm. 'I've had a vintage champagne set aside for this day for quite some time.'

'OK, I understand. That's up to you.' How pleasant of him. My clients aren't generally disposed to acts of celebration after their divorces, but Harvey's a one-off.

'Now, come on, what do I need to know?'

'That the chances of the divorce being ratified are ninety-eight to ninety-nine per cent. I've only got one small area of doubt.'

'Bollocks to that, Will.' His mobile rings. 'I'm in no doubt that you're going to pull this off. I'm not even contemplating the alternative. Sorry, hang on a sec.'

Harvey walks out of the room with his phone clamped to his ear. A minute later he returns. 'Now, what was that doubt?'

'It concerns the judge.' I explain that even in situations like ours, when both sides go into the FDR satisfied with the agreement, judges still have to look closely at the figures to satisfy themselves. They cannot force any changes, but if they feel that one side is being harshly treated they might ask some questions and suggest the odd amendment. Without too obviously covering myself in praise, I suggest to Harvey that our judge might decide that this is one such case.

'What would that mean?' he asks.

'That the other side might press for more money. That would spin us out a little longer and might cost you a little more, but it wouldn't be the end of the world.'

'Right.' Harvey is not amused by this piece of information. 'Well, I don't want to go anywhere near the end of the world and it's your job to see to that. Hang on . . .' His mobile phone is ringing again, though this time with a different ring tone to indicate a text message. He reads it, smiles, then looks up. 'Excellent. Will, I'm satisfied that you'll take us sailing through the ordeal on Wednesday. One other question, though.'

'Go on.'

'This whole thing in court. Is there any chance of it overrunning? I mean, there's no chance of it stretching into Thursday, is there?'

'None whatsoever.'

'Good. I'm out of here on Wednesday night – for a cheeky ten days on this little battleship of mine on the Mediterranean. I don't intend to miss a minute of it.'

'You'll be fine, Harvey. Don't worry.'

'Good.'

There's a knock on the door and Clare comes in. 'Sorry to interrupt. There's a call for you, Harvey, in the lounge. Do you want to take it in here?'

'No, that's all right.'

Harvey leaves me alone with my coffee and his *FT*. I call Sam on my mobile. The list of the judges for Wednesday is available at two o'clock and I may as well impress Harvey by furnishing him with the most up-to-date information. This doesn't prove possible, though: my mobile dies on me, leaving me with nothing but the information that the battery has run out. I try calling Sam again, but again my line goes dead.

I get up and walk over to the view of East London, but all I want to do is find out who Harvey's judge will be. I try my mobile a third time. Not even a ringing tone. I sit down and start sideways-reading Harvey's newspaper.

I could use Harvey's mobile. It's sitting there next to his *FT*. I might as well. After all, the call is on his behalf. I pick up the phone without a second's thought and look at the small screen. The text message he just received is still on it. This is embarrassing, but I look at the message nevertheless.

I read it again, trying to comprehend the words in

front of me. This is no longer embarrassing: it is extra-ordinary. The content of the message is unbelievable. I put the phone down as if it's burning my fingers. My mind is racing.

Outside, I can hear Harvey's voice. He is still on the phone. I can't hear his words, but the tone suggests he's mid-conversation. That's enough for me. I pick up the mobile again, read the message one last time and memorise it: 'H. We're home and dry. The judge is a pushover. Gx.'

I replace the mobile in the exact position from which I picked it up and replay the words in my mind until they're indelible. 'H. We're home and dry. The judge is a pushover. Gx.'

I continue to replay the words in my head throughout the remainder of my meeting with Harvey and the short journey out of his offices, down in the lift and out of the building. Then I write it on a scrap of paper, and phone Jake.

'Jake, we need to talk.'

'Brilliant. It's been too long, and I've been dying to ask you about that new programme Jenny's in. It's shit, isn't it?'

'Shut up. I'm serious.'

'What's up?'

'Can't tell you now. Can you be in the Dolphin tonight? Half past eight?'

'Yup.'

'And Lauren?'

'I think so.'

'She's got to be there.'

'OK. But seriously, Will, that programme's shit, isn't it?'

'Yes, Jake, you're right. See you later.'

31

'I don't know what you lot will think of this,' I say to my small audience, 'but I've decided it's time to commit professional suicide.'

We're in the Dolphin. There is a somewhat surreal air to the proceedings because we're not the sort of people to arrange last minute top-secret gatherings to discuss matters so deadly serious that they can't be mentioned on the phone. That probably explains why Jake is maintaining an unprecedented level of quiet. He is holding hands with Lauren on my left, and Alex is on my right. In a childish buzz of excitement this afternoon, I rang Alex and invited him along. I could hardly leave him out of the fun and I decided his judgement as a lawyer might be valuable at a time when mine may have deserted me. It helps that, with five days remaining until she joins him at the altar, Steph is tied up in table plans, marquee specifications and a list of the lists of responsibilities from which Alex has escaped.

'Right, are you all sitting comfortably?' I clear my throat. 'I know this sounds ridiculous, and I'm not sure of any of it, but I think I've unwittingly become part of a plan to rob Lauren of a large sum of money. I can't explain it any other way.'

I begin my tale: the White case, the details of current divorce law, my stay of execution in being allowed to continue to represent Harvey Goode, Harvey's long-held confidence that the case would go our way, and my unexpected success against an uncharacteristically invertebrate Georgina McKnight. Jake, Lauren and Alex sit in silence, sipping their drinks. Their incomprehension only partially lifts when I deliver my hammer-blow final line: the text message.

'So what are you saying?' asks Lauren.

'I'm wondering who you think Gx might be.'

'No,' says Alex, 'you're telling us that you think Gx is Georgina, kiss.'

'I thought that's what you were getting at,' says Lauren. 'The fucking bitch. You're saying she's in collusion with Harvey?'

'I don't know, but who else whose name begins with G would find out the identity of the judge the minute it's released?'

'It might be the judge of another case,' says Alex.

'Might be anything.'

'If there is really something dodgy going on, how much do you think she might be stealing from me, Will?' asks Lauren.

'There are two ways of looking at it.' I take a long gulp of my beer, then explain that if the conspiracy theory is wrong, Georgina is simply doing a poor job and Lauren is only losing a mere – I laugh at the absurdity of the sum – £95,000. But Georgina isn't a poor lawyer, and she should be sailing in there on the White-case ticket. And thus the conspiracy theory: 'I reckon she could deliver you at least six million more than you're getting now.'

'Jesus Christ.' Lauren lets her forehead drop on to Jake's shoulder. 'It's so much money it's almost funny. Just imagine, I wouldn't even have to be a bankrupt!'

Even Alex is stunned into silence.

'Six million pounds!' Lauren whispers, in disbelief. 'Six million pounds!' She shakes Jake's shoulder. 'Six million! I wouldn't even have to rely on you to pay the rent. The fucking bitch.'

'But, Will,' says Jake, 'isn't it Georgina who's committing career suicide here? Surely this will ruin her reputation.'

'Not really. It'll be just one dud in a CV of explosive successes. People will assume that, because it's Georgina, Lauren's case wasn't strong and that no better deal was available.'

'What are you thinking of doing?' asks Alex.

'I don't know, but I want to ask Lauren one thing. How did you come to have Georgina representing you?'

'Ah. Oh, Lord. I see what you mean. I've known her for ages. Funnily enough I thought we were friends. About three days after I got my letter from you, Will, I had a phone call from Georgina. She'd rung for a gossip, it seemed. I'd barely told anyone about the divorce but I told her then. Since we were on the subject, I also asked if she could recommend a good divorce lawyer, and I was surprised when she recommended herself. I said that that didn't seem right, given that she also knew Harvey. She said she'd never liked him and that she'd love to represent me. I was easily persuaded. I wasn't feeling very strong at the time.'

'Right, well, that's good enough for me,' I say. And it is. 'What do you think, Alex?'

'I think Lauren should change her solicitor and start the whole divorce procedure again. Agreed, Lauren?'

'I don't know. How long would it take to get it all done, Will?'

'Not much less than three months. Probably more.'

Lauren shakes her head in dismay. 'I'd almost certainly lose my business. I need to come up with around thirty thousand a month just to keep the bank onside. I don't know what to do, Will. Should I sacrifice my business for the possibility of a huge jackpot?'

'Possibly, but here's the problem. I'm probably out of a job anyway, but if you do that, I definitely am.' I explain my predicament: if we start again, Lauren will presumably get a decent lawyer who isn't bent and will hoover up an infinitely larger percentage of the contents of Harvey's bank account. That would be seen as a major defeat for Mellstrom Roberts and for me. Harvey is worth far more to the firm than I am, so I'd be an easy sacrifice.

'Well, we could just leave it, then,' says Lauren. 'I'm going to get a great little payday whatever happens. Harvey and the bitch Georgina may be taking us to the cleaners, but I'll get enough to keep my business alive. And you'd get to keep your job.'

'Sorry, Lauren, we can't do that.' I'm sounding unusually sensible here, but I've thought it through too completely to be diverted. 'It's sweet of you to think of me, but the point of this settlement is not to have you staving off bankruptcy and struggling to pay the rent. Harvey is too big a shit to be allowed to get away with it. It's downright illegal, and I don't want to be party to it. We're talking millions of pounds here that are rightfully yours, Lauren, and it's not just because some stroke of luck found you in a wealthy marriage. The law used to discriminate against women like you, but you're a sleeping partner in a big business and you're allowed your rightful share of it.'

'So what do you suggest?'

'We've got until the court case on Wednesday morning. I think we try to find something that proves Harvey and Georgina are in this together. I'm not sure how we do that – we could play him at his own game, get a private eye to follow him and take pictures. Maybe we could have a rifle through his Chiswick house when he's not there, that sort of thing.'

'I've still got my keys,' she says brightly.

'Good.'

'Sounds a bit Famous Five for me,' says Jake.

'I know, but think of the lashings of ginger beer when it works,' I reply.

'Hang on a sec, Will,' Alex says apprehensively. 'If we do find something to prove the Harvey-Georgina thing, your job's buggered. You're supposed to be on Harvey's side, not exposing him for perverting the course of justice.'

'You're right, of course. And I haven't cracked that

part of the equation yet. All I can think of is this: my overriding duty as a lawyer is to the court above the client.'

'And when has that ever had anything to do with anything?'

'Never, as far as I can remember.'

'Well, you're being brave, scrupulous and amazingly honest. You're going way out of your depth and you're going to lose your job.'

'Maybe, but at least this way I get to feel good about myself.'

'Will,' says Jake, 'you could have kept quiet about this and you'd have been made a salaried partner. You could have secured your future.'

'I know, Jake.'

I'm back at home. It's eleven thirty when I get an answer from Jenny.

'Will? Is that you?'

'Yup.'

'You're kidding me!' She goes quiet. 'Will!' She goes quiet again. 'Will! You hate me, you write me nasty poems. You ignore me for two whole months. You don't ring me up. What on earth do you want?'

'To say sorry for that poem. I was drunk.'

'Apology accepted. Never before has anyone been so horrible to me in such an entertaining way. It was quite classy, actually.'

'Oh, good. I'll write you another.'

'No, you don't have to go that far.' She chuckles. We

are both, I sense, somewhat uncertain and overcome. 'Are you drunk now?'

'No, just driven home.'

'Then tell me why you're ringing. I don't believe you've suddenly decided you want to apologise for four lines of rhyming abuse.'

'You're right. I'm ringing because I wanted to say how much I've been enjoying *Food of Love*.'

'You cheeky fucker.'

'Honestly.'

'Bollocks. The show's shit and you know it. Go on, why are you calling?'

I pause before answering. 'I need you tomorrow evening.'

'Are we going to Amalfi?'

'No. I need to hook you up with the lovely Harvey Goode again.'

'You're joking!'

'I'm serious.'

'That's a big favour to ask of someone you don't like any more who shat on you from such a great height.'

'I know. But you're wrong if you think I don't like you.' My voice falters. I hadn't intended to be so up-front at this stage.

'Oh.' She pauses. 'What's in it for me?'

'The knowledge that you'll have played a major part in Harvey's downfall.'

'Ah.' She appears intrigued, but I haven't hooked her yet. 'You're sounding interesting at last.'

'How kind of you.'

'But ... Hello? You're his lawyer. I thought that meant you're on his side.'

I tell the whole tale again, concluding with an explanation of the Famous Five heist that has just been cooked up in the pub. Jenny's role, I explain, is to provide the all-important element of distraction. If she can tempt Harvey out for a drink, the rest of us can pay his house a visit. And Harvey, with his unique set of moral values and an undisguised fondness for Jenny Joffee, is likely to be tempted.

'OK, I'll do it,' says Jenny. 'It's too exciting to say no.'

'Fantastic.'

'What are his numbers?'

'I thought he gave you his card.'

'You think I'd keep a card belonging to a bastard like that?'

'S'pose not. I'll text you first thing in the morning.'

'Great.' With the business side of the conversation now completed, we find ourselves in an awkward silence.

'D'you want to meet us all for a drink in the Dolphin afterwards?' I ask, finally. 'I think you'll have earned it.'

'That would be really nice.'

'Good.'

'Just one thing, though, Will,' her voice softens, 'I'm a bit worried about you. Are you sure you know what you're doing? Are you going to be all right?'

'No. But don't forget I'm a man of unrivalled bravery.'

'Just take care.'

'You too, good luck tomorrow.'

'Thanks . . .' She goes quiet again. 'It's good to hear from you, Will.'

'It was good to have an excuse to ring you.'

'Don't feel you need an excuse next time.' She hangs up.

32

By Tuesday afternoon, I'm sitting in my office beset by stage fright. The wheels are in motion and there is no turning back.

This morning, Jenny left a message with Sam: 'It's on' – a drink in the West End this evening at eight. Alex, Jake, Lauren and I are to meet at the Old Ship, a pub on the Thames a few hundred yards from Harvey's house, at 7.45 p.m.

My pre-match nerves are not helped by Sam's excitement at having Jenny Joffee on the phone again. 'Come on, come on!' she said. 'What's going on?'

'Absolutely nothing, I'm sorry to say.'

'Are you going to take her back, Will?'

'I don't think that's for me to decide.'

'Well, what I want to know is whether she knows how awful her new programme is and whether she's going to look after you a bit better this time.'

I tried to explain to her that I didn't think there was going to be another time and that it was probably me who messed up last time anyway, but I was interrupted by Simon, who wanted to congratulate me on having done an excellent job with Harvey. 'To think we had all that trouble with you and Mrs Goode and those photographs!' he scoffed. 'And here you are now. Who'd have thought it?'

If only you knew, Simon, if only you knew . . .

Alex's response to the call to arms, meanwhile, was at the other end of the spectrum from mine. While I sat at my desk feeling all jelly-legged, he had turned all gung-ho and daredevil. By midday he had fixed up a private eye to tail Harvey with a long lens for twenty-four hours. A couple of hours later he rang to ask whether I thought we should be wearing gloves – 'you know, black leather ones like the Saint would have worn' – for our nocturnal visit. This didn't seem unreasonable, I said, but a little while later he was debating the necessity for balaclavas and a get-away car.

The use of a private eye seems increasingly hopeless. The likelihood of Harvey being caught on camera with Georgina in the twenty-four-hour window of opportunity is negligible, especially with the lovely Jenny booked in at the most obvious time when they could be caught at a cosy tête-à-tête. This puts more pressure on our visit to Harvey's house. We'll need to be lucky.

At least Jake can be relied on to take the edge off any nervousness. Alex is already in the Old Ship when I arrive, wearing black jeans and a black polo-neck. A pair of black leather gloves is lying on the table in front of him. He's been watching too many spy movies. The sight of him makes Jake burst into laughter when he and Lauren walk in twenty minutes later.

'You're late,' says Alex, more seriously than necessary.

'Sorry, mate. We forgot to synchronise our watches. Nice gloves, though. Where are yours, Will?'

'Ah, yes . . .' I haven't any.

'Well, take a look at these,' says Jake, and, with a flourish, he pulls out a huge pair of red ski mittens. 'This is the pair I usually wear for breaking into multi-millionaires' houses.'

'Very funny,' says Alex.

'Sorry, guys,' says Lauren. 'I couldn't persuade him to leave them behind.'

'Come on, we'd better get going,' says our leader.

'Don't we need to hear from Jenny first?' asks Lauren.

'I have already.' I tap my mobile phone. 'Got a text message just now. Your lovely husband is with her as we speak.'

'Haven't I got time for a drink?' asks Jake.

'No.'

'Not even a quick vodka martini, shaken not stirred?'

'No, you prat.'

We leave the pub in a state of heightened excitement. We're not an imposing collection of crime fighters, bravely championing the cause of moral rectitude, yet we are about to break into the house of a man who is very powerful and, given what we know of his contempt for the law, probably dangerous too.

We turn right along the side of the Thames, up a short rise in the road, past another pub called the Black Horse and down a gentle slope the other side. Here, Lauren rummages in her handbag for the keys and stops outside a magnificent three-storey white house, which has a clear view over the road to the river beyond. It is set back behind a neatly cut lawn and a three-foot-high, chalk-white brick wall with a tall, ornate gate in the middle. I find myself gasping at the grandeur.

'Lauren's gone up in the world since she moved in with you, hasn't she?' I say to Jake.

'She's never been happier,' he replies, and turns to Lauren, who is muttering to herself, rattling her key-ring and thrusting different keys one by one into the same keyhole. She then takes a step back. 'Shit! Why the hell didn't I think of that?'

'What's the problem?' asks Alex.

'The bastard's had the locks changed.'

'Oh, fuck.'

'Oh, fuck indeed.'

'Can you try again?' I ask, clutching a broken straw.

'I already have.'

Silence falls among us.

'How long have we got?' Lauren asks me, a trace of hope in her voice.

'Dunno, but we're OK until Jenny rings to say Harvey's left her. We don't know if he'll come straight back here but I reckon we've got at least an hour.'

'Good.' Lauren marches past us and out of the gate. 'Come on.'

'Where are we going, sweetie?' asks Jake, following her like an obedient spaniel.

'Hammersmith, to get some keys from the house-keeper.'

'Why don't we ring her?'

'I haven't got her number on me.'

'What if she's not in?'

'I don't know.'

Jake and Lauren disappear round the corner to where his car is parked and set off to save our mission. Alex and I retrace our steps to the Black Horse where he buys us both a pint of rather nice bitter, which we sip, looking regularly at our watches, acknowledging that time is running out and that the game, which was always stacked against us, is slipping away.

'Nervous?' Alex asks.

'A bit. But I'm sure I'd feel worse if it was only four days until my wedding.'

'No, you wouldn't.'

'Why?'

Alex shrugs.

'Go on, tell me.'

'I'm a bit nervous about whether you'll remember the rings, but I can't wait to be married to Steph.'

'It is amazing, though.'

'I know. Like Bobby and Pam in *Dallas*: always meant to be together, even when they weren't.'

'I wasn't referring to any of your sad eighties heroes.'

'Oh. What did you mean, then?'

'It's amazing because you were the one who wouldn't settle down, the one who didn't want a girlfriend, or only wanted a girlfriend for a week until the next one came along. And then you only wanted the next one for half an hour because you'd already spotted the one after that.' Alex is fidgeting with a green Heineken ashtray.

'Don't get me wrong, I'm really, really happy for you and Steph, but I've never understood it and I want to know how you could go from being the playboy of West London to engagement and marriage to Steph inside six months.'

'Six months and six days, actually.'

'Whatever.'

'Six months and six days on Saturday, that is.'

'Stop avoiding the issue.'

'OK!' He looks up. 'You really want to squeeze this out of me, don't you?'

'Yes!'

'I thought we were breaking into Harvey's house tonight, not questioning if I'm suitable to be a husband.'

'I'm not questioning that.' I take a deep breath, 'But as your best man, wouldn't it be irresponsible not to know what you think you're doing getting married?'

'Hmm.' Alex isn't impressed by the direction of the conversation. He picks up the ashtray and spins it again.

'I mean that. I want to get married one day myself, but only if I'm so dazzled by someone that I simply have to spend the rest of my life with her, not because I've got to a stage in life where it turns out to be the done thing to get hitched.'

'Is that what being a divorce lawyer has taught you?' He puts down the ashtray and looks at me with sudden interest.

'No, it's what Jenny Joffee taught me.' Somehow this

conversation has extracted something intimate from me rather than its intended source.

Alex looks into my eyes. 'Is that why you think I'm getting married?' he asks slowly.

'No. Not really. I'm envious of you. I simply want my envy to be for the right reason.'

'Fair enough.' Alex raises his arms and leans back in his chair, indicating that any potential confrontation has been deflected. 'What you're saying's probably what half the congregation will be thinking on Saturday anyway. Is it going to last? Has Alex really changed? Well, here's your explanation. I don't think I was happy the way I was before, perceived as eternally single or the eternal scoundrel. It was a role I created, then found myself having to play up to. But this'll make you laugh – I was jealous of you when you were going out with Jenny.'

'Really?'

'Yeah. That was the sort of thing I wanted and couldn't get. I guess that's why I always behaved the way I did. It made me feel a little better about myself, I suppose, as if I was desirable, as if I was OK.' He fidgets uneasily with the ashtray again.

'Alex, put the ashtray down!' I say. 'Carry on. This is fascinating.'

'OK. Well, all that playboy of West London stuff may have made my life exciting but it wasn't very honest. It was pretty cowardly of me to pretend to be something I wasn't. I could never have been as honest with myself as you or Jake.'

'Alex, I can promise you I'm not perpetually single out of a desire to be honest to myself.'

'I know. But you didn't take the other extreme like me. And look at Jake. Until Lauren came along, he joked about being a loser. I couldn't have done that. Will, the point is not that I'm being dishonest with myself now by turning my back on the way I was before. I was being dishonest before. I know that's not very cool, but at least I can be proud of the way I am now.'

I find myself smirking as I watch Alex stewing in the heat of his own confession. 'What's so funny?' he asks.

'That it's taken you over thirteen years to tell me anything half as intimate as that. It was almost worth waiting for!'

'Well, don't expect anything else inside the next thirteen.'

'Can I ask just one more thing?'

'You can try, but I might start playing with the ashtray again.'

'After all those years with all those hundreds of thousands of women, what was it about Steph that made you stop?'

'She was just completely different, allowed me to be myself.'

'Are you trying to say you fell in love with her?'

'Will!' He picks up the ashtray and starts spinning it again, intent on shutting out my question.

'Go on, Alex, say it.' I snatch the ashtray from him and hold it above my head. 'Say it. It's not that hard.'

'I can't.'

'Why not?'

'Because Jake and Lauren are here. Come on, let's go.'

Finally, now, our mission is going to plan. The house-keeper was at home, Jake and Lauren have her key and this time it works. The new code to switch off the alarm – also provided by the housekeeper – works too. An hour later than planned, we are standing in the hall of Harvey's house, staring at the portraits that fill the walls, overwhelmed by our surroundings and wondering what to do next.

'Jake and I will look upstairs,' says Lauren, taking charge. 'The study is through that door. You and Alex start there.'

'What exactly are we looking for?' asks Jake.

'We don't really know,' I reply. 'That's where this plan is flawed. Anything connecting Harvey and Georgina will do, anything like that you can find.'

Alex and I push open the door to Harvey's study, a long, wood-panelled room with an antique mahogany desk overlooked by a large portrait of Sir Winston Churchill. It would be helpful if there was also a framed photograph on his desk of him and Georgina looking lovingly into each other's eyes, but it isn't going to be that easy.

We wander down the room like tourists, taking in the splendour. No clues to the Harvey-Georgina axis are to be found this way either, so we decide to tackle the sets of drawers either side of the desk.

'Fuck,' exclaims Alex under his breath. 'I've forgotten my glasses.' He fumbles around through the drawers, pulling out papers and letters and putting them up to within an inch of his nose. 'This is fucking ridiculous.'

So after a while, we change sides of the desk and I sift through the same papers that Alex has just had on the end of his nose, looking for headed paper with the name of Georgina's firm at the top. I discover instead the contents of what is clearly Harvey's motoring drawer: MOT certificates, vehicle ownership forms, insurance documents and receipts for garage repairs. I then find house and property documents, investment fund bro-chures, health insurance and medical details and return to my initial set of drawers to equity holdings, dividend accounts, horse-racing syndicates, everything except a link to Georgina McKnight.

'I give up,' Alex announces.

'So do I,' I reply. 'Let's try somewhere else.'

We turn off the study lights, cross the hall and find ourselves in a magnificent sitting-room which opens into the garden. It is filled with antique furniture from what appears to be imperial India and a huge grand piano.

'He never went near that bloody piano,' says Lauren, startling us, standing in the doorway. 'I tried to get rid of it but he liked it because he thought it looked good. Any luck in the study?'

'None at all.'

'None here either. We'd better keep moving.'

We scatter a second time. Alex and I find ourselves

rummaging through a second, smaller sitting-room containing a huge television, then a dining room, with the growing feeling that we are going through the motions now. There is no trace of Georgina. It is also far later than I had intended us still to be in the house.

'Shit!' Suddenly Jake's voice echoes through the house. 'Come and look at this! Jesus!'

Alex and I rush from the dining room and follow Jake's voice. We find him and Lauren in the kitchen.

'Feast your eyes on this boys,' he says triumphantly. 'I think we might have cracked it! I was looking through a pile of letters and found this envelope of travel documents.' He is brandishing a British Airways receipt. It shows two people booked business class to Nice on the 18.45 flight tomorrow. The first name on the document is H. Goode, the name immediately below it is G. McKnight.

'The tickets are in the envelope,' says Jake proudly, 'but this is what you need, isn't it?'

'The bastard! I can't believe it.' Lauren is walking round the kitchen as if in a daze. 'You were right, Will! You were bloody well right.'

'Jesus Christ, we've got him! Yes!'

We cheer ourselves exultantly, triumph mixed with a distinct sense of disbelief. In the midst of all this, I hear my mobile phone beeping.

'Hey, guys, shut up!' There's panic in my voice. 'It's a message from Jenny. Harvey's left the bar and is coming home. I don't know how this has happened, but the message was sent twenty minutes ago. I think a rapid exit is required.'

And so to Jenny again. We leave Harvey's house at full speed and pile into Jake's car, then drive via the Hammersmith housekeeper to the Dolphin. All four of us are shaken by what we have just done and while we're in the car brief silences are punctuated with inane giggles, uncontrollable laughter and further exclamations of disbelief. Twice I take out from my inside pocket the travel document, a single sheet of printed paper whose significance is inestimable. Something extraordinary will now happen tomorrow and I am hurtling towards an uncertain, albeit dramatic, end. On top of all this, Jenny, the lovely, colluding, conniving Jenny, is waiting for me in the pub.

When we walk in, hers is the first face I see. The others all seem to be a blur. She looks excited, adventurous, pleased with herself, pleased to see me. She looks like the Jenny I've missed. Her hair is cut a little shorter than it was when I last saw her and is pushed behind her ears. And her eyes appear to emit delight.

'You clever thing,' I say to her. 'You did a brilliant job.' Then I stoop forward uncertainly for a kiss, to be greeted full on the lips.

'And what about you?' she asks. 'How did it go?'

'It couldn't have gone better. We've got him, Jenny!'

'Fantastic!' Her eyes widen with triumph. Beautiful, smiling eyes. For a moment I'm lost in them. It's a pleasant way to go missing.

'How was Harvey?' I ask eventually. 'Did he make a pass at you?'

'He's slightly too smooth for that. But I guess if I took up his invitation to go to New York with him he might.'

'The dirty bastard! Look, I've got slightly bad news. It's drinks all round for everyone except me.'

'Why?' Jenny looks wonderfully concerned.

'Jake, will you look after Jenny?' Then I explain to her: 'I've got to go home and prepare for my finest hour in court tomorrow.'

'Do you really have to?' she asks persuasively.

'I do. Well . . . why . . .' We're looking at each other and, for all today's planning, I hadn't considered what to do when Jenny's mission was complete.

Now we're silent, wondering what to do next. 'Why doesn't Jenny come to the wedding on Saturday?' asks Alex, leaping to the rescue, unusually intuitively. 'If that's all right by you, of course, Will.'

Jenny looks up at me. 'D'you fancy it?' I ask.

'Bloody love to.'

'Brilliant. See you Saturday.' I turn to Jake and Lauren, 'I'll see you two in court tomorrow.'

With that, I take six steps in the direction of the door then decide I have to plant another kiss on Jenny's lips before I go. And I do and, maybe I'm wrong and over-excited, but it appears to me that it is received rather gratefully.

I remain on a high in the taxi home and during the two hours I spend slumped in my dilapidated sofa, A4 notepad in front of me, supposedly fine-tuning 'my finest hour in court' as I ostentatiously described it. Eventually I go to bed, but for the second night running my mind is far too active to allow me any rest. Last night trepidation kept me awake but tonight I'm wound up in a tingle of excitement.

I suspected it would come, Jenny, I just didn't know it would take so long for the after-effects of our relationship to wreak some terrible affliction on me. Two and a bit months later you have given me insomnia.

33

I am in the office at eight o'clock, all efficiency, glugging coffee, yawning broadly, working efficiently towards a deadline. At 10.30 a.m. in the family division of the High Court, 42–9 High Holborn, the financial-dispute resolution hearing of Harvey and Lauren's divorce is due to be held and their divorce ratified. I have two and a half hours to fix the outcome.

My first job is to ring Lauren and brief her. Then she will call Georgina to say that she has changed her mind and decided to attend court.

My next call is to Simon, who isn't yet in the office. As intended, I click on to his voicemail: 'Simon, Will here. Something's come up last minute with the Harvey Goode case. I'm concerned that there might be some tricks afoot. If possible, I'd appreciate it if you could attend too.'

My third call also goes to a voicemail – to my frustration. Giles Preston, one of the court reporters for the Press Association, is not a man I know well and I'd rather speak to him in person, as I explain at the start of my message: 'I can't tell you any more as I'm sure you understand,' I try to sound tantalising, 'but I wanted to alert you to the fact that it'll probably be worth your while pitching up at ten thirty for Goode v. Goode. You won't be allowed in, but wait outside afterwards.'

I make two photocopies of the British Airways document, then slide one into the top drawer of my desk. Finally I skim-read a couple of law books, and make a few basic notes.

By half past eight I'm ready to leave the office, keen to avoid Simon and a thunderous inquisition. I switch off my mobile for the same reason and set off on foot through New Square and Chancery Lane. It is one of those cool, clear late-summer days with the fresh bite of September, and I'm happy to duck into a coffee shop on High Holborn, to read a newspaper and wait.

By nine thirty I'm outside the court building, cursing that the doors don't open for another half-hour. To kill time, I put another call through to Giles Preston but there is still no answer. I may just have to cope without him.

Ten o'clock. The glass doors slide apart and I go through security. A glance at the court lists shows that Goode v. Goode is to be heard in Court Fourteen by Judge Perry, the apparent pushover. I have never appeared before him, never even seen him; I just hope he's pushed over by us rather than them.

Court Fourteen is on the fifth floor; I follow the signs to it. The building is white-walled, with purple-flecked carpet, clinical-looking and characterless. People are starting to arrive, but the building is still quiet. No one is about, and I duck inside the door of the courtroom.

It is smallish, with five rows of long imitation-wood

tables and red swivel chairs in front of a platform on which the judge and the clerk of the court sit. There are two doors behind the judge's chair and I make straight for them, wondering which will lead to the judge's room. There is no answer when I knock at the first, but at the second I am asked to enter.

Judge Perry is a district judge, a smallish man with thinning grey hair and lines etched into his brow. He is sitting in a leather armchair in front of a window, reading his briefing notes. He is wearing half-moon glasses and peers over the top of them at me.

'Good morning, sir. My name is Will Tennant. I'm acting on behalf of Harvey Goode, whose FDR you're dealing with this morning.'

'Yes?' He sounds uninterested.

'There's an element of the dispute that I would like to discuss with you, sir.'

'Mr Tennant, I'm sure you know perfectly well that there is a time and place for such discussion and that is in the courtroom.'

'Yes, sir.' The judge is refusing to raise his eyes from his reading, but I press on regardless. 'I can only say that this is an unusual case that I think you need to hear of in advance.'

'Mr Tennant,' his tone is flat and dry, not remotely encouraging, 'I will be the judge of what I hear in advance and the answer is that, in advance, I hear nothing. It is highly irregular for a representative to come and see me like this before court begins. If there is a matter of law that you wish to discuss out of court, then I shall happily do so, but only, of course, if the other side is represented. I'm sure you must know all this, Mr Tennant. Now, may I suggest you leave before you compromise your position further.'

'Certainly, sir. I apologise. Can I please just leave this with you?' Judge Perry is apparently immersed in his reading. Nevertheless I remove from my briefcase the photocopy of the British Airways document and leave it on the coffee table by the door.

I have almost closed it when I turn back with a second thought. 'Two more things, sir.' I resolutely await the judge's attention. Eventually he thrusts away his papers in frustration and bawls, 'Tennant! What are you still doing here?'

'First,' I reply, with as much calm as I can muster, 'you may be interested to hear that Mrs Goode is a co-founder of Intertalk. And second, her solicitor has spread the word that you're a pushover.'

With that I close the door smartly behind me before the pushover has a chance to reply.

Outside the courtroom, the white corridor is coming to life. Georgina McKnight is standing half-way down it, looking bored and superior. I wonder if she's looking forward to her holiday; I also wonder what she looks like when she's not wearing today's cleavage-revealing black trouser suit and is stretched out on Harvey's yacht in her bikini. Sometimes you can't help yourself.

'Pleasure to see you, Georgina.' Which, in certain ways, it is.

'Let's hope so,' she replies curtly. 'For some reason, my client has decided to turn up.'

'Oh, really?' For once I'm ahead of her in the curious game I discovered rather late that we're playing. And for once she doesn't know.

There are still fifteen uneasy minutes to wait before the courtroom opens. Lauren and Jake arrive next, Lauren looking nervous and Jake as serious as he can, making a point of barely acknowledging me. Harvey arrives afterwards, pristine in one of his light grey Savile Row suits. He raises half an eyebrow at Georgina, no more, and doesn't look remotely flustered until I guide him into a consultation room. Then he turns on me. 'What the fuck's going on?'

'What do you mean?'

'What the fuck are *they* doing here? Why's Lauren here? I thought this was going to be straightforward, that no one needed to come. And your fucking friend, why's he here?'

'I don't know, Harvey. Mrs Goode has every right to be here. Jake won't come into the courtroom, though.'

Harvey paces up and down aggressively and it is no surprise to see that his forehead vein has joined us for the morning. I am infinitely happier in here with Harvey's wrath, though, because I don't want to see Simon until we are all in court – and I don't know how I would handle Giles Preston if – on the off-chance that he turned up – he greeted me in front of my client and my boss.

At exactly ten thirty, an usher in the corridor announces: 'Could all parties associated with the Goode case please now go to Court Fourteen.' My hour is nigh and the cast assembles. I lead Harvey down the corridor, passing Jake, then Giles Preston, who is standing nonchalantly by the door. He looks as if he has dashed in straight out of bed: his collar is rumpled and his hair untidy. Then Simon breezes up next to me.

'Will,' he says, under his breath, 'what on earth is all this about? And why on earth did you nod at Preston?'

'Just wait, Simon,' is all I can say. 'I'm confident it'll all be OK.' But my confidence is slipping fast. What on earth am I doing here, impaling myself on the sword of justice? What alternative career could I pursue? I should have addressed such thoughts earlier, though, because Judge Perry is in his seat on the platform, waiting for us to sit down.

We assemble in the front row before him, Lauren and Georgina on the right, Simon, myself and Harvey on the left. We are greeted first by Judge Perry, then by a tense silence.

The judge clears his throat. 'Is it the case that both sides are already in agreement?' he asks. We murmur acknowledgement, and Georgina presents him with a copy of our financial settlement.

There is a further silence while Judge Perry studies it. He says nothing.

I don't know if it's just me who feels the tension but, judging by Simon's heavy breathing and the throbbing forehead vein on my right, it is not.

Eventually Judge Perry looks up. 'Mrs Goode.' He looks over his glasses at Lauren.

'Yes, sir?'

'Are you sure you're happy with this settlement?'

'I think so, sir.'

'Hmm.' The judge's eyes return to the document and we're back in the awkward silence until he looks up again. 'Does anyone else have anything to say about this agreement?'

This is my moment and I have no option but to grab it. 'Yes, sir,' I reply. Simon and Harvey stare at me in horror. 'Sir.' I hear a level of confidence in my voice as I speak, which surprises me, and I lean down to pick a file of papers out of my briefcase.

'Will, what the hell are you doing?' mutters Simon through clenched teeth next to me.

I ignore my employer and address the judge again: 'Sir, I refer you to the Law Society code of conduct, guide to professional conduct for solicitors, rule 21.01. It reads thus: "While under a duty to do their best for a client, a solicitor must never deceive or mislead the court."'

'Yes, Mr Tennant. I'm aware of the code of conduct. Your point, please?'

'Sir, I'm wondering whether the code has been adhered to here.'

'Mr Tennant, having reviewed the terms of the proposed financial settlement agreed between Mr and Mrs Goode, I should say that your duty to your client has been impeccable.'

'Yes, but . . .'

'Sir,' Simon is bolt upright alongside me, 'we are,

indeed, extremely content with the terms of the settlement and have nothing further to say on the matter.'

'That would not appear to be the case, Mr Henderson.'

Thank you, Judge Perry, for offering me a tiny scrap
of help.

'May I request, then,' Simon isn't giving up, 'that the
court adjourns briefly while Mr Tennant, our client and
I confirm this.'

'I think we will hear what Mr Tennant has to say
first.' Simon slumps in his chair, and all eyes are now
back on me. 'Mr Tennant,' Judge Perry continues, 'as I
have suggested, I'm inclined to think that you have made
an astonishingly good settlement for your client.'

'Thank you, sir. In fact, that is what I wish to draw
your attention to. Is the settlement not *too* good?'

Simon sits up again like an attentive schoolboy. 'Sir,
I must object.'

'Objection overruled. Now, Mr Tennant, it is certainly
the first time in my recollection that anyone before me
has questioned a settlement that so clearly favours their
own client. But I take your point and so I must ask you,
Miss McKnight,' he now addresses Georgina, 'are you
of the opinion that your client has a fair and equitable
settlement?'

There is a heavy silence as Georgina contemplates
her response. For the first time since I've known her,
she appears to be something other than 100 per cent
in control. 'Of course I am, sir.'

'Miss McKnight, when there is an agreement between
two sides in a matrimonial settlement, then I am loath

to question it. However, I have looked closely at the papers for the Goode settlement. Please tell me, is it not generally the case that in a divorce where one party has the wealth of Mr Goode, the other tends to receive more than seven hundred and forty-five thousand pounds?'

'Yes, sir, but only marginally so and there are unusual circumstances.'

'Then, Miss McKnight, would it not perhaps be best to adjourn this hearing until the end of the day while we consider these unusual circumstances and, if everyone is still satisfied, settle the FDR then?'

'I'm sure we can conclude this to everyone's satisfaction now.'

'Would you be in a position to come back at five o'clock, Miss McKnight?'

'If absolutely necessary, which I do not believe it is. I think we would be wasting everyone's time, sir, including your own.'

'It's kind of you to think of me, Miss McKnight, but I shall be here in court as ever. Where will you be?'

'Well, I had intended to be leaving to go on holiday.'

'How interesting, Miss McKnight. That will be all for the moment. Now, if I may address Mrs Goode again, please.' Lauren sits forward nervously. 'Mrs Goode, I ask you a second time, are you still of the opinion that you have a fair and equitable settlement?'

'That was the only opinion that I could come to,' Lauren speaks in the quiet, studied manner I first heard in my flat all those months ago, 'because that was the information I was given by my solicitor.'

'But would you agree, Mrs Goode, that it is not ideal to employ a solicitor who is on the point of spending a holiday with the husband you are divorcing?'

Suddenly the tense quiet of the courtroom is broken and pockets of noise and objection erupt on both sides of the court. Simon and Harvey turn to me, Simon's face pale, Harvey's red, his vein hopping up and down as if bursting to get out. Simon looks bemused, Harvey as if he might explode. 'You fucking bastard, Tennant,' is what he says.

Simon looks through me as if he doesn't know me: 'Harvey, is it true?'

'It's fucking bollocks.'

Judge Perry watches in apparent amusement; eventually he demands quiet. 'I will repeat my last question to Mrs Goode. Would you agree, Mrs Goode, that it is not ideal to employ a solicitor who is on the point of spending a holiday with the husband you are divorcing?'

'I would, sir.'

'May I conclude, then, that you were not aware that this foreign liaison was to take place?'

'Yes, you may, sir.'

'Thank you, Mrs Goode. Now, Mr Tennant,' he turns to me, utterly in control, 'is it this to which you were referring when you said that there had been an infringement of the Law Society's code of conduct?'

'It is indeed, sir.'

'Very interesting. Now, Mr Henderson,' the judge turns to Simon, 'if you have something to say, I would be happy to listen.'

'Thank you, sir.' Simon pats down his side-parting. 'Sir, I would like first to apologise for any misinformation that may have come your way through my colleague, Mr Tennant, or any other party. However, the idea that our client, Mr Goode, is shortly to holiday with Miss McKnight is a dangerous one and it has implications, as I believe you are suggesting. However, it is also untrue.'

'Really, Mr Henderson?' Judge Perry seems about as impressed with Simon as he was with me in his room earlier. 'In that case, I would like to invite a representative from each side to approach me to view some evidence.'

Simon and Georgina step up towards the judge, who shows them a sheet of paper. I feel pretty confident that it is the photocopy I made in my office earlier this morning. I also feel pretty confident that we are home and dry. Not even Harvey, who is whispering threateningly in my ear, can shift my feeling of success. I probably will 'fucking pay for it', as he insists, but so will he.

Simon and Georgina return to their seats, Simon looking as though he's had six of the best from the headmaster. Georgina manages a defiant smile, which disappears the moment Judge Perry commands quiet. Again he clears his throat. 'Mr Goode and Mrs Goode,' he speaks slowly and clearly so that his words cannot be lost, 'this is a most reprehensible business. To my knowledge it is unprecedented and the view I take of it could not be dimmer. Mrs Goode, I understand that you are enthusiastic to cut all your ties to Mr Goode, and I sympathise with you in that, but I cannot resolve your financial dispute today. The suggestion that there has been an extreme contravention of procedure is too strong. If this causes a problem, please say so, because I am entitled to make arrangements for an interim payment to be made. Would that be helpful to you?'

'It certainly would, sir.' There is a note of glee in Lauren's voice that I have never heard before.

'How much do you need?'

'A hundred thousand pounds would be nice.'

Harvey's shoulders sink.

'Oh,' Judge Perry allows himself a conservative chuckle, 'I wasn't expecting *that* sort of figure, but in the circumstances, I see no reason why you're not entitled to it. Do you, Miss McKnight?'

'No, sir.' Georgina is wearing that defiant smile again.

'Good. I'm pleased to see that you haven't parted entirely with your senses, Miss McKnight.' Judge Perry looks at her sternly over the rims of his glasses. 'However, I am profoundly disappointed by what has come to light. It seems that you may have been acting here for the opposition and, in so doing, you have failed in your duty to both your client and the court. I hope, for your sake, that you will be able to prove that this is not the case. Otherwise a dynamic and flourishing legal career will have been prematurely snuffed out. I have no option but to refer your handling of this case to the solicitors' disciplinary tribunal. It is for your employers, Chilton Shaw, to decide whether or not to suspend you until any tribunal is completed, but I must insist that all Mrs Goode's legal fees are withheld until we know whether or not you did anything that was worth her paying for.

'Now, Mr Goode, if your forthcoming holiday is not as relaxing as you had intended, I suspect you can only hold yourself responsible. It seems that you set out to mislead the court and cheat your wife of what was rightfully hers. You should take note that this is certain to stand against you when negotiations for your financial settlement are resumed.

'Mr Henderson, whether or not your firm wishes to continue to represent Mr Goode is a question that you must answer yourselves. I do, however, wish to commend the conduct of Mr Tennant in this. It may have been highly irregular and a little abrasive, but it would be wrong for it to be viewed with disdain. He was certainly no pushover.' And he allows himself another little chuckle.

'Finally, I return to you, Mrs Goode, the victim here. It is my firm recommendation that you choose different solicitors to represent you from henceforth. I would hope that they are far more ambitious with the financial settlement you negotiate. May I ask, did Miss McKnight ever mention the White case to you?'

'No, sir, she did not.'

'I thought not. Well, the White case may prove helpful. It is not for me to deliver anything conclusive here, but I wouldn't be surprised if the figure you were about to settle for with Miss McKnight turns out to be some ten times too small.' Ten times too small! I'm sure the sides of Judge Perry's mouth turned up as he said that. 'Right, that is the end of this odious business. This court is now dismissed.'

Judge Perry rises and exits through the door behind him, leaving in his wake the sound of Lauren shrieking loudly to everyone and no one in particular, 'Ten times too small! Did you hear what he said? Ten times! I can't believe it!'

Without a word to anyone, Georgina breaks for the courtroom exit, flings open the door and almost knocks over Giles Preston, who is waiting outside. She is followed hotly by Harvey, and we are treated to a furious exchange between them as they disappear down the corridor. Simon weighs up the situation and moves pretty fast. 'Wait here, back in a minute,' he tells me breathlessly, then sets off in pursuit.

It's just the victors who remain – if I can be called that, but I certainly feel like it. Then Giles and Jake join us, demanding to know all. Lauren wraps herself round Jake and shrieks: 'Ten times too small! Can you believe it, Jake? We're going to be fucking rich!'

After some persuasion, however, she slows down and relays what has just happened. Given that officially I am still representing Harvey, I'm not supposed to speak to the press, but I butt in occasionally when her version of the truth becomes a little too over-elated. Giles scribbles furiously in his notepad, muttering that maybe it was worth getting out of bed for this after all. I decide to make one official statement, an ill-disguised attempt to secure my future by extolling the virtues of

Mellstrom Roberts and telling Giles how fervently I hope to continue working there. But Giles is already heavily on my side and not only does he promise to mention this in his story, but he is understanding when I tell him that there is not the remotest chance of him finding out how the British Airways travel document came into the judge's hands.

Just as we're about to leave, Simon walks back into the courtroom, puffing. 'Will, can we have a word?'

'Sure.' But I don't move to a quiet corner as I suspect Simon was hoping I would. I don't want to be sacked just yet, so I remain exactly where I am. At least while the Press Association is within earshot, my future is safe.

'Will . . .' Simon seems stuck for words. 'That was a magnificent thing you did just now. It was highly irregular and you've pissed off Harvey Goode something rotten, but it was magnificent, and, Mr Preston, I want you to let that be known. It's not something I'd encourage you to do too often, Will, we tend to find that the firm works best on a policy of holding on to our clients, but as a one-off it was admirable, your own little footnote in legal history. Well done. You'll go a long way with the firm. You've done us proud.'

34

Within two and a half days, Simon had broken his word. All it took was a short, sharp exchange of words on my mobile and that was it. I wasn't shocked: the only surprise for me was that it had taken him so long.

And those intervening two and a half days were almost worth it. After court on Wednesday, I had no option but to join Lauren and Jake in celebrating our triumph, and never made it back to the office. We started off with a bottle of champagne that we bought from an off-licence. Then when the pubs opened we consumed another in a wine bar, another in a different bar, and thus it continued all day, long into a warm, wonderful evening, large chunks of which I can't recollect. What I will never forget, though, was how the combination of exhaustion, relief and giddy success transplanted me to an emotional heaven. I remained there the following morning when, hung-over, I was greeted with newspaper headlines so absurdly praiseworthy that they proved more effective than a fistful of paracetamol in clearing my head.

The *Guardian* had me as the basement story on their front page with a headline that read: 'Lawyer Puts Conscience Before Pay Cheque'. *The Times* had me stretched across the top of page five with: 'Strange Case of Solicitor Stuck on Moral High Ground'. The *Daily Telegraph* and the *Independent* were more interested in the future of Harvey Goode, though they, too, had fun at the expense of the legal profession, portraying me as an extraordinary beast never previously seen in the law courts, the 'white knight' solicitor who put the interests of justice before the interests of his client. And everyone included the descriptive snapshot of Harvey storming out of the court in the shouting match with Georgina.

That morning my mobile phone went berserk with friends, colleagues and a couple of journalists, and I fielded their calls from my dilapidated sofa, bathing in my moment of glory and wondering if Jenny would ring.

Sure enough, she was on the phone shortly before midday, full of praise, telling me that she was proud of me and lauding me in a sufficiently adulatory tone to keep me on my emotional high for the rest of the day.

And it was easy to remain there, given that I had the day off. I had always planned to take the Thursday and Friday before Alex's wedding as holiday, to stand by him as best man and help inject the necessary light relief as his hour at the altar approached. On the Thursday evening we drove to Upper Heynington, near Banbury, where the wedding was to take place and on Friday morning I awoke in the hotel where we were staying to find – as I expected – that I had been shifted out of the spotlight. It was Alex and Steph's moment of glory now, and while my story was still running, albeit considerably smaller, in Friday morning's newspapers, the focus of the news had shifted on to Harvey, his future, his libido, and the mystery of his whereabouts. Unsurprisingly, no one could find him.

My only dealing with the office through all this was a phone call on Thursday from Sam, who asked if I was all right and then informed me that everyone was talking about me, the general conclusion being that I was 'off my fucking rocker'. In fact, she said, I was apparently 'so far off it that it'd be a miracle if I ever found it again'.

Finally, though, came the call from Simon, shortly before six o'clock on Friday. It was a rather beautiful evening and we had already consumed a couple of glasses of Pimm's on the veranda of the golf club where the wedding reception was to be held. Alex and I were in the marquee, moving the last of the tables into place, when my mobile rang.

In his rather distant, weighty manner, Simon informed me that there had been a board meeting at which my performance in the Goode case had been the main item on the agenda. There was neither sympathy nor compassion in his voice when he told me that the board had reached the unanimous conclusion that my position with the firm was no longer tenable. When should I come in to clear my desk? I asked. There was no need, he replied. Sam had been instructed to box up my possessions and have them sent round in a taxi on Monday. After that it seemed hardly worth asking such questions as: isn't this a different story from the one you gave the press on Wednesday? Or:

could this decision be related to the fact that Harvey Goode is worth more to Mellstrom Roberts than little old me? Or: where do you think we should go for my leaving party?

Alex and I then moved the last table and returned to the jug of Pimm's on the veranda. Alex's sympathy was unnecessary and we were soon talking about my career as a divorce lawyer as you do the passing of a grand old relative. My death, we agreed, was sad but expected and, boy, didn't I have a good innings!

It hurt more than I let on, of course, but only marginally. There had been too much else to occupy my mind – Harvey, Georgina, the wedding, Jenny, primarily Jenny, I suppose – to let my all-too-predictable sacking bring me clattering to earth. But my disappointment was certainly strong enough to have me punching Giles Preston's phone number into my mobile. He was surprisingly unenthusiastic and, though he said he would certainly put out this latest 'snippet' on the news wires, he explained that the story had pretty much burned out. He also told me that early newspaper deadlines on Fridays make late Friday stories notoriously hard to get into print and that Mellstrom Roberts were probably all too aware of this, which was why they had elected to sack me when they did. The clever bastards.

Alex and I ordered another jug of Pimm's, then had another at our hotel. By the time we had finished it, our conversation had moved away from me and back to Alex. This shaped the extraordinary events of the previous days rather nicely. It felt good that just as Alex was about to embark on his marriage, I was renouncing a career spent picking such unions to pieces.

35

'You're a saint!' Jake is grinning at me. We're standing outside the church – Jake, Alex and I – greeting the wedding guests as they arrive. Before us, a pergola of blooming jasmine hangs over the path, and behind us the church, a smallish, beautiful piece of Cotswold-stone architecture, is cloaked in warm sunlight. The twitter of pre-nuptial excitement flows towards the doors and the guests respond to Alex either with a 'Good luck' or an expression that suggests he is about to come face to face with his Maker. They also bestow on me a variety of comments: 'Congratulations!'

'What you've done is fantastic!'

'The tossers you work for clearly don't know what they're losing.'

'I'm so proud of you!'

'I hope you feel really good about yourself!'

And I do. The news of my sacking has spread throughout the wedding party. Almost every guest who knows me – and quite a few who don't – is aware of my fate and determined to hail me as some sort of post-modern super-hero. I am taken aback by this, but I'm not going to argue. I never knew that being sacked could feel so good. Given the choice right now to be in run-of-the-mill employment or sacked and famous, I think I'd choose the latter. The novelty will no doubt have worn off by Monday morning when I'm alone in my flat with the rest of my life stretching in front of me and nothing to fill it with, but today, on the moral high ground, I might suffer from the odd pang of vertigo, but I have a pleasant view of the world.

It is also a good place to meet Jenny, who is one of the last into the church, looking delicate, bare-shouldered, in a pink silk dress with a black Japanese orchid print. I don't think I've ever seen her look so striking – in this petite, feminine way – and I feel a ripple of self-consciousness as she approaches me.

'What an incredible few days you've had, sweetie,' she says when she's standing in front of me. 'I heard about your bastard employers. Are you OK?'

'Surprisingly fine, actually.'

'Oh, good. I've been worried.' She's talking quietly, intimately, specifically to me, and to the exclusion of Alex and Jake. 'What are you going to do with your life?'

'Dunno. We'll talk about that later. Definitely something new.'

'We've both got a lot of reassessing to do, I think, sweetie.'

'Really?'

'Yes, I'll tell you about that later too.'

'Tell me now.'

'Certainly not. You've got a job to do. Good luck.' She gives me a tweak under my ribs – the tweak she used to give me six months ago. I watch her disappear into the church, and when I turn round, Alex and Jake are raising their eyebrows suggestively.

As the wedding day develops, three different identities are thrust upon me. I am Will, the best man, the guy who brings with him the rings and, apparently, a speech littered with side-splitting one-liners; I am Will, notorious hero and victim of the legal system; and I am Will who is foolishly allowing himself to nurture an increasing obsession for the girl who dumped him – and you don't need to be a divorce lawyer to know how clever *that* is. I guess this all makes me a multi-faceted and therefore more-than-usually fascinating person, although my third identity barely surfaces.

During the wedding service Alex and Steph look so good together it's a wonder that anyone (me, that is) questioned whether they were suited for wedlock, and I do a fine job in not forgetting the rings. Yet this is what surprises me: for the first time ever at a wedding, I find myself so swept up and enchanted by the enormity and romance of one person saying, 'I will,' to another that the questions that usually fill my head on these occasions evaporate. Do this couple really know what they're doing? How do they know they know? Will it last? Why them and not me? Why do brides feel obliged to wear crowns on their heads? For once, I don't care.

I'm not completely soft-focus, though. Just briefly, I pause on the thought that I once proposed to today's bride – and that it is probably a good thing she said no. During the first hymn, I also find myself casting an eye round for Jenny. I see her on the far side of the congregation and she flashes me a smile. During the second hymn, I re-engage eye-contact, and enough warm glances are exchanged thereafter to create an understanding that I know where she is and she knows where I am and that this somehow seems important.

After the service, hardly a glimpse of Jenny is possible as I am borne along on a wave of love, harmony and hysteria, and Nicky the nurse seems permanently attached to my arm. I understand that, as best man, it is my duty to walk back up the aisle with the chief bridesmaid on my arm, but I had no idea that her duty was to hang on to me for dear life once we were outside.

At the golf club, champagne is on hand and we encounter the photographer, Chris, who seems to take his job rather too seriously. After half an hour, Alex is fed up and Steph is trying to calm him down. The vicar who joined Alex and Steph had said that no man should put them asunder, and I feel obliged to take him at his word and usher Chris away. This is a popular move, particularly with Nicky the nurse.

'Come on,' she says, 'let's get a drink,' and ushers me through to the marquee where the other guests are chatting. There's no doubting that Nicky isn't looking at all bad. I knew she was tall and quite large in bone structure, but I hadn't guessed what her tight-fitting bridesmaid's dress is making so apparent, that she's also perfectly formed. She's good company too, and moves straight into a string of half-decent jokes about the worst best-man speeches she has ever heard.

Talking to Nicky is more like talking to a boy than a girl. Girls aren't supposed to do irrelevant, amusing chat, but she is so good at it that I lose track of Jenny. In the middle of another of Nicky's anecdotes – 'Did you know that Steph's stepfather was the second husband of one of the hostesses on *The Golden Shot*?' – I decide I need to find her. 'Sorry, Nicky,' I say.

'That's OK. I'll see you at dinner anyway. We're sitting next to each other.'

'Great.' And for some reason I flash her a wink.

It is easy to spot the soft pink silk of Jenny's dress on the other side of the marquee. She is on her own, pretending to be busy.

'Are you all right?' I ask.

'No. Poor old me, you're not looking after me very well.'

'Well—'

'Will!' she interrupts. 'I'm joking. I'm a big girl now, and you're too important today to talk to me.'

'You little tease!' I say drily. 'So, what's up? I'm dying to know about this reassessing we're going to be doing.'

'I'll give you a little taster.' She puts her champagne glass to her lips and sips. And I know I've got to calm down because the way she does that is suddenly erotic. 'I've given up my job too. Decided to come clean. Couldn't stand taking everyone for a ride any more so I followed your lead and opted for the honest route. I was offered another series of *Food of Love* – for some reason Channel Five liked it – but I've said no.'

'Wow! Well done, you.'

'It feels great.'

'What'll you do instead?'

'Dunno. Something a bit more true to myself. I quite fancy doing a programme about penguins.'

'Serious?'

'Well, sort of. I've only had a couple of days to think about it.'

'Great. Will our Richard play the lead role?'

'Of course. Will you visit him with me some time soon?'

'You're on.'

And after that frustratingly short yet thoroughly welcome exchange, we are separated again. It is dinner time and because I am on the table with the bride, the groom, their parents and anyone else of particular importance to them, Jenny is not seated with me.

I have Nicky on one side of me and Lauren on the other and this is all extremely convivial, especially with Nicky being such an expert at ensuring my glass is never empty. I had intended to hold back on the alcohol until after my speech, but it's already too late.

'Interesting evening for you, my saviour, isn't it?' asks Lauren quietly, half-way through our main course.

'What are you referring to?'

'Jenny.'

'How do you mean?'

'You don't have to be a shrink,' she says, under

her breath, 'to spot that you're still pretty fond of her.'

'I'm not very good at disguising it, am I?'

'No, but I don't think that matters.'

'Why?'

'Because she's still pretty fond of you.'

'What makes you think that?' I can feel a smirk forming.

'She told me.'

'What did she say?'

'Nice stuff. Just hints, nothing definite. She said she'd missed you and that being around you again made her realise that. She also said she'd aged a bit since you split up. Her "feelings towards commitment have changed", is how she put it.'

'And did she ask you to pass that on to me?'

'No, but girls tend to know what information is intended for passing on and when a secret is exactly that.' She raises an eyebrow significantly.

'Her feelings towards commitment have changed?'

'That's what she said.' Lauren slaps my thigh in an uncharacteristically ballsy way and exaggerates her American accent. 'Enjoy yourself tonight, buddy-boy, you certainly deserve it.'

I deserve it?

I scan the tables for Jenny, and catch sight of her dress again. She's chatting to a man on her left, then breaks into laughter.

Meanwhile, a microphone is being moved into position for the speeches. I pick up my notes in my right hand, straighten my tie, then refill my wine glass, and wait my turn to speak.

When Alex has finished, to roars of acclaim from the audience, I'm greeted with a loud whoop of anticipation, which surprises me, and as I stand in front of the microphone on the edge of the dance-floor, I find myself searching again for a fleeting glance from the girl in pink silk. Then I clear my throat, wait for silence to fall and begin.

My opening is the easy bit: the protocol, the thankyous, the kind words about the bridesmaids, more thankyous. I can hardly get that bit wrong; if only it were the same hereon in. I start by talking about role models and how, in his formative years, Alex trawled the depths of seventies and eighties culture and eventually settled on Meatloaf. I throw in the odd joke about Alex's weight and his taste in music and, though this only gets me the odd chuckle, I don't mind because this speech isn't intended to win any awards for light humour. I'm possibly committing an unforgivable sin here, but what I really want to say is something important I have learned from Alex.

So I adopt a quiet tone and talk about the new respect I have developed for him. Alex, I explain, recognised love when it came into his life and responded appropriately. My audience are no longer twittering or chuckling: they are staring up at me in stunned silence.

'What Alex realised,' I continue, 'is that he didn't have to be his Meatloaf character any more. It can be too easy to get stuck in the roles we create for ourselves and Alex had a role about as well-defined as anyone's. I'm not saying that his was an act or an affectation – he'll always be a larger-than-life exuberant character. He'll probably always have that nice, cuddly waistline and, unless Steph can work miracles, he'll always have a God-awful taste in music. But what he demonstrated is that we shouldn't be afraid to adapt and grow as people beyond the identities with which we feel safe.

'I always thought that Alex would be the last man on earth to get married; he had enough role models – the Six-Million Dollar Man, Scott Tracey of *Thunderbirds*, Jesus of Nazareth – who were single. And I'm sure he won't mind my telling you that when he announced that he'd got engaged, I thought it a joke, that it would be just another short chapter in the rock opera in which he has played out his life. But it has given me immense pleasure to discover I was wrong. Love hasn't changed him, it's just made him strong enough to discover more about the person he is.' I stop here and the silence is complete.

'I hope I'm not disappointing those who were hoping to be regaled with the six-in-a-bed-in-Budapest story or the one about Alex, the Thai trapeze artist and the farmyard animals. But I think everyone who is lucky enough to know Alex will find him likeable, lovable and roguish without any persuasion from me. So I'd like you all to toast the man who made the journey from Meatloaf to marriage. Alex isn't quite Meatloaf any more and anyone who's listened to their old *Bat out of Hell* LP recently will know he's infinitely the better for it.

'So, ladies and gentlemen, will you please stand for a toast; to my fine and admirable friend, Alex, the man from the rock opera, and to Steph who, thank goodness, saved him from it.'

I'm greeted with a wave of applause so loud and long I'm almost embarrassed. Then Alex approaches me and wraps me in a huge hug and only after that can I shrink back into the safety of my chair and my wine, and soak up the acclaim.

The music starts up, Alex and Steph are dancing, I feel exhausted, excited, and suddenly rather drunk and this pleasing sensation intensifies when Jenny plonks herself in the chair vacated by Lauren. 'That was amazing,' she says.

'You didn't think it was too heavy and serious?'

'Not at all. What you said about adapting and growing with someone was lovely.'

'Do you think anyone understood what I was going on about?' I'm fishing for something here.

'I know I did.' She's looking into my eyes having swallowed the bait. 'I understood it perfectly. It was wonderful hearing thoughts like that come from you.'

'Was it wonderful enough to make you want to dance with me?'

'Easily.'

So we join the gyrating horde on the dance-floor, and I can't help thinking how happy Jenny seems to be. When our hands touch or our bodies brush gently, she responds as if it were entirely natural and expected. And as the faint brushing and hints of contact increase so much so that the touching is clearly not just a string of happy coincidences, Jenny starts looking up to me with a sincerity that suggests that maybe the intentions are hers too and I know already the fate that awaits me, that I won't be able to resist finding out.

We're dancing closer and closer when she turns away, then moves backwards into me so that the silk pink dress is gliding against me. Instinctively, my arms close round her midriff, and I stoop to kiss her below her left ear. 'Would you mind if I kissed you?' I whisper.

'I'll only mind if you wait any longer.'

So here we are, kissing on the dance-floor, twirling to the music, then kissing each other again. We break for another glass of wine, barely talking but squeezing each other's hand and holding each other's gaze. But there is a heavenly togetherness on the dance-floor to which we return, a confederacy of couples of which we are now part. Jake and Lauren hug us and tell us how happy they are for us, followed by Peter and Di, then Alex and Steph. It doesn't get any better than this.

'They're not bad, weddings, are they?' says Jenny softly, into my right ear.

Not bad at all. And suddenly everything seems to make sense. I feel embraced by a sense of clarity.

'Come on,' I whisper. I lead Jenny off the dance-floor and between the tables to the exit. In keeping with the current state of perfection in my world, it is a clear, twinkly, starry night with a nearly full moon casting a beautiful silver glow across the golf course.

'Where are we going?' Jenny asks.

'Never you mind.'

I kiss the top of her head and lead her past the clubhouse, then a hundred yards down an incline so that we are on the eighteenth fairway. We stop on the green, a romantic little corner on the edge of deep woodland, guarded by hydrangeas whose petals have begun to fall and have created a carpet of deep pink.

'Will, what's all this about?' Jenny asks, laughing.

'Come here.' I face her, take both her hands and sink down on to one knee, drawing Jenny down with me so that she is crouching in front of me. 'Jenny, I know this has come out of nowhere, it's only just come to me, but it makes perfect sense. Let's not work out where we're going to be in our relationship this time or how we're going to get there and how quickly. All that was me last time, my fault. It was all wrong and I don't want to make that mistake again. Let's just be together, stay together, and know that's where we belong. Please, Jenny, will you be my wife? The place we should be is together, you and me. So, please, Jenny, will you marry me?'

Jenny stares at me, frozen, her face betraying nothing, the quiet broken only by the distant beat of the music in the marquee. I look into her eyes for a sign of acceptance, but their focus has changed and they are looking straight through me. She withdraws her hands, stands up and walks three steps away.

'Jenny?'

'I don't know what to say.'

'Say yes.'

'I can't.' Her voice is barely audible. 'You lovely,

foolish man.' She crouches in front of me again and strokes my cheek. 'I can't, Will. How can I possibly?'

'By just saying yes!'

'I can't. I'm so sorry.'

'But, Jenny—'

'Why are you asking me this, Will?'

'Well, we could do with some new cutlery and a dinner service, couldn't we?'

'Will! Don't joke. Not now, of all times.' She sounds frustrated now. She stands up again, paces away, and another silence falls between us. I cover my face with my hands. I was soaring so high I hadn't considered that a crash landing might be close. I screw up my eyes and see 'failure' written before me.

'Why, Will?' she asks again. 'Why did you want to do this?'

'Alex and Steph have just done it. Why can't we?' I know immediately how hopeless that sounds and Jenny does too.

'Will,' she replies, 'you just don't like being left behind.'

'That's bollocks.'

'It's true. Look, if no one else was married, if all your mates were going out together, boyfriend and girlfriend, like they were back in their twenties, would you still want to get married?' I contemplate my answer – for too long. 'There you are! Will, you don't really want to marry me. You just don't like the feeling of being the one left behind.'

'Sure, I don't like being left behind.' I'm still on one

knee and Jenny is only a few feet from me, but suddenly we seem miles apart. Yet I have to make my point. 'But not the way you think. It's not the marriage I want, or the marquee or the cutlery or even that I'd be treated normally at dinner parties. It's something else. I've watched Alex and Steph today, I've seen the way they look at each other, respond to each other, their joy in each other. And I admit I'm jealous of that. It looks brilliant and, yes, I want a bit of it too.'

'What makes you think we've got what Alex and Steph have got?'

'How do you know what they've got? How do I know what it feels like to be Alex and Steph?'

'Exactly! So just wait, Will, until you do.'

Good weddings are like great pieces of music: they have rhythm, pace, quiet moments that have you spellbound, and crashing great crescendos. They sweep you up and carry you along and at the end you feel you've been on a long emotional journey. I had been in tune with this one, but now I can't even hear the music.

An hour after the scene on the green, I am sitting in the marquee, my arms propped on my knees and, but for the glass of red in my hand and the half-bottle in front of me, I am alone. You can carry on drinking, and I've been working hard at that over the last hour, but it's amazing how a proposal sobers you up, especially when it's turned down. And I've certainly got manifold experience of that now. Was Icarus drunk when he flew too close to the sun?

Outside, the wedding noise is still raging, but it no longer sounds like sweet music. It's a chaotic cacophony that has been transported on to the golf-club drive where the bride and groom are departing. I can identify raucous chants roared out by boozy breath, and cackling laughter. 'Bye, Bye, Baby,' is the only clear lyric among the discord, an ugly monotone rendition. Did they really intend to combine 'Auld Lang Syne' and the Bay City Rollers?

'Hiya.'

I turn. Nicky is standing behind me. 'Can I join you?' she asks.

'I don't think I'm worth joining.'

'I know.' She pulls up a chair so it is touching mine. 'Is there anything you want to talk about?'

'I don't think so.'

'If you're miserable, you're not very good at covering it up.'

She catches my gaze. I've avoided looking anyone in the eye since my return from the eighteenth green, so I turn away. 'I'm a complete idiot, that's all.' My attempt to sound defiant isn't convincing. 'I've fucked it up. So stupid! Had it all and chucked it away. What a fool I am.'

'No, you're not. Come here.' She stretches an arm round me and draws me maternally towards her, so that my head is resting against her blonde hair in the curve of her neck.

Some other guests filter back into the marquee, arm-in-arm or in raucous groups, and Jenny is among them.

But she walks in alone, slowly, dejectedly, head slightly bowed, her arms loose by her sides.

'Come here,' Nicky whispers to me. 'Come here.' She rubs my back gently and kisses me lightly on the head. 'Come here.'

36

In my bed in the hotel in Upper Heynington. A sheets-and-blankets bed with a sorry hangover brewing inside it. I don't need to move to confirm that it is about to thunder down on me. On the right side of the bed there is a white plastic tray with a kettle, tea-bags, sugar sachets and those annoying little plastic containers that spill milk on you when you open them. I could make a cup of tea, but that would mean sitting up, which is out of the question.

I remain motionless, and let the follies of last night rattle across my brain. How are the mighty fallen! As for me, that's another matter.

I swivel round, with the utmost care, and contemplate the blonde head lying next to mine. How could I not have noticed before the little waves at the ends of the tresses? I could stroke them, show them some sort of affection and gratitude for the fact that they have come to be lying here next to me. But I think I should let their owner sleep on peacefully. If she's going to continue to hang around in beds and hotel rooms with me, she should be allowed to sleep, relax and get used to the idea that she may be here to stay.

On the left side of the bed, my blonde bedmate's side,

is the red display of a digital clock: 9.46 a.m. Quite a comprehensive stay, I'd say, from the bedmate: no obvious sign of displeasure to be lying here, no mad dash for the door. But I'll not be counting the minutes this time. I'll not be wondering what it feels like to be Alex and Steph . . . 9.48, 9.49 . . . She's here and that's all that counts. It's uplifting enough. Why risk going any higher?

Dishevelled remnants lie on the floor. Shoes and socks, a shirt, trousers doing the splits, and a tie falling like a hangman's noose from the wardrobe door handle. Disorder. An ugly reflection of the chaos gathering in my brain.

And yet there's a smooth pool of calm too. There, folded carefully over the chair in front of a window: a pink silk dress, with a black Japanese orchid print.